Never The Best

A SAVANNAH'S BEST BOOK

MAYA ALDEN

NEVER THE BEST

MAYA ALDEN

.

Trigger Warning

This book contains themes and subject matter that may be difficult or triggering for some readers.

The story delves into the emotional and psychological impact of bullying, fat-shaming, and body image issues. It explores the lasting scars caused by being ridiculed and ostracized for one's appearance during childhood and how those experiences contribute to the development of an eating disorder in the protagonist.

The book references disordered eating behaviors, including starvation and restrictive eating, as well as the challenges of body dysmorphia and the struggles of living with internalized shame and self-hatred.

While the story aims to handle these subjects with care and sensitivity, readers who are sensitive to discussions of eating disorders, body image, or bullying should proceed with caution. If any of these themes resonate deeply with your own experiences or may be upsetting, please consider whether this story is the right choice for you at this time.

Your well-being is important. Please take care of yourself as you read.

If you or someone you know is struggling with an eating disorder or body image concerns, help is available.

National Eating Disorders Association (NEDA) – Call or text (800) 931-2237 or visit nationaleatingdisorders.org

Crisis Text Line – Text HOME to 741741 for free, 24/7 support

BEAT (UK Eating Disorder Charity) – Visit beateatingdisorders.org.uk for resources and support

ANAD (National Association of Anorexia Nervosa and Associated Disorders) – Call their helpline at (888) 375-7767 or visit anad.org

CHAPTER 1
Rhett

"Y'all owe me. I got in there," I chuckled, my arm around Sage. "Or rather in *her*."

Sage groaned. "You're such an asshole, Rhett."

"I know, darlin'." Sage and I had been dating on and off for a couple of years. I was her first, and she was mine, but we weren't planning on being each other's last. We were seventeen, and life was too short or maybe too long to be stuck with the same girl forever.

"I can't believe you fucked Fat Pearl," Gary said in awe.

"You said I couldn't do it, and I showed you I could. She was easy. Real easy."

She wasn't. She'd made me work for it. Pearl was naïve but not stupid—in fact, she was brilliant. I had gotten close to her because of our shared love of reading, and we'd started a book club for two. In three months, I'd read more books I loved than ever before.

"How the heck did you do it? She doesn't even talk to anyone," Larry wondered.

"Did you have to roll her in flour to find the wet spot?" Gary cackled.

A part of me wanted to tell Gary to shut the fuck up. But Rhett Vanderbilt, the cool dude and future playboy, was too young and too much of a douche to fuck with his carefully curated image of callous cruelty.

"It was virgin pussy, wasn't it? Bet she was tight," Larry leered.

She was a virgin, sweet, and, fuck...sensuous. I, who prided myself on having slept with more girls than any other guy in my circle of friends, had been shocked at how sex could be emotional and beautiful, even while it was dirty. I wanted her again and again and again. But I couldn't have her because choosing Pearl as my girlfriend would shatter my standing in the high school hierarchy.

"She was a bet, and yeah, she was tight, so it made up for... you know, how she looks," I said, but the words tasted like ash in my mouth. Pearl had looked stunning naked, with silky skin, amazing tits, and an ass that was made for—I reined in my thoughts before I got a hard-on just thinking about her. "Now, pony up, assholes. Hundred bucks from each of you."

That was when I heard Sage gasp.

I turned and saw Pearl standing by my pool gate, clutching a copy of The Grapes of Wrath. *A few days earlier, she had told me she wanted me to read it and was convinced that I would love it.*

There was no chance that she hadn't heard me, because her

beautiful, usually happy face was pale, and there were tears in her deep gray eyes. I wanted to apologize, but then Gary laughed, "Hey, Fat Pearl, my friend here give it to you good or what?"

I should've told him to shut up. I wanted to, but I didn't.

"You lucky girl," Sage added, joining in the fun. "Well, savor it, 'cause that's the last time someone like Rhett is going to fuck your big ass."

"What are you doin' here, Bumblebee?" I knew she hated the nickname she'd gotten when she was a kid, dressed for Halloween as a bumblebee, and it had stuck. She'd been round and roly-poly. It was cruel, but that was life, yeah? "You come here for round two? I don't do seconds, so you should run along."

She held up the book in her hand and then shook her head before turning around and leaving.

I'd never in my life seen someone look as devastated as she did—not until then, or since. She was crushed. I had done that.

I woke up sweating, breathing hard. The nightmare swarmed inside me, making me nauseous.

I sat up, my heart pounding.

I'd had the same memory show up in my dreams on and off for years, but they'd become more frequent since Pearl Beaumont had returned to Savannah.

I looked at the clock on my bedside table. It was four in the morning. I could get another two hours of sleep before getting ready for the day, but I knew that wasn't going to happen. If Josie was in bed with me, I could've fucked her to get some respite, but I hadn't been spending the night with her or fucking her for a while now.

How differently had my life turned out than I thought it would. When I was a seventeen-year-old asshole playing with the feelings of nice girls like Pearl—okay, so maybe only one nice girl; the others were sophisticated, like my fiancée Josie and my friend Sage—I'd thought I'd have the world at my feet.

On paper, I did.

I had a thriving business. Between the family wealth and my consulting firm, the Vanderbilt Trust had only increased in size. The Vanderbilts of Savannah were old-money aristocrats, our wealth a legacy carefully tended across generations. I now not only ran a successful business but also oversaw my family's extensive portfolio, ensuring our fortune remained as formidable as our reputation.

Personally, my life was a shitshow.

Four months ago, Josie became pregnant with my baby. I'd had no choice but to propose to her, and we got engaged. Hell, the engagement party was in a week.

I'd known Josie all my life. We grew up together, and since she ended her engagement with Dylan Rafferty a year ago, she'd become part of my friends' circle, and one night, when I'd had too much to drink, we had sex. That led to us casually dating, *and* I knocked her up. Before she crossed the twelve-week mark, though, she'd had a miscarriage. I'd been traveling and found out by text from my mother because Josie had been so distraught.

My first thought had been about the innocent child we'd

lost, and it wasn't until I saw Josie back home did I wished I'd waited to propose to her, as my Aunt Hattie had suggested. But Josie had told everyone and their mother, especially mine, that she was knocked up, and there was no way around that. A part of me wondered if she'd trapped me. A part of me wondered if she'd even been pregnant and then *conveniently* lost the baby. That thought made me feel like the seventeen-year-old prick I used to be. I wasn't *that* boy anymore. Also, Josie had been so devastated that I'd pushed the thought out of my head. I couldn't break off my engagement to a woman who had been expecting my baby and had cried for days after she lost the pregnancy. So, I let the status quo remain. We were now going to have an opulent engagement party and get married in a year.

I ran a hand through my hair and closed my eyes.

I'd always wanted to marry for love like my friend Royal recently had.

Royal Legere had married his best friend's sister after what had seemed like an untenable and unending courtship. He was happy with Nevaeh, and as I'd stood with Noah, Nevaeh's brother, as co-best man, I'd wondered if I'd be lucky enough to find the love of my life. Now, I knew that would never happen. I'd marry Josie and have the kind of marriage that so many men around me did—the kind Gary had entered with his father's business partner's daughter, Dixie May. The way Sage had been with the man her parents had deemed "appropriate"—the one she eventually had to divorce after ending up in the emergency room following yet another fight that turned physical.

The sad thing about my situation was that I'd always known I didn't want what my parents had—a marriage based on what was suitable for the family.

George and Dolores Vanderbilt had a cold relationship, communicating only to discuss logistics around their appearances in society. That would now be my life, my marriage.

I didn't want that, I silently screamed inside my head. I wanted...*more* out of life. I wanted a partner, a lover, a friend —someone who I trusted with myself. With Josie, it was all surface. The sex had been *okay*. The first drunken night hadn't been memorable, as they never are. After that, it had been missionary all the way.

But I hadn't been planning to marry her, so I didn't care. But now we were engaged, and we were not compatible in bed. Josie wanted the lights out and to think about goddamn England while I fucked her. She didn't participate. She didn't make love. She faked her orgasms. She did what she had to do to make me think I was a great lover—but I wasn't an idiot, and I knew that Josie wasn't interested in sex, at least not with me. And that was fine. I just didn't want her to be my wife. I liked sex. I enjoyed it. I'd had a lot of it—but since Josie, the whole fucking thing, pun intended, was a barren wasteland.

"Why don't you join Belle?" Royal suggested when I'd told him that I was going to lose my mind being engaged to a woman who thought her duty was to be a serviceable hole for me.

Belle was a sex club in Savannah that no one talked about,

6

but everyone knew about. A journalist had recently written a scandalous story about a senator who'd been a regular member.

Beau Bodine had been a member until he'd gotten married—for love. If that man could fall in love, that meant it was possible for anyone.

"I don't want to have sex with strangers. I want to have good sex with my spouse."

"Then I suggest you change your spouse," Royal advised.

He didn't like Josie. Hell, none of the people I considered true friends did. Damn it, I didn't even like Josie.

"You know I can't do that," I muttered.

The Vances, Josie's family, and Vanderbilts shared deeply-rooted business ties that spanned generations, intertwined through land holdings, real estate ventures, and joint investments. The Vances, known for their real estate development firm, had often partnered with the Vanderbilts to transform Savannah's historic properties into modern, lucrative ventures. It was a relationship built on old Southern alliances—equal parts mutual benefit and social expectation. This marriage was going to cement that alliance. My father and hers were fucking ecstatic.

"I don't get it, Rhett." Royal shook his head. "You're a grown-ass man; live your life on your own terms."

That was easier said than done, though, Royal *had* done it. He'd walked away from his family and only continued to have contact because of his grandmother. Once she passed, he'd stopped having anything to do with the Hilton Head Legeres. But I couldn't do that. Family was important to me.

My parents, my sister, and everyone expected me to behave like a Vanderbilt, and I had no choice.

Since I wasn't getting any sleep, I got out of bed and decided to go for an early run. The air outside was heavy with the faint scent of azaleas and jasmine, the first signs of Savannah waking from winter. The pale blush of dawn was just beginning to bleed into the dark sky, and the streets were still quiet, save for the occasional hum of a distant car or the rhythmic chirp of crickets that hadn't yet surrendered to the coming day.

I lived in the historic district, in the kind of house that tourists liked to snap pictures of—the one that made you think of long-dead cotton barons and gala balls under gaslit chandeliers. It was old-money Savannah through and through, with Greek Revival columns and wrought-iron railings that seemed too delicate to hold up under the weight of their age. The house had been in my family for generations, and though I owned it now, it felt more like a museum I was tasked with maintaining than a home. I grew up in this house, and when I was ready to find a place of my own, my father suggested I live here. My parents had moved to live on an expansive estate in the countryside in Richmond Hill, where we went to celebrate the holidays, as we'd have a full house with aunts and uncles and cousins. Their estate had an old plantation-style home and acres of land, including stables, a small lake, and even the remnants of old rice fields and outbuildings. I fucking hated that place almost as much as I hated the house I lived in.

As I turned off my street and headed toward Forsyth

Park, the cobblestones beneath my feet felt slick with dew. The sprawling trees arched above me, their limbs heavy with foliage that swayed gently in the early morning breeze. The park was quiet at this hour, save for the occasional dog walker or a vendor setting up to sell fresh-cut flowers from a cart.

I fell into an easy rhythm, the steady slap of my sneakers against the pavement merged with the soft murmur of a world slowly waking up. Running usually cleared my head, but not today. My thoughts kept looping back to Pearl as they always did after the dream. Or was it a nightmare?

I hadn't meant to, but my route took me toward my Aunt Hattie's property on the edge of town. Harriet "Hattie" Odum's home was sprawling, old plantation-style, and surrounded by acres of land she'd somehow managed to keep intact despite all the encroachments of modern development. It felt a little frozen in time, like out of a Flannery O'Connor story.

Since Pearl returned to Savannah, she was staying in a small cottage just beyond the line of camellias that bordered the estate. It was small, tucked back near the garden where Aunt Hattie's roses would bloom in a riot of color later in the season. It was embraced by a wraparound porch with a couple of wicker chairs, a swing, and pale blue shutters the color of the Savannah River on a bright, sunny day. I didn't slow down, but my eyes lingered, as did my thoughts.

I found it remarkable that she was closer to Aunt Hattie than I was, despite Pearl living in California for several years. Pearl left Savannah after high school and studied at Stanford.

No one blamed me for shaming her—everyone accused her of trying to fuck above her station, not societally, since the Beaumonts were as old and wealthy as the Vanderbilts—no, it was because of how she looked. The plump, dull girl deserved to be used for a bet. That had shamed me even more. Aunt Hattie hadn't been reticent in telling me what a terrible human being she thought I was. But I'd been a young buck then and had not paid much attention to my crazy aunt. However, what I did stained my life—and me. I carried it with me like my own scarlet letter, carved into my soul. Now, fifteen years had passed, and the guilt was steady, my need for redemption growing just as firmly. And since Pearl was back in Savannah, I wanted nothing more than to make right the wrongs I'd done her.

I could only do that if she talked to me, which she didn't. I'd tried, and she'd given me a blank look, said nothing, and extricated herself from my presence. Pearl had always had a spine of steel, and I had nothing but regret for what I did while high on youth and arrogance. Unlike me, she wasn't going to submit to familial pressure. She'd once told me, when I'd been wooing her for that dumb bet, that she didn't want any part of the Savannah society we'd grown up in. She'd said it with a fire in her eyes, a rare defiance that had fascinated me.

"All that legacy nonsense," she'd said, sitting cross-legged on the edge of the dock at her family's summer house by the river where we used to meet up, where ultimately she'd given me her virginity. "It's not a legacy, Rhett—it's just an excuse to

cling to a rotten past. You can call it Southern tradition if you want, but that doesn't make it any less dark."

I'd argued with her; of course, I did. At seventeen, I'd been so sure of myself, so convinced that it was our responsibility—our duty—to carry on what our families had built. *"You can't just turn your back on it, Pearl. It's our history. It's who we are."*

She'd laughed, low and bitter. *"Are you sure? Our history is that of exploitation and slavery, of Jim Crow and the Klan."*

"That was years ago; you can't hold us responsible for the sins of our ancestors."

"You sure about that, Rhett? Look at how we live, look at our lives and those of the less fortunate. Have we really moved past the past?"

I thought I was protecting a legacy worth preserving, but maybe I'd only been hiding behind the weight of tradition. The conversation had stuck with me, even after all these years, though I didn't want to admit why. Maybe it was because she'd been one of the few people brave enough to challenge me—or maybe because deep down, I'd known she was right. It was because of Pearl that I now contributed heavily to the ACLU, the Southern Poverty Law Center, Planned Parenthood, and several other non-profit organizations my family would be shocked to learn I even knew about.

As I ran past her little cottage, I wondered who she had grown into. What had the past fifteen years done for her and to her?

She looked different, that's for sure. No one would dare call Pearl big now. She was slender and elegant. Her auburn hair was cut in a sophisticated style and made her look like the finance executive she was. She wore skirt suits to work—I'd noticed that when I saw her at Savannah Lace. She worked there, and I'd been to the office a few times to meet with the CEO, who had contracted Vanderbilt Finance for a project. She elevated her five-foot-five body with high heels. She had an air of insouciance about her. I hadn't seen her at any of the society events since she'd moved back three months ago—her brother, Cash, who I occasionally met at the country club, had told me how disappointed he, his wife, and his mother were that Pearl continued to shun society and embarrass them.

"How on earth is she doing that?" I demanded.

"She refuses to behave like a Beaumont," Cash lamented. "Caroline has tried to get her to meet some women to socialize with, but she refuses, and hangs out with that Nina Davenport suffragette gang."

Nina Davenport was the CEO of Savannah Lace, an all-woman design and architecture firm where Pearl was the director of finance.

"Suffrage was a long time ago, Cash, since women have been voting since the 19th Amendment was ratified in 1920. Nina is a brilliant CEO, and Savanah Lace is involved with some of the biggest projects we've seen in this city," I remarked, annoyed with Cash. I had tremendous respect for Nina. My Aunt Hattie and she were close friends, and I would not have anyone tarnish their names.

"Oh, please, don't tell me you, too, believe in that nonsense."

"It's not nonsense, Cash, it's called progress."

I had learned from my aunt that Pearl was close to Cash's teenage daughters, which pissed off his wife, Caroline, as much as it did Cash. They worried that their daughters would become like their aunt. *They should be so lucky.*

When I saw a light flicker on in Pearl's cottage, I felt like a creepy lecher, so I picked up my pace, not wanting to be caught gawking at her home.

The cool morning air stung my lungs as I pushed harder, like I could outrun the memory of her or the feeling in my chest that told me I still hadn't figured out how to be the kind of man who was worthy of her forgiveness.

CHAPTER 2
Pearl

"**I**t was virgin pussy, wasn't it? Bet she was tight," Larry the Creep said.

"*She* was *a bet, and yeah, she was tight, so it made up for...you know, how she looks," Rhett claimed. "Now, pony up, assholes. Hundred bucks from each of you."*

I stood by the pool listening to Rhett crush my faith in humanity, my hands clutching a copy of The Grapes of Wrath, *a book I was going to give him as a gift because we'd bonded over our love of Steinbeck.*

After this point, the nightmare always changed, transforming from reality into dream-like surrealism. Sometimes, he'd see me and laugh. Other times, I'd struggle to move. There were times I'd run and run and run until I collapsed. Sometimes, I'd wake up and cry.

So, seeing the man who took my virginity sitting across from me in a meeting room was nothing short of a waking nightmare. What made this worse than any nightmare was that Rhett hadn't just been my first love—he was the one who had taken my innocence, shattered my trust, and destroyed my belief in people.

I was humiliated—as anyone would be—to find out that my first time had been the result of a bet. Rhett had won three hundred dollars from his friends—and then the whole school and everyone who was anyone in our age group in Savannah found out he'd won the title of "Cool Playboy." Ultimately, to Rhett, that was what a sixteen-year-old's innocence was worth—three hundred measly dollars and a bump to his already soaring reputation.

Now, you may say, that happened fifteen years ago, Pearl, get over yourself. But how do you get over what derailed your life? Because *after* he announced to his friends that he'd had the chubby girl—and had probably rolled her over in flour to find the wet spot—my life in Savannah became miserable. I went from fat to foolish in seconds. It got so bad that, after high school, I ran from my city and home. Rhett went from jock and straight-A student to Harvard, to fame as a finance guru.

It was in that capacity that I had to meet with him in a professional setting. I left Savannah to study at Stanford. I mean, what else was a girl with no friends going to do in high school but study all the time? My GPA and SAT scores had been outstanding, and I got into several Ivy League schools. I chose Stanford because a lot of the Savannah set went to schools on the East Coast.

After I graduated, I worked in LA for several years. When my Aunt Hattie's friend Nina Davenport wanted to hire a Director of Finance for her architecture and design firm, Savannah Lace, I decided to return home because Savannah was still where I felt I belonged. Right now, I wasn't sure if I had made a big, fat mistake—almost as *fat* as I used to be.

I'd been back for two weeks, and it had been a shitshow.

It started with hearing *everything* about Rhett Vanderbilt's upcoming engagement party to Josie Vance: high school mean girl, blonde Barbie—you get the picture?

Now, Aunt Hattie was confident that the marriage wouldn't last; Josie was on her second fiancé, but this was Rhett's first walk down the proverbial aisle. I'd seen the engagement photos. They looked so cute together—an *ideal* couple. When narcissism meets assholery, you know their children were going to be *fucked* up.

Hattie was my mother's third cousin by marriage. As was the norm in the South, she was *also* Rhett's *actual* aunt, his mother's sister. After what happened with Rhett, she sort of adopted me. She was the one who told me to get the hell out of Dodge and go to college far, far away. She'd been there for me more than my mother or brother ever had. She became my guardian angel, my source of strength after what Rhett did.

My father had passed away when I was nine years old, so he, thankfully, hadn't had to deal with the rumors and innuendos of when Fat Pearl, fondly called Bumblebee (there was once a Halloween costume that Mama insisted I wear), had foolishly set her sights on Rhett Vanderbilt. He'd done what he was supposed to; taken advantage of my stupid ass and discarded me in public. As these things always went, it was the girl's fault. She was the fool, the slut, the whore. The boy? Well, he was just doing his duty, sticking his dick into whomever let him.

"If you grind your teeth any harder, there will be none left for you to chew your food," whispered Layla Warren, my boss and Savannah Lace's Chief Financial Officer.

I grinned.

Layla knew my history with Rhett; in fact, she and our CEO, Nina Davenport, had checked with me to see if I was okay working with Rhett's financial consulting firm. As Savannah Lace grew, we had to navigate new financial regulations and overhaul our systems and policies to stay compliant. This was where Vanderbilt Finance stepped in. Rhett had built a company that specialized not only in wealth management but also in helping businesses streamline their processes, policies, and systems to ensure they conformed to ever-evolving regulations.

"I'm just listening to all the fabulous things Vanderbilt Finance is going to do for us," I remarked.

Rhett, who had been talking, paused. "Do you have a question?"

I smiled broadly, even though seeing him hurt in places I'd thought had healed.

I'd never let him know that seeing him now was devastating, that it made the hole inside me—the one he'd helped create—bigger and deeper. I had been so young, so naïve, and he'd destroyed all of that, and then continued to do so.

Five years after he won *the* bet, he tried to apologize—

though calling it an apology would be generous. It wasn't your typical "*I'm sorry.*" It was more like, "*I'm sorry, and you should be grateful I'm even bothering to say it.*" When I didn't immediately fall at his feet to forgive him, he had the audacity to accuse me of being rude, as if I should've been honored by his half-assed attempt to excuse the mess he'd made of my life.

Because of Rhett, my trust issues were as vast and impassable as the Grand Canyon. I dated, but always cautiously—so cautiously, in fact, that the possibility of a real relationship never even existed. I had sex, but it was always casual, deliberately so. I mainly chose men I didn't know, who I met through apps like Tinder, where anonymity felt safer. And even now, after losing so much weight, I still insisted on keeping the lights off during sex. It wasn't about how I looked anymore, it was about the fear that someone might judge my body, the same way I still silently did myself, because no matter what the scale said, my mirror told me I was fat and ugly.

My weight loss, however, had not been intentional, and came at a significant cost. My eating disorder was born from the humiliation I suffered as a child and teenager because of my weight. The fear of being seen as obese took root so deeply that I starved myself to have some semblance of control. For years, food was the enemy, every bite a battle-ground between guilt and survival. It took countless therapy sessions to unlearn those thoughts, to see food as nourish-ment instead of punishment, and to remind myself that my worth had nothing to do with a number on a scale. The journey I was on was long, painful, and never-ending. I fought hard, sometimes every day, to reclaim my life.

But I had triggers, and when I got depressed or anxious, my first response was to stop eating.

My life was a constant balancing act—and even though I played the part of the confident, size-six, tough bitch, the truth was that, when I looked at my body, all I ever saw was Fat Pearl. Body dysmorphia was a relentless, insidious voice in my head, always whispering that I wasn't good enough, wasn't thin enough—wasn't *enough*, period.

Some days, I could silence the self-loathing by drowning it out with logic and self-compassion. Other days, it consumed me. Even after all the progress I'd made, old wounds still lingered beneath the surface, waiting for the right moment to remind me they were never truly gone.

So, let no one tell you that all wounds heal over time, because some deep ones never do. Mine hadn't. But I was adept at masking; I wouldn't let people see me as weak, not ever again. I wouldn't allow it. My entire life had become about wearing armor to protect myself, to never be vulnerable again.

"I was just telling Layla how excited I am about working with your team," I lied. He wouldn't know I was lying because he, like everyone else, only saw in me what I allowed them to.

It was also not my first lie to Rhett that day.

He had come into my office before the meeting to ask me how I felt about Savannah Lace hiring his company. My response and demeanor were SoCal breezy.

"According to Layla, your team does excellent work. I'm looking forward to working with y'all," I deliberately misunderstood what he was asking.

He cleared his throat. *"I meant,"* he paused and took a deep breath, *"I want to talk about what happened."*

"When?" I asked, my affected confusion evident.

"Come on, Pearl, you know—"

"Are we talking about high school here?" I cracked my face to look amused.

He flushed. *"Yes, Pearl, we are. What I did was...I regret it so much and—"*

"Good God, you're still on about that?" I laughed with what he'd assume was humor. I waved a hand. *"Let it go, Rhett. We're here to work together, yeah? So, that's what we'll do. I don't have a problem with it. Do you?"*

"No. I just...I wanted to be considerate of your feelings."

Now, you want to be considerate, you piece of shit!

"It's been fifteen years, Rhett; I can assure you that my feelings are not stuck in the sixteenth year of my life." Only if that were true!

He looked at me in disbelief.

"Is there anything else?" I asked sweetly, then looked at my phone, which beeped and saved me from telling him I wanted to rip him a new one. *"Layla needs me for a minute before we meet."*

Rhett shook his head, looking shocked. I loved seeing that look on his face because he didn't know what was up or down.

I walked out of my office and called out for Rachel, Nina's EA, and Savannah Lace's receptionist. *"Rachel, can you take*

Mr. Vanderbilt to the Jasmine Conference Room?" I smiled at Rhett. "See you in fifteen."

Now, Rhett looked at me speculatively, still unsure about what to make of me. I was an enigma to him. Aunt Hattie had said that I had surprised everyone in Savannah with my arrival. Since returning, I know I was seen with curiosity. I'd heard all the snarky remarks.

"She's the one who used to be overweight."

"Rhett Vanderbilt slept with her?"

"It was a bet, and she gave it away to him. She was a virgin."

"She's gorgeous, so why wouldn't Rhett want to go with her?"

"She used to be fat."

I hated how people felt that I was now acceptable, including my mother, because I'd lost a few pounds at the expense of my health, mental and physical. The truth was that I hadn't been obese, not even in the least. I had been a size fourteen, which was the average size for women in the United States of America—but in Savannah society, where all the Belles worked hard to fit into designer sample sizes their Mama picked up during Paris and Milan fashion weeks, I stuck out like a *big* sore thumb.

I cringed when people said, "*You're so lucky to be so thin.*"

That wasn't why I was lucky; I was lucky because I was alive.

When I was twenty, I nearly died. I didn't like to think about it, much less talk about it, but the memory had a way of creeping up on me when I least expected it—like now, while I watched Rhett.

I lost so much that day by his pool—but the most insidious thing his words and actions had done was change my identity from being a chubby girl to being...well, someone who fed herself the bare minimum while running on caffeine and self-hate.

I'd gotten so good at hiding it, so good at smiling and insisting I was just *"too busy to eat."*

I believed I was fine, even as my clothes hung loose on my shrinking frame, even though my reflection continued to look the same to me—fat, ugly, hideous.

Then, one day, my body finally gave out.

"What do you think, Pearl?" Nina asked me, making me snap out of the past and into the present.

I had been listening with one ear, a skill I'd picked up as a kid who didn't want to hear what people were saying about her but couldn't help herself, and listened to them all the same, breaking her tender heart.

"I think that we need a strategy that combines new hardware with the implementation of new policies—if we do one without the other, we're going to be playing catch-up."

Rhett nodded and took a document from his colleague, whose name I didn't catch. "That's exactly our recommendation as well." He smiled at me. "We've done quite a few such projects, and trying to implement new regulations without the right IT systems will create more issues and lead to policy violations. Here is a list of companies we've worked with in the past who have agreed to speak with you, if you want more insight."

He slid the document in front of Layla and me. I picked it up and scanned it.

He was good at what he did, I had to give him that. I had worked with several consultants in my years as a finance professional, and he was one of the best—as was his team. They were en pointe and weren't trying to fleece the client or push projects to increase their billable hours. Well, even though, as a teenager, he had the morals of a worm, in business, he seemed to have integrity.

After the meeting was over, Rhett walked with me to my office. I wish he hadn't. I needed to tighten the chain links on my armor as they had come loose at the impact of seeing him again, up close and personal.

"Aunt Hattie is very grateful that you're staying close to her," he said casually as I stepped into my office and glanced back at him, my gaze making it clear I was wondering: *What the fuck do you want?*

"I'm the one who's grateful."

"Cash said you didn't want to live on the Beaumont Estate."

"Are we making small talk, Rhett?" I went around my desk and sat down on my leather office chair. I swiveled, my ponytail swishing on my back as I did. At work, I tied my shoulder-length hair into a ponytail. When I was younger, I used to leave it loose as a way to hide my face. I forced myself not to do that anymore.

"I just wanted to say thank you for being there with Aunt Hattie."

"I don't need you to thank me."

He tucked his hands in his slacks and looked at me with keen eyes.

He was a handsome man, no denying that. We were about the same age—just past thirty, still navigating who we were. I'd seen him around town enough to know he wore a suit well, but today, he was dressed more casually: slacks and a crisp blue-and-white striped dress shirt that made his eyes look like brilliant azure. His hair was freshly cut and styled with just enough precision to look polished without feeling rigid. And, of course, his shoes had red soles—because Rhett Vanderbilt couldn't help but be a walking fashion statement.

But it was his hands that I'd watched the most. They were big and strong.

I remembered those hands, even though I didn't want to. I remembered them touching my untrained body—coaxing an orgasm out of me, which surprised both of us.

"It doesn't always happen," he told me in awe. "I'm so glad it happened for you. And, fuck, Pearl, you look so beautiful flushed like this."

"Can we do it again?" I asked breathlessly.

"Let me try something."

"What?"

"I'm going to eat your pussy. I...I've never done that before."

"Before I forget, congratulations on your engagement," I trilled. "You and Josie make a lovely couple."

He arched an eyebrow. "Do we?"

"Absolutely. I always thought you'd end up together. She was so keen on you."

He looked confused. "Really?"

"Oh, yes, she was one of your floozies who often told me that...." I shut the fuck up. What was I doing? Why was I talking about the past? Why was I letting Rhett bait me into exposing old scars and scratching them open?

"Told you what?" he coaxed.

I shrugged lazily. "Doesn't matter, and I honestly can't even remember; it's been so many years. Is there anything else I can do for you? I have a meeting shortly."

Rhett nodded. "Yeah, me too. Ah, it's good to see you, Pearl. You...look nice."

"Well, I'm a size six now, so I fit right into Savannah society." Bitterness edged my voice, sharp and unrelenting. I was nice-looking now—acceptable—because I'd lost weight. But no one cared who I was on the inside. No one cared that, once upon a time, my heart had stopped beating. That I had technically died because I'd been starving myself, unable to stand the sight of my reflection. And even now, even after everything, I still struggled to look in the mirror.

He looked hurt, and I wanted to throw something at him.

"I didn't mean it like that, Pearl. It's good to see you thriving in a professional setting."

"Of course, you did. Now, if you'll excuse me." I tried to keep my voice light, but I knew it wasn't working. My therapist had warned me that going to Savannah would trigger me

—that old struggles would resurface, and I'd known that seeing Rhett would be a test to see how far I'd come, if at all.

CHAPTER 3
Rhett

"So, did you hear that Bessie Simons is getting a divorce?" Josie announced.

"She found her husband diddling the maid," said Gary's wife, Dixie May, giggling.

Yep, her name was Dixie May, a perfect summation of her: old Southern money, perfectly polished exterior, with a talent for gossip that could turn even the smallest detail into a full-blown scandal.

"But then Bessie put on all that weight after she had kids; what did she expect would happen?" Josie shook her head, disgusted.

"I don't think a woman who has children and puts on weight should have her spouse cheat on her because of it," my friend Sage interjected.

Sage used to be one of the mean girls, but as we grew up, we both developed a conscience. She was a lawyer and a partner at her father's fancy white-shoe law firm, *but* she also

27

did a lot of pro bono work. We'd gotten closer over the past years as we found ourselves morally drifting away from the friends we grew up with.

"Oh, come on, Sage, we're not talking about *your* marriage," Josie said sweetly, but I knew she was.

Josie didn't like my friendship with Sage and was jealous of it, and God knew why. Sage and I were *not* sexually involved, hadn't been since high school, since...Pearl. Somehow, that one incident had changed a lot of lives, mine and Sage's included, and I hated to think it, but I knew Pearl's as well. One stupid, heartless mistake had damaged Pearl—but it had helped Sage and me grow up and strive to become better people. It took a few years for us to get our heads straightened—and, even though we still hung out with our old friends, we'd expanded our circles.

I spent time with Royal Legere and his close friend Noah Carter, men who had more on their minds than conforming to Savannah society. They were older than me and, in so many ways, wiser. My father, an archaic patriarch, obviously didn't approve of either man. Royal had broken off from the Legere family, and Noah, well, he had been investigated for bribing a senator, *and* there had been that sex tape with his wife that pretty much everyone had seen. Somehow, he and his wife Stella didn't seem to care what people said or thought, and I aspired to be just like them when I grew up—*if* I did.

"Since I don't have any children, I know you're not talking about my marriage," Sage clipped, "or my divorce."

"Well, we were talking about cheating spouses," Josie said, almost waspishly.

That, unfortunately, had been Sage's spouse, though their divorce came about for more reasons than her husband's inability to keep it in his pants.

"Josie," I interjected, a hint of warning in my tone, one she picked up on but, alas, Dixie May didn't.

"Sleeping with help, it's such a cliché," Dixie May declared heatedly.

The cliché, I thought, was all of us gathered at The Olde Pink House for dinner, talking about *other* people and their sordid lives.

This was Josie's favorite restaurant, and not because it was elegant, not because it was a stately 18th-century mansion that dripped with Southern charm. Fuck, no. Josie liked coming here because it was the *place* to be seen.

"Is that Governor Abernathy?" Josie asked, lowering her voice.

I looked around the dimly lit dining room, which had flickering candlelight and low-hanging chandeliers. The walls were a soft blush pink, offset by mahogany paneling.

I found her quarry.

"Yes, I believe so," I acknowledged.

"We should go say hello to him. You know, he's coming to our engagement party."

"Maybe later," I prevaricated. I had no intention of approaching Abernathy. Sure, my father and Josie's knew him well, but I didn't, *and* I also didn't care to know the asshole, who was more corrupt than the previous guy who used to have his job, which I didn't think was possible.

Thankfully, before Josie could argue, Gary launched into a story about the Governor.

I ignored what he said and looked out through the restaurant's tall windows, into the gaslit glow of Abercorn Street, where my office was located.

You could hear the faint hum of Savannah's post-work crowd filtering in and out of nearby bars. The street bustled with conversations, punctuated by bursts of laughter from nearby tables. I wondered if *they* were all talking about some woman and her sordid divorce. What pissed me off was how excited Josie was about this woman getting cheated on. My future wife was not about solidarity with women. Instead, she was all about crushing them and making them feel smaller.

I was relieved when the waiter came to take our drink order—because I desperately needed alcoholic fortification. Maybe Royal was right; I should end this engagement. I could barely stand talking to this woman, how would I stay married to her?

But my father wouldn't stand for it—hers wouldn't, either. It would be a scandal.

When you were born and raised a certain way, breaking free of that mold was damn near impossible. The hardest part, though? I'd never even thought about the life I wanted to live—I had no clue what that life looked like. I wasn't living by design, I was living by default. You do A, then B, then C. You follow the same well-trodden path everyone else before you had walked—right up until the end. In the meantime, you made a lot of money, got married, had kids, and worked tirelessly to expand the family legacy and protect the almighty reputation. It was the formula, and God help you if you tried to deviate.

The waiter took our drink orders—an Old Fashioned for me, Josie's usual Sauvignon Blanc, a martini for Sage, a Jack for Gary, and an obnoxiously complicated drink for Dixie May because she had to be a fucking nuisance.

"I don't care what anyone says." Dixie May delicately adjusted the napkin in her lap. "Carol Ann shouldn't be hosting the Historical Society Gala this year. Everyone knows she's just doing it to climb her way up. You can't make up for a tacky pedigree, no matter how much money you marry into."

Gary chuckled, a loud, booming sound that turned a few heads from nearby tables. "Well, Carol Ann's husband didn't seem too worried about pedigree when he bought her that monstrosity of a diamond ring. My God, it looks like he got it from a Vegas pawnshop."

"Gary, please," Dixie May scolded with a laugh, her pearls practically vibrating with the effort. "We don't talk about such things so openly."

Apparently, we did, and Sage concurred. "Only behind her back," she muttered, just loud enough for me to hear. I glanced at her and smirked.

Sage wasn't much for Savannah's social politics any

longer. She had developed a sharp tongue that occasionally made these dinners tolerable for both of us. Tonight, though, even she looked like she'd rather be anywhere else. Just like me.

She'd married for *family* validation, and where had that left her? She was divorced and embarrassed in society because her ex-husband was parading a new belle, a pregnant one, around town. So, the rumor went, that Sage couldn't give him children, which was why he'd simply had to find another woman to impregnate. But Sage was still part of this life, and since she worked at her father's firm, she was, as she said, *trapped*, just like I was.

Josie leaned forward, her elbow grazing my arm. "Oh, Rhett, didn't your Aunt Hattie host the gala a few years ago? Now, that was a proper event. Everything was so tasteful."

The server came then, and Sage and I grabbed our drinks like we were crawling in the desert, looking for hydration.

"Aunt Hattie didn't." I downed half my drink in one go. "That was Mama."

"Well, she's such a class act, darlin'." Josie fluttered her eyelashes. My mother loved her.

I didn't have much else to add, and truthfully, I didn't care. Mama's gala had been just as pretentious as this dinner.

What the fuck was I doing with my life?

"People like Carol Ann don't get Savannah," Dixie May drawled. "They think you can just throw money at things and suddenly have culture. It's insulting, really."

"When the fuck can we stop talking about Carol Ann?" Sage whispered in my ear.

I chuckled softly, and Josie glared at me.

She'd tried to get Sage to sit across from me, but we'd managed to sit next to one another. In fact, Sage had agreed to come to dinner only because I *begged*; I couldn't *not* go. Josie would make so much fucking noise about it that it would drive me up the freaking wall—well, I was here, and that was precisely how I felt, crazy and up a wall.

The server returned. "Have y'all had a chance to look at the menu?" he asked, his tone polite but efficient.

"We'll need another minute." Josie flashed him her brightest, most polished smile. I could tell by the way his smile tightened that he'd probably seen a dozen "Josies" tonight, all with the same perfect hair, perfect clothes, and perfect expectations. He was past this shit.

You and me both, bud!

I opened the menu but barely looked at it. I already knew what I wanted—pecan-crusted grouper, one of their specialties—but I kept the menu in my hands, more as a shield than anything else. The conversation continued without me.

"Speaking of people who don't get Savannah," Gary chimed in, "did you hear about the renovations they're doing at the old Habersham house? It's gonna be some kind of boutique hotel now. Can you imagine?"

Dixie May gasped theatrically. "A hotel? That house is practically sacred!"

"It's Gabe Rhodes buying up properties to please his wife," Josie claimed. "Savannah Lace is getting that architecture contract. I still don't understand why Aurora still works, you know? I mean, she's married into the Rhodes fortune."

"Maybe because she likes to work?" Sage suggested.

"Oh, please. I'm sure it's because they have an airtight prenup. You know Betsy Rhodes, she wouldn't have let her son marry someone like Aurora without one," Josie continued as she perused the menu.

"And what does that mean?" I asked. The hell with it. I wasn't going to let her make racist remarks around me. I knew Gabe and Aurora, and liked them very much. I also knew Betsy Rhodes, and she'd fuck Josie up for the comment she just made.

"Just that she doesn't come from our circles, darlin'," Josie dropped condescension like magnolia petals in a summer storm.

"And what the fuck does that mean?" I persisted.

"Rhett," Josie rage whispered, "language, *please*. I just meant that she isn't like *us*."

"I hope to fucking God you weren't saying that 'cause she's not white," I challenged.

Josie looked aghast. "I'd never...stop being crass, Rhett. What's gotten into you?" she tittered self-consciously. Her fiancé wasn't behaving like a well-trained pet.

Yeah, that *was disconcerting; not* you *making racist remarks.*

"You owe me a freaking case of Burgundy for dragging me here," Sage muttered into my ear.

"What's it that you both keep talkin' hush-hush about?" Josie flashed angry eyes.

34

"Can we order?" I replied with a non-sequitur. "I'm hungry, Josie."

Josie took a deep breath and gathered herself. Christ!

She straightened and smiled warmly at me. It was completely fake. "Rhett, what do you think of what's happenin' with the Haversham house?"

She was as subtle as a honking goose in church with her effort to show me that she was changing the topic.

"I think Savannah's gonna do what Savannah always does." I offered a neutral shrug. "People will complain about it for a while, and then they'll show up to the grand opening like nothing happened."

Gary laughed, but Dixie May gave me a look like I'd missed the point entirely. Josie, to her credit, didn't push, though I could tell she was annoyed. It wasn't the first time I'd failed one of her subtle *"show the world we're together because we think alike"* prompts, and it wouldn't be the last.

The waiter returned, pen poised to take our orders, and Josie went first, choosing the salmon with a side of asparagus. I ordered the grouper, as I'd decided, Sage picked the scallops, and Gary went for the filet mignon. Dixie May spent an unbearable amount of time asking detailed questions about the preparation of the duck before finally settling on it, her voice dripping with the kind of condescension reserved for someone who'd never had to work a day in their life. She could give Meg Ryan in *When Harry Met Sally* a run for her money when it came to ordering off the menu.

As the waiter walked away, the conversation circled back

to someone new, and I zoned out, letting everyone's voices blur into the background. My eyes drifted to the window, where the faint glow of the streetlights bathed the sidewalk in a soft, golden hue.

A group of young professionals in suits and pencil skirts laughed as they crossed the street, heading toward one of the nearby bars.

My heart began to beat fast when I saw one of them was Pearl, along with Luna Steele and Aurora Rhodes, from Savannah Lace. They were laughing, and I envied how happy she looked.

"Rhett," Josie said again, her voice sharp enough to pull me back. "Are you even listening?"

"Of course," I lied, sitting up straighter and forcing a smile.

"Oh my God," Dixie May gasped, "speak of the devil, Aurora Rhodes just walked in, darlin'."

"With Pearl Beaumont and Luna Steele?" Josie curled her nose. "I can't stand either of them. Luna is just so...you know, *masculine*. Look at how she dresses like a biker bimbo."

"Pearl's looking good, though." Gary grinned at me. "You remember that time when you won the bet that—"

"Gary, leave it be," I cut him off. I didn't need the conversation to turn to Pearl.

"Oh God, yes, you were the one who took her virginity and—" Dixie May's eyes were bright with excitement, her malicious intention evident.

"Can we not talk about *that*?" Josie interrupted her friend. Her problem wasn't the bet, it was that I had slept with someone before her. Christ but my fiancée was a nightmare.

CHAPTER 4
Pearl

W hen Aurora and Luna suggested drinks after work, I'd agreed enthusiastically. Still, the minute I stepped into The Olde Pink House, the air immediately wrapped around me like a suffocating, perfumed cloud of history and wealth, probably because I saw Rhett at a table *with* Josie and his despicable friends from high school. Was he still hanging out with them? He hadn't grown up one bit, had he?

My pulse quickened, the sound of it roaring in my ears. It wasn't just seeing Rhett—it was seeing all of them, that same kind of group dynamic that had surrounded me by the pool fifteen years ago. Sage's polished exterior, Gray's biting comments, the casual cruelty disguised as humor. All of it came rushing back, as vivid as if it had happened yesterday.

I could still hear their voices mocking me and could still see Rhett's smirk as he told me he didn't do seconds.

I hadn't been in Savannah for more than a week here and

there in the past fifteen years, and I'd mostly avoided public places. Now, I lived here again, worked here, I couldn't possibly hide. What did it say about the progress I'd made emotionally, that one whiff of the past, and my stomach was coiled into knots?

An emergency session with my therapist was in my very near future, for sure. I knew when I needed help, and after almost dying from not getting it before, I wasn't going to take that chance again. I didn't want to die. I wanted to live. I wanted to thrive. I couldn't do that if I kept getting triggered.

Once again, I wondered if I'd made a mistake moving to Savannah, thinking that I could handle it.

The hostess led us toward the bar, a polished mahogany centerpiece flanked by high-backed stools. This arrangement worked fine for us; we didn't want a table, not that we'd get one. As usual, the restaurant was packed, a blur of elegant couples and well-dressed groups laughing over cocktails— Savannah's finest.

"Pearl?" Aurora's voice snapped me back to the present. "All okay?"

I forced a smile, nodding as I slid onto one of the stools. "Yeah, just looking around. Is that the Governor?" I smoothly changed the topic. I wanted, very badly, to tuck my tail between my legs and run the hell out of there. I'd been hungry a minute ago, now, my appetite had vanished.

"Sure is." Luna arched an eyebrow. "Let's hope he doesn't see us; I'm in no mood to hear him talk about how I need to convince Lev to run for office."

Lev was Luna's older brother by eleven months, so they were Irish twins. Lev managed the Steele lumber business. I had met him once, and it was evident that the siblings were close.

"Doesn't he know Lev at all?" Aurora shook her head. "Speaking of Lev, he's donating to Betsy's charity, so it looks like we can open another women's shelter."

The indomitable Betsy Rhodes was Aurora's mother-in-law and a force of nature, which was why she was friends with women like Nina Davenport and Aunt Hattie.

"Lev will say it's a nice tax deduction." Luna grinned.

Aurora laughed. "He wants to pretend he's a big bad businessman, but he's a softie."

"He is *not* a softie, Aurora," Luna reminded her friend. "He likes Betsy, and I think he's also a little afraid of her, so when she said, write a check, he wrote one."

Once we got menus from the bartender, Aurora and Luna dove straight into a conversation about a new architecture project they'd been assigned at the firm. They discussed the adaptive reuse concept, where Savannah Lace was turning an old textile warehouse into a modern co-working space. They were passionate about architecture as they talked with their hands. Luna's bracelets jangled every time she pointed to make a case.

But I couldn't focus. My eyes kept darting to Rhett's table, where Josie was leaning into him. I caught Gary gesturing with his fork, Dixie May laughing, and Rhett, who was swirling a drink in his hand as if he didn't have a care in the world.

"Pearl, sweetheart, what would you like?" Luna asked, obviously not for the first time.

I looked down at the cocktail menu in front of me and flipped it open. I skimmed over the drinks without really seeing them. My chest felt tight, my hands a little shaky. The thought of food, of eating anything at all while *they* were here, while they could look over and see me, felt unbearable.

I settled on a glass of bubbly. It wasn't about wanting the wine—I didn't even particularly like it. But it felt safe. It gave me something to hold, something to sip on in small amounts. It wouldn't make me feel full, and it avoided awkward questions like, *"Why aren't you drinking?"* or, even worse, *"Are you an alcoholic?"*

What could I say? I was *like* an alcoholic, only my chronic condition was diagnosed as anorexia. And, like alcoholism, you didn't just get over it. It stayed with you, lurking in the corners of your mind, whispering doubts and lies on the bad days. Even on the good days, when I felt strong and healthy, it was there—a quiet, dormant presence I had to keep in check. Therapy helped, self-awareness helped, but the truth was, it was a lifelong battle. You didn't cure it; you managed it, one meal, one choice, one thought at a time.

Aurora ordered a Negroni, Luna went for a Manhattan, and they both continued talking, including me here and there.

I tried to listen, I really did.

They debated the pros and cons of keeping some of the old architectural features intact, whether it was worth reinforcing the original beams or if it would be easier and more efficient to replace them entirely. It was fascinating, but I couldn't fully connect. The past was inundating me and sending all the wrong signals to my brain.

The bartender set my wine down, and I took a sip, the cold liquid burning slightly in my empty stomach. I hadn't eaten since lunch—just a salad, light enough that I didn't have to think about it—and the thought of ordering off the menu now made me sick. What if *they* saw me eating? What if they whispered and laughed like they had back then? It was irrational, I knew that, but *fear* didn't care.

Luna's voice broke through my haze. "Pearl, what do you think? Is it worth saving the original windows, or would it look better with modern frames?"

"Oh," I said, fumbling for an answer because I was pretty distracted. "From a finance perspective, I think refurbishing the originals would be more expensive than buying new ones. From an aesthetic perspective, the old windows have more character."

Luna grinned. "I like finance people like you who actually understand the business and look beyond the dollars and cents."

Aurora rolled her eyes good-naturedly. "She says that now, but when I go to her to get the budget approved, she's gonna give me hell."

I tried to smile, to focus on the warmth of their banter, but the truth was, I felt like I was crumbling. My fingers tightened around the stem of my wineglass as I snuck another glance toward the dining room. Rhett was speaking, and Josie watched him like he hung the moon.

They were in love, weren't they? Made sense. He'd proposed to her, regardless of what Aunt Hattie said about Josie having *trapped* Rhett. Women didn't do that anymore, especially since men didn't have to marry a woman who was, as the old timers would say, *in the family way.*

"I need some nosh," Luna mumbled, perusing the menu. "Should we get some appetizers to share?"

I nodded in relief. This way, no one would notice that I wasn't ordering food, or ordering it and not eating anything. I hated that *they* still had this power over me, that just being in the same room as *them* could send me spiraling back into old habits, erecting familiar defenses. I hated that the idea of eating made me feel exposed and vulnerable. Most of all, I hated that no matter how far I'd come, part of me was still that sixteen-year-old girl by the pool, wishing the ground would swallow her whole.

I managed to nibble on a truffle fry. If Luna or Aurora noticed that I wasn't eating much, they didn't comment.

We'd just gotten the check and dropped our credit cards for the bartender to split the bill when Dixie May came up to us. Her husband, Gary, who I hated with a passion, trailed behind her, grinning that easy, leering grin that made my insides cave in. I remembered it well.

"Hey, Fat Pearl, my friend here give it to you good or what?"

"Well, if it isn't the Savannah Lace ladies," Dixie May said, her voice dripping with false sweetness as she stopped in front of us. "And, my word, Pearl, can't believe you moved back to Savannah. I mean...we didn't expect you'd come back, did we, Gary?"

Gary winked at me. "You're lookin' good, Bumblebee."

Before I could answer—not that I particularly wanted to —Luna glared at Gary. "What did you call her?" she demanded.

Gary shrugged. "You know that used to be her nickname?"

"Are you fuckin' kidding me?" Luna stood up. She was in full biker bitch gear. Jangly bracelets, a skull on her leather belt that was around the loops of dark skinny jeans, and a tank top that showed her muscles and the tattoo of a dragon on her right arm.

"What? It's an adorable nickname." Dixie May fluttered her eyelashes, her smile widening just enough to make it clear she thought she had the upper hand.

"You were three years our juniors in high school, but even I know there's nothing adorable about that name." Luna crossed her arms over her leather jacket and fixed Dixie May with a threatening smirk. "Now, Dixie May, as I recall, you had a nickname as well. What was it?"

Dixie May went pale.

Aurora gave everyone a serene look. "You know, bumble-bees are pretty amazing, right?" She continued as if she were speaking in a David Attenborough documentary. "By all accounts, they shouldn't even be able to fly. Aerodynamically, their bodies are too big, their wings too small, but they do it anyway. They defy the odds just by being themselves."

Luna grinned, catching on. "Yeah, Pearl. Maybe you've

been looking at it all wrong. Bumblebees don't give a damn what anyone thinks; they just buzz around, making the world a little sweeter."

Aurora nodded. "Exactly. Bumblebees are resilient. They're badass. And honestly? The world would fall apart without them."

"Badass Bumblebee." Luna smiled and then turned to sign the credit card receipt the bartender had left with our bill. "Now, that's a nickname that I can get behind."

"That's not why she was called that," Dixie May, who was dumber than a rock, murmured. "But *anywhoo*, I saw you here and just had to come by." She turned and waved, and since hell was a real thing, Sage, Josie, and Rhett joined us.

Hellos and how do you dos were dropped.

"Pearl, Rhett and I are so glad that you're coming to our engagement party." Josie all but slithered all over her fiancé. "You know, your mother was worried that you wouldn't show up because of that...*unpleasant* business in high school."

Rhett's jaw clenched.

My mother was Josie's Godmother because her mother and mine were friends—yeah, welcome to the incestuous ways of Savannah society.

Birdie Beaumont, my mama, was the mean girl of her time and a sidekick of the main mean girl, Suellen Vance, Josie's mama. Rhett's mother, Dolores Vanderbilt, completed the evil axis of Savannah Society, who never failed to tell me how I was *less* than their children.

"Tess is so fit. She does Pilates every day. You should go to the gym with her, Pearl." Dolores would show off about her daughter when she met my mother and me at a clothing store, where I was trying on size 12-14 dresses.

"Are you going to eat the whole slice of pie? Bless your heart, Pearl. My Josie keeps her figure by being careful about what she puts inside her mouth," Suellen once told me in public at a party. There had been a lot of snickering.

"I wish you were more like Josie," my mother, Birdie, said over and over.

In fact, she still said it. Now, I could ignore it. *Then*, it had been devastating.

"We have to go," Luna muttered loud enough for everyone and God to hear her. "Christ on a crutch, sometimes I feel like half this city's floozy population hasn't left high school."

I held back a laugh. I loved Luna. She said things people thought but didn't have the guts to say. But Luna's attitude was, *"I'm outta fucks, ladies. I'm so the wrong person to fuck with."*

Aurora chuckled.

And then, to my surprise, Sage smiled at me. "Truer words haven't been said."

"Excuse me?" Josie was incensed and looked up at Rhett.

"You are excused," I said, smiling widely.

Luna was right—we weren't in high school anymore. I was thirty-one, an independent and intelligent professional, and emotionally healthy...well, most of the time. At least, I was when I wasn't living in Savannah.

"How dare you?" Josie's eyes lit up with anger, but she kept her voice down. It wouldn't do for *nice* Josie Vance to let her temper show in public. It'd be in the gossip airwaves how she lost her temper when talking to Pearl Beaumont at The Olde Pink House while Governor Abernathy was dining five tables away. Ah, the scandal!

"Just because you managed to lose some weight doesn't change the fact that you are—"

"Stop." The single word from Rhett was sharp enough to cut through the din of the restaurant and silence Josie, who looked up at him in confusion.

I was confused, too. I thought Rhett would be on her side.

"Give it a rest, will you, Josie," Sage mocked flatly. "It's not cute anymore, not that it ever was. And you, too, Dixie May. You came here to see if you could get a rise out of Pearl, and all you got is an ass-kicking."

Luna, Aurora, and I couldn't help but smile, and I saw that Rhett's lips had curved up as well. Gary, who should be defending his wife, had his hands tucked in his pockets, amused *and* drunk.

Dixie May's mouth snapped shut, her eyes widening in surprise. "I beg your pardon?"

"You heard me." Sage didn't bother keeping her voice low. "We're not sixteen anymore, and you're not the head mean girl; what you are is a *Karen*."

The room felt like it had tilted slightly. Sage, the girl who had been part of the gang that made my life hell, along with Josie and Dixie May, was defending me? She wasn't smiling, wasn't trying to soften the blow. She simply looked at Dixie May like she was tired of the entire act and wasn't afraid to show it.

Before Dixie May could recover, Rhett moved closer to his fiancée. He glanced at Dixie May, then at me, he was clearly not pleased.

"Josie, let's go." He put his hand on her arm and began to steer her away from us.

"But—" Josie protested.

"Now," he clipped.

It wasn't loud, but it was enough. Josie straightened, her eyes flashing indignation. Dixie May looked cowed and, without another word, grabbed Gary's arm and stalked to the exit.

For a moment, I was frozen, my heart hammering in my chest as I watched them leave the restaurant. I didn't know whether to cry or laugh or just run out of the restaurant.

"You okay?" Aurora put a tentative hand on my shoulder.

I nodded, swallowing hard. "Yeah, I think so."

But I wasn't merely *okay*. For the first time since I'd come back to Savannah, I felt supported. By Aurora and Luna, who had stood their ground without hesitation. By Sage, who had surprised me more than anyone. Even by Rhett, who, despite everything, had told his fiancée to shut up.

It wasn't enough to make me want to eat a three-course meal—but it was enough that I managed to have some pieces of smoked gouda before I went to bed that night.

CHAPTER 5

Rhett

"Yes, sir, I understand." I managed not to sigh too loudly after my father was finished lecturing me about the *incident* at The Olde Pink House.

The Great George Vanderbilt was all about appearances and maintaining the family name.

I struggled with his values more now than I had growing up. I was supposed to manage the family wealth and live like he had—doing absolutely nothing but checking on stocks, bonds, and investments, spending my time in a country club, and occasionally nabbing a mistress that my wife would overlook because that was how it worked.

When I decided to use my Harvard finance degree to build a company, my father scoffed but *allowed* me to do it, saying everyone needed a hobby. Now that Vanderbilt Finance was a successful consulting firm, he talked about it like it *was* the family business. It wasn't.

I had done what I was supposed to do: expand the generational wealth, and considering I was not merely investing money but building a company gave me comfort. Vanderbilt Finance employed hundreds of people across multiple offices in several Southern states, with a portfolio that included not just wealth management but high-level financial consulting and corporate restructuring. We didn't only handle the money of Savannah's elite—we helped companies streamline their operations, ensure regulatory compliance, and set themselves up for long-term growth. It was about more than profit, it was about being privileged to help those who worked at my company to live fulfilling lives—that was what I was most proud of, for being the source of employment for so many.

And yet, despite all of that, my father still found ways to act as though my success was *his* accomplishment, casually dropping hints at parties about how he'd *encouraged* me to take the initiative to *steer the family legacy into the modern age*. The reality was that George Vanderbilt hadn't lifted a finger beyond cashing his monthly trust fund distributions and ordering me around like I was some kind of PR Manager for the Vanderbilt name. The reality also was that I let him.

"Rhett, we cannot have such public scenes. You *must* talk to Josie. She's a good girl, yeah? She just needs a little training. Tessa had the same issues with Macon, but he sorted her out."

I controlled my temper. My brother-in-law, Macon, in my opinion, emotionally abused Tessa. I had tried to talk to her about it, but she couldn't or wouldn't see it; after all,

she'd only seen a patriarchal marriage, where love was trans-
actional, where silence was a weapon, and where apologies
were unidirectional, from the wife to the husband. Our
parents' relationship had set the bar so low that Macon's
manipulations seemed normal—acceptable, even. She
mistook his control for care, his criticism for guidance, and
his coldness for strength. It made me sick to watch, but no
matter how I tried to open her eyes to it, she told me, "*You
don't understand him like I do.*"

Macon probably reminded her of our father. They were
similar in how they thought about and treated women.
Hadn't I been raised in the same manner? Women were
ornamental and dispensable. It had taken growing up and
expanding my emotional intelligence to unlearn all that crap.

I respected women—not for what they did for men or
how they looked on a man's arm but for who they were. *But*
there was a time when I didn't, and wasn't that the source of
my endless nightmares featuring Pearl?

I snapped back to the conversation with my father,
clenching my jaw to keep my irritation from showing. "Yes,
sir."

"Good." He thoughtfully leaned back in his leather chair
with the kind of self-satisfied smirk that made me want to
walk out of his study and never come back. "Now, I hear
that Luna Steele and Aurora Rhodes were there to witness
the disaster. Luna Steele is...well, let's not get into that. But I
hope you understand how important it is to smooth things
over with the Rhodes family. Aurora Rhodes is married to
Gabe Rhodes, and you know what that means in Savannah."

I knew exactly what that meant. The Rhodes family wasn't merely old money—they were *ancient* money, so entrenched in Savannah society that even my father had to tread carefully around them. Their name was on buildings, schools, and foundations all over the city. To George Vanderbilt, upsetting a Rhodes wasn't just bad manners—it was a social catastrophe.

"Now, we all know she's just some floozy who married into the family, but it appears that she has her mother-in-law's ear," my father continued, "and you know Atticus does whatever Betsy wants. If they hear about this, there will be hell to pay."

I doubted it. I knew Gabe Rhodes, and he didn't give a shit about societal bullshit, not since he decided to tell the world to fuck itself, and married a woman who was an architect, half-black, and not from our elite circle. Betsy cared even less; she always had, but was still a power unto herself, thanks to the backing of the Rhodes name and money.

"Aurora is not the type to go running, complaining to Betsy about every run-in she has with someone." I looked at my glass of scotch, wondering how it would feel to throw it against the wall behind my father where the portrait of my grandfather, George Vanderbilt the Second, hung.

"Now, Dixie May is an airhead, we all know that, but I thought Josie had more sense. You need to do better with her, Rhett." My father's tone took on that faux-paternal quality he used when he was *teaching* me. "You need to make sure she understands how to behave, *and* you need to make it right with Aurora. You make Josie send that woman flowers, write a note, whatever she needs to do. We can't afford to have the Rhodes thinking poorly of us."

"I don't think it was Aurora who she offended." No, I didn't want to hurl this heavy glass on the wall but rather into my father's face. "It was Pearl Beaumont."

My father waved a hand. "No one cares about the Beaumonts, especially *her*. You know, Cash has made some lousy decisions of late, and I hear that Pearl signed away her entire inheritance."

I knew about Cash's poor investments but not about Pearl giving up her inheritance. Was that why she was staying with Aunt Hattie?

I knew Cash well enough to know he wouldn't share those kinds of details with me. He'd rather complain about his sister than show any gratitude for the fact that she'd given him her share of the family wealth. The Beaumonts of the past had made their fortune in real estate, though I'd never dealt with them from a business perspective. I recalled that Pearl's father had passed away when she was still a child, leaving the estate in the hands of trustees who mismanaged it —only for Cash to continue the decline when it eventually fell to him. They weren't the first old-money Savannah family to squander a legacy until there was nothing left for the next generation, and they certainly wouldn't be the last.

"She's staying with Hattie, who we all know is fuckin' crazy," my father continued.

He *never* liked Aunt Hattie, my mother's younger sister. Big surprise there. Harriett "Hattie" Odom was what old, white Southern men called a *problematic* woman. In Savannah, she commanded respect and loyalty, her presence as steady and unyielding as the ancient live oaks. She was fiercely independent and unapologetically strong. She had carved her place in Savannah society through her intelligence, wit, and unwavering sense of self. She was equal parts charm and steel, capable of delivering a razor-sharp observation with a honey-sweet tone.

Unlike other society belles, Hattie never married. She remained single and managed her father's steel mills with him. When he passed, she sold it all and had invested her part of the buyout wisely, so it had grown. Her investments included Pearl's new employer, Savannah Lace, where she sat on the board to support her friend, Nina Davenport.

Unlike the indomitable Harriet Odom, my father had invested my mother's share of the steel mills in ventures that were probably as unwise as Cash Beaumont's.

I wondered if my father realized that, without me, the Vanderbilts would be having the same financial issues as the Beaumonts. If he did, he never thanked me. But then, men like him pretended they were winners even when they were losing.

"This the girl you slept with in high school, isn't it?" he sneered. "Just shows her loose morals."

"And mine," I instantly countered.

My father cocked an eyebrow.

"*We* had sex—*I* was involved."

"You're a man," my father scoffed.

Like hell I'd been a man then. The way I'd behaved with Pearl had not been *manly* at all.

"Anyway." Father looked at his watch. "Time to head to The Alabaster."

I rose, wanting very much not to go to my engagement party. Josie and her mother, along with mine and, in fact, Pearl's, who was Josie's godmother, planned the damn thing and had been making it more elaborate by the minute ever since she got knocked up. They'd chosen, thanks to the Vance fortune, Savannah's most luxurious hotel and a landmark of old Southern grandeur as the venue for the debacle our lives together were going to be.

"Yes, sir," I clipped.

He put his arm around me. "You know, son, you did right with Josie. The Vances are the right kind of family. And like I said, with a little bit of training, I'm sure she'll make you a good wife."

I should've left it right there, but I didn't; I couldn't. "And what does a good wife mean, sir?"

He gave me a look like I'd asked the stupidest question in the world. His arm tightened around my shoulders, a mock show of camaraderie that felt more like a trap.

"A good wife knows her place." His voice dripped with superiority and condescension. "She supports her husband. She knows when to keep her mouth shut. She knows how to look pretty on his arm at events, and how to run a home without bothering him about the details. And if she's smart —well, smart enough—she'll give you sons who know how to carry on the family name."

I stiffened under the weight of his arm, disgust curling in my stomach, almost choking me. His words were so matter-of-fact, as if this was just the way the world worked, like he couldn't fathom there was anything wrong with his worldview.

"Right."

He chuckled as he continued, "Son, these days, women keep saying they want more—a career, their own lives— whatever the hell that means. Let me give you some advice. You don't marry a woman who wants to be *more than* your wife. You marry her *to be* your wife, to complement you. If she starts chasing things outside the marriage, she'll make your life miserable. Mark my words—too much ambition in a wife is a recipe for disaster."

He clapped me on the shoulder as if he'd just passed down tremendous fatherly wisdom. "You'll see, in time, that I'm right. Josie's got the right breeding for this. She just needs a little guidance. That's your job, Rhett."

I didn't reply. What could I possibly say when he acted like we'd just had a perfectly normal conversation? In my father's mind, my job wasn't just to uphold the family name and fortune—it was to mold my wife into some Stepford ideal that would fit neatly into his warped sense of tradition.

"Josie just needs a tighter leash. A Vanderbilt wife needs to understand her place."

God, I hated the way my father talked about women like they were accessories to be managed and displayed; their value tied entirely to how well they played their roles.

"Yes, sir," I lied, shrugging his arm away, because I wanted to break it, as I opened his office door so we could go to the parlor and collect our women, and then head to fuck my life up in front of Savannah society.

"See that you take care of this," he replied, dismissing me with a jerk of his chin as though I were one of his underlings instead of his son.

Making an excuse, I walked out onto the verandah instead of going to Josie because I needed a fucking breather. The air was thick with the smell of blooming magnolias, and the distant hum of cicadas filled the quiet. I wanted to loosen my bowtie, but I knew someone would admonish me for that. It was fucking hot and humid, and I was in a tux that felt too tight and uncomfortable, even though it was tailormade for me.

CHAPTER 6

Pearl

"Wasn't Josie engaged to Dylan Whatsisname?" Rose Dixon, one of Aunt Hattie's friends and, in fact, Gabe Rhodes' cousin, mused as she sipped champagne.

Rose was a few years older than me, so I didn't know her well. But since moving to Savannah, I'd seen more of her. She was close to Aurora, who wasn't at Rhett and Josie's engagement party. Aurora and her husband, Gabe, were in New York, along with their family, celebrating Gabe's daughter Sophie's birthday, combining it with college tours to make the trip extra special.

"Dylan Rafferty," Aunt Hattie provided with a smirk. "He was smart, cheated on her, made sure she dumped him, and then left for Europe, where I hear he's living a charmed life in southern France with a French girl he married."

I arched a brow and offered a sly smile. *"Comme c'est*

charmant." I swirled the champagne in my glass. *How nice for him!*

Hattie tilted her head and replied, "*Mais bien sûr,*" before taking another delicate sip of her champagne. *But of course.*

"So, Dylan dodged a bullet, which I see Rhett walked right in front of?" Rose murmured.

I doubted that. They seemed perfect for each other. *Narcissist weds asshole—a marriage made in Savannah society heaven.*

"Oh, she made sure of that. She got knocked up," Hattie remarked.

I sighed. "Aunt Hattie, stop saying stuff like that and starting unfounded rumors."

"Hush, Pearl, this is good gossip," Rosie admonished. "I have not heard about this. Hit me, Hattie."

"Christ," I groaned. "Why is it that everyone in Savannah gossips so ferociously?"

"Darlin', it's like breathin' for us." Rose fluttered her eyelashes dramatically.

"No shit," I retorted dryly.

Aunt Hattie smacked my arm playfully. "Now, Pearl, be a good girl and take the gossip with grace."

I gave out an exaggerated sigh. "Fine. Go on, Queen Gossip."

"Well, after her engagement ended, she began hanging out with Rhett for emotional support. They got drunk one night and had sex. Then, they dated for a few weeks. When

Rhett was all but ready to dump her bony, shapeless ass, she told him she was knocked up; *bless her heart.*"

"That timing is suspect," Rose concurred. "But Rhett's a big boy. Wasn't he suited up?"

"She brought the suit," Aunt Hattie said with satisfaction.

"How do you know?" I demanded wryly.

"My nephew talks to me." Aunt Hattie grinned.

"You think she sabotaged the rubbers?" Rose was loving every second of this conversation. She had her own real estate business and obviously didn't like women like Josie.

From what I could see, there was a stark divide between the women who worked and those who were only interested in getting married in Savannah—either side couldn't stand the other. I saw nothing wrong with a woman who wanted to make an advantageous marriage (like this was a scene from *Pride and Prejudice),* but I didn't want to be mocked for my choices, either. So, I stayed out of that discussion, if I could help it.

"Actually, I don't know, and neither does Rhett, *but* then she had a miscarriage right after all the announcements were made," Aunt Hattie explained.

"The poor thing," I exclaimed.

"*Please,*" Aunt Hattie muttered, "if she was even pregnant, I'd eat my favorite fascinator."

"She wouldn't lie about that!" I protested.

I had grown up with Josie, so I knew she could be a malicious bitch—but to lie about a baby? *No.* I didn't believe that at all.

"Oh, I could absolutely see her doing that. I mean, think about it," Rose considered. "Women like her are waiting to get married, and she wasted five years of her life with Dylan. Now, she's past her prime—"

"She's my age," I protested.

"Past her prime by Savannah standards," Rose expounded. "I know because I'm almost a dried-up old hag at thirty-four. I love my life and am not interested in getting married."

"That's because you have that friends-with-benefits relationship with...what's his name? That hunky blonde who works for Gabe?" Aunt Hattie queried.

The music changed from classical to jazz. That would be for Rhett, I thought. He was a jazz lover, had been when....

Stop thinking about the past, Pearl! That way lies pain.

"Devon." Rose dropped her empty glass of champagne on the tray of a passing server and picked up a fresh one. She lowered her voice. "So, Hattie, how do you know she lied about the baby?"

I was still nursing my first and only glass. I hated being here, seeing Rhett celebrating getting married, and there was no way I could force food down my throat.

Aunt Hattie gave her a sly look and said in a bad German Gestapo accent, "We have our ways."

"Come on, spill, woman!" Rose demanded good naturedly.

Aunt Hattie only laughed.

I loved Aunt Hattie. She was the embodiment of Southern grace, with her silver-streaked chestnut hair swept into an elegant chignon, and a timeless beauty that had only deepened with age. She was a tall woman who carried herself with the kind of regal poise that turned heads in every room. Her sharp, intelligent eyes missed nothing, and the faintest trace of a knowing smile often played at the corners of her perfectly painted lips.

She knew how to play the game in society, which is why she knew most of what was going on. I didn't aspire to be her, but I was glad I was not on her bad side.

"Does the family know?" I asked.

"Even if they did, they wouldn't believe it. Saint Josie can do no wrong."

"Does Rhett know?" Rose mused.

"He doesn't want to believe it." Aunt Hattie sounded sad. "He's so busy being a Vanderbilt and being controlled by that asshole father of his that he doesn't know how to live his life for himself. I hate that the boy cannot see himself."

"Parents have a strong hold on us," Rose muttered. "I spent a lifetime tryin' to please my mama, and you know she ain't never gonna be happy with me until I'm married and pregnant."

"But you're not going to let them force you into a marriage," Aunt Hattie pointed out.

The music soared and then started to drop off. I thought it was going to be time for announcements and speeches. We'd hear from the happy couple's parents and then the couple themselves, who'd share stories about how they met and how much they loved each other.

Shoot me the fuck now!

"I came close a few years ago...very close." Rose took a deep breath.

"What happened?" I asked.

"*Thankfully*, he dumped me."

"He didn't dump her; she made him," Aunt Hattie explained to me with a twinkle in her eyes.

"How did you do that?" I was curious as hell.

"I made sure he saw Devon fucking my brains out," Rose said happily.

"I want to be just like you when I grow up," I blurted out.

We laughed, and eyes turned to look at us.

One set was *his*.

"Well, a woman has needs," Aunt Hattie declared.

Having been single her whole life, Aunt Hattie lived life to the fullest and had many lovers, some discreet and others not so much.

She reached out to straighten my neckline with a gentle, almost absent-minded touch. "You look gorgeous."

"Thank you." I looked down at my dark blue dress, hoping that it didn't make me look fat. Even now, after all these years, I worried about what people would say, the Savannah people, that is.

"Hello, hello," Suellen, Josie's mother's, voice crackled loudly, followed by the tapping of a finger on a microphone.

"Well," Hattie drawled, her voice low and rich, "looks like the show's about to begin. Try not to roll your eyes too hard, ladies; someone might notice."

Rose and I giggled.

I listened to the speeches and the stories about how Josie and Rhett, the loves of each other's lives, had met with a smile on my face, even though everything inside me was shriveling to see Rhett celebrating life with another woman.

I didn't *love* Rhett, no, he made sure to destroy that innocent affection—but he'd been my first lover, and right here was a reminder of *that*. He'd treated me like dirt but was elevating Josie as his future wife in society. He'd taken my virginity as part of a bet, but he'd given Josie a big fat diamond ring. He'd ridiculed my body and was now with a thin woman.

Now, I was a size six, which by societal standards was considered slim—but when I looked in the mirror, that's not what I saw. I saw every flaw magnified, every imperfection glaring back at me like an accusation.

According to my therapist, having been ridiculed by the boy who I'd given my virginity to, on top of being constantly reminded of it by my mother, classmates, and everyone in society, had led to my body dysmorphia.

My therapist had tried to teach me how to challenge those thoughts, to separate reality from the distorted image my mind conjured up. "*The mirror isn't a fact, Pearl*," she'd said more than once. "*It's a filter. Your brain is showing you what it fears, not what's true.*" But fear was powerful, and it whispered things I couldn't ignore, not when I was standing here feeling every single one of my old wounds rip open.

Rhett had made sure I knew my body was unacceptable back then *after* I'd let him see me naked. God! I'd been so scared he wouldn't find me attractive. We'd been in our family's summerhouse. He'd been sweet, kind, loving, affectionate, everything that I'd ever dreamed a first lover would be. He told me I was beautiful. He was the first person to do so.

To find out after that he'd lied—that it had all been a game, and in reality, he found me hideous, and my *tight virgin hole* was what made it bearable to fuck me—well, that was a poison that got into my bloodstream. That day by the pool had been the beginning of my unraveling, the moment I'd started to honestly believe that my body wasn't good enough.

"Rhett is the best partner a girl could ask for," Josie spoke into the microphone as she looked into Rhett's eyes. They looked perfect together. Beautiful. Confident. I'd bet none of them looked in the mirror or their plate of food and wondered how they could disappear into nothingness.

"I'm the luckiest girl in the world," Josie continued.

"And he's the unluckiest," Aunt Hattie murmured.

Rose chuckled. "You know what they say about marriage?"

We both waited for her to tell us.

"Life is short, marriage is long, drink up."

"That's what Shirley MacLaine said in a movie," Aunt Hattie complained. "You stole it."

"You bet I did, but it's quite apropos."

Rhett came to the microphone then, and his presence silenced the room. He was a handsome man. He had blue eyes, was well-built, and had hair that always looked casually styled but perfect. And that face? God had spent extra time

carving that one up. He looked, not hyperbole here, like a
Greek god.

"I want to thank all of you for coming to celebrate this
occasion with Josie and me. We're grateful for your blessings
and your friendship," he spoke with quiet grace. His voice
was sexy, audiobook dirty hero hot. Josie had landed herself
one hunk of a man.

I could guarantee he was good in bed. If he'd been so
caring and concerned about my pleasure *then* when he was
seventeen, now in his early thirties, after way more experience than most men thanks to how he looked and who he
was, I was sure he'd only gotten better.

Did he remember me? Did he remember my first time?
And if he did, how did he feel about it? Was he disgusted
that he'd had to have sex with someone as huge as me? The
thought twisted in my mind, sharp and relentless, as my eyes
drifted down to my body.

Even now, I couldn't stop the flood of self-criticism. My
thighs felt massive, like they didn't belong to me. My stomach, though flat by most standards, felt convex, pushing
outward in a way that seemed grotesque. My breasts were
too big—not in the way society deemed attractive, but in a
way that made me feel awkward.

The mirror was my enemy. Despite years of therapy, I
avoided it whenever I could, especially when I was naked.
Seeing myself fully exposed wasn't just unpleasant—it was a
trigger, a doorway to the darkest parts of my mind. The
irony wasn't lost on me: the one thing I could never escape
—my own body—was what made me feel the most emotion-

ally unbalanced. It wasn't fair. How could a part of me so intrinsic, so inescapable, feel so foreign and wrong?

No matter how much progress I thought I'd made, in moments like these, I felt like I was back at square one. A war waged inside me, and the battlefield was my reflection.

My hands shook, and I breathed slowly, remembering the tips and tricks I had in my emotional stability toolbox. I focused on what I knew deep down: that Josie's body had nothing to do with mine, that Rhett's choices didn't define my value. I was stronger than my old insecurities, and I wouldn't let them claw their way back into my psyche.

"As you know, Josie and I grew up together, and it's wonderful to see so many of our friends from childhood."

I raised my eyes and found him looking at me all the way across the ballroom.

"I thank each one of you for coming tonight. I hope that after dinner, we can catch up with a drink—and talk about days past, bring up the good memories, make amends where needed."

Josie looked at him squarely and tilted her chin as if asking him to say what she wanted him to.

Rhett cleared his throat. "I'm a fortunate man to be engaged to this beautiful and wonderful woman." He slid an arm around Josie and looked into her eyes.

She went on tiptoe and kissed him.

The crowd clapped.

I blinked hard, trying to hold back the tears that threatened to spill.

"Your body is not the problem, Pearl. It's the story you've

told yourself—the story Rhett's words planted in your mind," I could hear my therapist's voice pulling me back from the edge. *"But your life isn't about Rhett. It never was. You're good enough, and that has nothing to do with him. You don't have to measure up to him, to them, or to anyone else. You're brave. You're free. You're Pearl Beaumont, and you are a warrior."*

I took a deep, shaky breath, forcing myself to straighten my posture.

I wasn't that girl by the pool anymore. I wasn't the joke, the bet, the girl who needed someone else's approval to feel whole.

I was ready to escape after the speeches because I'd had enough. I was walking out of the restroom when I bumped into Sage. I sighed. This evening was *not* getting better.

Sage smiled at me eagerly. "Pearl, it's so nice to see you."

My patience was thin, my nerves frayed. "Can we cut the crap, yeah? We're alone here, and no one can hear you, so you don't have to pretend that—"

"I'm so sorry," she blurted out, speaking over me. "I was horrible to you. It has...it has haunted me. Rhett, too. I am really sorry, Pearl."

Her eyes filled with tears, and I took a step back, away from her. "What game are you playing?" I didn't trust this woman, not at all.

She looked at me sadly. "I'm not. I swear." She jerked her head to a door that led outside, where several guests were spread out. "Please, can I have a few minutes of your time?"

She looked so sincere and devastated that I didn't have the heart to turn her down. I nodded. We stepped outside and found a quiet corner with tables and chairs. We sat at one.

Sage rubbed her hands together. She looked good, like she always had. She never had to worry about her weight. She also looked older—more than I did, in fact.

"You know I got married," she began, "to a guy who was supposed to be *perfect,* he came with the Savannah society stamp of approval."

I folded my arms and leaned back. She wanted to talk, I'd let her.

"The marriage was a disaster. We were toxic. We fought. We threw things at each other. We...were physically abusive."

"Oh my God. I'm so sorry." I put a hand on her shoulder, hating that anyone had to experience physical abuse.

"We *both* were. Though he was stronger than me," Sage said, and then tears started to flow down her cheeks. "Even now, you want to comfort me? What I said to you and about you, Pearl, you should be applauding that terrible things happened to me because I definitely deserved it."

I pulled my hand away from her and frowned. "No one deserves that. And how would my enjoying your tragedy improve my situation?"

Sage plucked a napkin from the holder on the table and wiped her eyes. "But even before that, Rhett and I...after what happened with you, we changed. I—"

"Sage, you were the one who told the girls on the debate team about what Rhett did," I reminded her.

Look, I was all about people apologizing, if that was their jam, but no way was she rewriting history.

"Yes," she admitted. "It was like, I'd already screwed up so go for bust." She shook her head in self-disgust. "But I grew up. So did Rhett."

I arched an eyebrow. "I doubt that. He's marrying Miss Josie Vance."

Sage laughed without humor. "I tried to tell him that he was entering the same kind of marriage I had—maybe less violent. That he'd eventually end up divorced like me or live unhappily until death did them part."

"Sage, what do you want to say to me?" I rose then. I wasn't here to be drawn into chit-chat about Rhett and Josie. I didn't want to be *that* woman who gossiped and wished ill on others.

"That I'm sorry. That what I did was wrong, horrible. That I'm a better person now, and I'm working to be even more so."

I nodded. "I'm happy for you, Sage."

She licked her lips, waiting for me to say the words I knew she wanted to hear.

"Thank you for being honest with me," I continued, "and because you have been so candid, so will I. Your apology does nothing to change my life—it doesn't amend what I was put through as a young woman and how it has defined my life in some very ugly ways. If you're expecting forgiveness from me, it's not coming. I can't forgive you, not because I'm carrying hate or anger for you, but because I can't condone what you did. You talk like you were oh so young and foolish, but Sage, we're both the same age. I never hurt you or anyone else on purpose, but all of you did what you did, maliciously and with the intent to harm me. So, I'm glad you're working on yourself, but you'll have to continue to do so without my involvement."

Sage nodded as if she understood, shame written over her face. "I understand. I...I hope we can be friends...or friendly."

I shook my head. "We can be acquaintances," I offered.

"I'll take it." She got up then, and nodded at me. "Thank you for hearing me out, Pearl. That was generous of you."

I felt like a petty bitch for not forgiving her and saying, "*Hey, it's okay, it's in the past.*" But that would be a lie, and I wouldn't, couldn't say it. I had to be honest with myself, and pretending like what was done to me was no big deal was not good for my mental health, which, since I came back to Savannah, was hanging by a thread.

CHAPTER 7

Rhett

"Lunch?" I asked Pearl as we walked out of a conference room at Savannah Lace.

I didn't really need to attend this meeting. I had an efficient team that could handle a project this size. However, I decided to take it on, which surprised some of my team members. They assumed it was because of my Aunt Hattie's closeness to Nina Davenport.

The truth was more straightforward. I was hoping and praying for a chance to apologize, truly this time, to Pearl. She'd never forgive me, I knew that, and I didn't deserve it either, but she needed to know that I'd been wrong, so very wrong. She needed to know that the flawed person, in our sordid history, was me, not her. And, I needed her to know that I wasn't *that* boy any longer, that I had become a decent man.

After Sage told me how her conversation with Pearl went, it was evident to me that the past preyed on Pearl as it did me. If I could in any way reduce that burden for her, I would.

But what will you do if she needs you to stay away from her? I didn't have an answer to that question, so I stayed on course.

Before Pearl could reply to my lunch request *and* most probably turn me down, I heard Nina Davenport, the CEO of Savannah Lace, say from behind me, "She can't, I'm afraid. There's a finance team lunch meeting, but I'd love to go with you."

I didn't miss the grateful look Pearl threw Nina's way.

How the hell was I going to make this right if I didn't get an opportunity to talk to Pearl? Apparently, no one gave a flying fuck, and I got it. The need to apologize was mine, and as always, I was pushing with a single-minded focus on what *I* needed. Perhaps Pearl didn't need me bugging her. *But* if only she'd give me some time, so I could....

"Where should we go?" Nina asked.

She was an imposing woman—tall, with sharp features softened just slightly by an elegant sweep of dark hair. Everything about her radiated control, from the tailored navy pantsuit she wore to the deliberate, measured way she spoke. Nina Davenport was Savannah, through and through—polished, commanding, and rooted in tradition, but smart enough to bend with the times.

"The Collins Quarter?" I suggested an eatery I'd been to a handful of times. It had a central location and a professional vibe. It was only a short walk from Savannah Lace, tucked along Bull Street.

Nina nodded. "Perfect. I'm in the mood for their smashed avocado toast, which is always en pointe."

As we walked, I glanced back over my shoulder to catch a glimpse of Pearl. Nina noticed out of the corner of her eye, but if she had an opinion, she didn't voice it. Instead, she strode ahead with confidence, knowing I'd follow.

The Collins Quarter was just busy enough to feel alive without being chaotic. The hum of conversation blended with soft jazz playing from overhead speakers, and spring sunlight poured in through tall windows, spreading warm shadowy patches across the polished wood floors. The smell of fresh coffee and herbs lingered in the air as servers in crisp white shirts moved efficiently between tables.

We were seated by the window. The server handed us menus, but I already knew what I was ordering—grilled chicken salad with lemon vinaigrette. Nina glanced at the menu briefly before closing it neatly and placing it on the edge of the table.

"Smashed avocado toast," she told the waiter. "Add a poached egg, please."

The waiter nodded and looked at me expectantly.

"Grilled chicken salad." I handed him my menu.

After he left, Nina turned her piercing blue eyes on me. "I think we both know this lunch isn't about the project, Rhett." Her tone was even but pointed.

I hesitated for a moment, unsure how to respond. Nina wasn't the type of woman you could sidestep with charm or vague answers. But I wasn't ready to *submit*, either. "No?"

Her lips curved. "Hattie and I have a bet. Want to hear about it?"

"No, thank you," I said seriously.

Nina snickered. "Okay, that's smart of you, considering your aunt is absolutely *one flew over the cuckoo's nest.*"

"You said it, not me." I raised my hands in a sign of peace, amused. She wasn't wrong about my aunt.

"Why are you here, Rhett? And don't tell me it's about the project because you and I both know you didn't need to take this one yourself."

I guess we're done with small talk, I thought with a sigh.

I leaned back in my chair, my gaze dropping to the tabletop for a moment before meeting hers again. Nina didn't flinch. She wasn't angry or accusing, just direct. I *usually* liked that about her.

"I want to apologize to Pearl," I admitted finally. "*Properly*, this time."

"What happened the last time?" she asked.

"I was disappointed that she didn't accept my apology since I got off my high horse and gave it to her," I said in self-deprecation.

"Oh, Rhett! Sometimes I forget that you used to be a spoiled rich boy like so many others continue to be."

I picked up the wooden saltshaker and then set it down. "I was more than spoiled, Nina; I was cruel and entitled. This wasn't just about buying a car I wanted, yeah? It was...." I shook my head, not sure how to tell her or anyone that inside me was this horrible feeling that, even though I'd worked on myself, I'd never be able to remove the taint of my youth that came from doing what I had to Pearl.

I felt the weight of her scrutiny. "Since I like you, despite your youthful indiscretions, what the fuck are you tryin' to achieve by stirrin' up things that Pearl clearly doesn't want to talk to you about?"

Like I said, Nina was *direct*. She didn't pussyfoot.

I opened my mouth to respond, but she held up a hand to stop me.

"Here is what I know. Pearl's working very hard to rebuild her life. She doesn't need you barging in with your guilt and good intentions, throwing her off balance. So, I'm going to ask you again—what are you trying to achieve?"

I swallowed hard, the words catching in my throat. Nina's gaze didn't waver. It wasn't angry or cruel—just firm, unrelenting. I felt like I was being dressed down by a professor who knew I hadn't done the assigned reading.

I sighed. "Do you know what happened when we were teenagers?"

Nina shook her head. "I've been busy building a company and have not been in tune with Savannah gossip. Hattie mentioned that Pearl left because of an incident involving you. I didn't pry."

She wouldn't. Even now, if I glossed over the past, she'd let it be. Nina wasn't one to dig into people's secrets; she was more interested in their present intentions.

"The incident *was* me," I began. "I was seventeen; Pearl's a year younger than me. I...we had sex. No, actually, we became friends...well, I was...*fuckin' hell*."

I ran a hand through my hair.

"Spit it out," Nina instructed.

I chuckled. "I convinced her that she could trust me, and then had sex with her. I won a bet doin' that."

Nina made a face. "Well, that's horrible and disgusting, even for an entitled son of a bitch."

"Oh, but it gets worse."

"How?" she prompted, her eyes narrow with disgust.

"I said some terrible things about her afterward...about her weight. She overheard me. *And* since I had done the *telling* in front of lots of other people, it ruined her reputation. She didn't deserve any of it, and I can't undo what I did. But I need her to know that I regret it. That I was wrong. I know I can't make it right, but I just...I want her to hear it from me."

Nina was silent for a moment, her sharp gaze never leaving mine. Finally, she crossed her legs with the grace of someone who could disarm an entire boardroom with a single glance.

"I appreciate your honesty." She continued to study me, probably trying to measure the truth behind my words. After a moment, she gave a slight, deliberate nod as if she'd found what she was looking for. "I believe you when you say you regret your actions. But what *you* need doesn't appear to align with what *she* needs—*or* wants. From where I'm sitting, it doesn't look like Pearl is ready to have this conversation with you."

"I just want her to know I've changed." My voice was

hoarse as I tamped down my emotions, my need to shake Nina so she'd understand where I was coming from.

Nina tilted her head slightly. "Maybe you have changed. And maybe, one day, Pearl will be ready to hear that. But it has to be on *her* terms, not *yours*. You can't bulldoze her into forgiving you, and you sure as hell can't do it where she works."

The server returned with our food, breaking the tension for a brief moment. I nodded politely as he set my salad in front of me, but I couldn't bring myself to pick up my fork.

Nina, on the other hand, picked up her knife and began slicing into her toast with the same precision she brought to this conversation. She didn't rush, didn't push. She let the silence hang for a moment before speaking again.

"For what it's worth"—she glanced up at me—"Rhett, I've always thought you were smart and driven, and more capable than your father gives you credit for. But that doesn't mean I'll stand by and let you hurt Pearl, even unintentionally."

I'd expected Nina to be protective of Pearl, but I hadn't expected her to handle me with such firm grace. She wasn't angry, she was measured and controlled. And she was right.

"Understood," I accepted quietly.

"Good." She gave me a small, approving smile. "Now, let's talk shop. So, how much is this upgrade going to cost me?"

I grinned. "Well, you know how they say that you have to spend money to make money?"

"That's what *they* say?"

"Yes, they most certainly do. Let me break it down for you." We talked shop, and Nina didn't bring up Pearl throughout the rest of our conversation.

When I walked her back to Savannah Lace, I didn't go inside the building as I wanted to—because Nina was right.

I had to respect Pearl's need for space and time.

I also had to accept the possibility that she might never give me the chance to apologize—and that I'd have to live with my guilt forever.

CHAPTER 8
Pearl

One of the fantastic things about leaving Savannah was not having to attend the Beaumont family dinners. If you lived in Los Angeles, no one expected you to show up for family time at the Beaumont estate, which always felt like a performance, one I had no interest in participating in.

Like always, the long mahogany dining table gleamed under the soft glow of the chandelier, and the sterling silverware was arranged as though we were expecting royalty instead of having just another suffocating family gathering.

My mother sat at the head of the table, her back as straight as the chair she'd occupied for the past forty years. Cash was at the other end, leaning into his self-appointed role as patriarch with all the smugness of someone who thought he'd inherited a throne instead of a crumbling family legacy.

I was seated between Alice and Madeline—my saving

grace at family events since they were born. I adored my nieces, and the feeling was mutual. They were clever, quick-witted, and full of teenage rebellion that kept their parents perpetually exasperated. Tonight, they were trying not to laugh too loudly at whatever it was that Alice whispered under her breath about Cash, who had just launched into another long-winded lecture about the problem with the youth of today expecting handouts.

It went along the lines of, *"In our day, we had to work for what we had...blah, blah, blah."*

All bullshit because Cash had inherited the family fortune, including most of mine, which I'd happily given away—and he'd still managed to fuck it up. He thought I didn't know, but I did. I was a freaking finance director, and as a Beaumont, I still got the quarterly reports. Cash, despite his name, wasn't good with money, but God, did he pretend he was.

"Girls," Caroline hissed, her pearl necklace catching the light as she shot us a withering glare, the same pearl necklace she'd be clutching any second now. "Stop tittering at the table. It's unseemly."

"Sorry, Mom." Alice did not sound remotely apologetic as she pressed her lips together to stifle a grin. Maddie elbowed me gently, her eyes sparkling with mischief.

"Honestly, Pearl," Cash said, turning his disapproving gaze on me. "Do you always have to encourage them? They need a role model, not a bad influence."

"I'm a bad influence?" I raised an eyebrow. "Pray, tell me, how?"

"Because you don't take anything seriously," he shot back, cutting into his steak with far more force than necessary. "And let's not even get started on your so-called career."

I felt Alice stiffen beside me, and Maddie's playful grin faded. I forced a smile, even as my chest tightened. "My so-called career pays my bills, Cash, since I gave you most of my inheritance, remember?"

I wasn't passive-aggressive; oh no, in the past decade, I'd become aggressive-aggressive. I refused to take any bullshit from anyone—at least on the surface. I was faking confidence and *hutzpah* until I actually had it.

Cash had called me in Los Angeles, saying that he needed me to reinvest my inheritance into the family business to save the Beaumont family name. He made it sound like it was my duty. Lucky for him, I didn't want to be burdened by the *family legacy*. The more I took from the Beaumont coffers, the more they'd try to control me.

I wished Cash had been honest with me and said that he'd overleveraged several properties, taken out massive loans, and made some terrible investments that hadn't paid off. Real estate was a volatile game, and Cash had bet big—on luxury condos during a downturn, on high-risk commercial developments that went belly-up, and even on a golf resort in the middle of nowhere that no one wanted to visit. Instead, he'd all but demanded that I *save* the business. He couldn't sell his part of the company because he had children, while I, the loser, didn't have any offspring to worry about.

Then, I'd helped him out with an open heart. Now, as I

watched Cash act like the king of the Beaumont empire, I wondered if I'd made a mistake by letting him throw *my* good money after bad. He hadn't saved the legacy. The quarterly reports told me the real story: unpaid debts, declining property values, shrinking margins. The empire was crumbling, and Cash had the nerve to sit here and act like I was the one who didn't take things seriously.

"Don't be defensive, Pearl," Mama chimed in. "Your brother is only trying to help. You wouldn't need to work at all if you'd simply made better choices. Now that you're not fat any longer, I thought you'd do the right thing and find yourself a beau, but—"

I set my fork down, the sharp clink against my plate louder than I'd intended. "Mama, we've discussed this enough times now for you to know how this conversation ends. Do we *really* need to do it all over again?"

Birdie Beaumont's lips pursed, an unmistakable and familiar sign of her displeasure with me. "I don't understand why you're so stubborn. There's nothing wrong with making a good match, Pearl. Josie has done quite well for herself, and she'll make an excellent wife for Rhett. Not everyone is content to...what is it you do again?"

"Mama, I work in finance, and I'm good at it. My goal in life is not to marry some wealthy, vapid Savannah socialite and spend my days planning luncheons and charity events." I loosened my grip on the stem of my wine glass before I broke the damn thing.

"Oh, but you think working for Nina Davenport is a

good thing?" Caroline now took over the *let's hammer on Pearl* part of the dinner.

This was the age-old battle that women participated in, weakening our gender's ability to succeed. "I don't know what your problem is with Nina having her own company—she's never insulted *your* choices or those of women who want to be homemakers."

"We're more than homemakers," Caroline ground out, her jaw tight. "We help the society at large."

"So does Nina. Savannah Lace employs a large number of people, and—"

"Enough!" Mama banged a hand on the table. We all stared at my mother. She pursed her lips and cleared her throat. "Pearl, I know you think you're being some fancy independent woman, but what you're being is lonely."

"I'm alone, Mama, not lonely."

Cash sighed, shaking his head. "You know, Pearl, if you'd just listen to us, you'd actually get somewhere."

Before I could speak, quiet Maddy mused innocently, "What does getting somewhere mean, Daddy?"

"That means," Cash said, trying to sound superior, "Pearl would be married and have kids by now. Instead, she chose to run away to the West Coast and now works for a company that is not considered serious in the field—just Nina's minions playing *Designing Women*."

The condescension was just too much. I knew I was about to lose my temper and say things I would regret, so I shut up. My stress levels were remarkably high right now, and I wanted to throw up the food I'd eaten.

"Daddy, I know Bianca Davenport, and she told me how her mother built that Savannah Lace from the ground up," Alice remarked. "Miss Davenport is smart, successful, and honestly, pretty admirable. I want to be just like her when I grow up."

Caroline was about to scream the house down when Mama put her *foot* down.

"Let's eat *one* meal in peace, shall we?" Mama's tone carried a familiar note of maternal disappointment. "I don't know, Pearl, we were doing fine before you came back to Savannah. Now, every time we meet as a family, it's like this,"

"Then, Mama, I, from now on, have a plausible reason to decline your future invitations to family dinners," I said without inflection, burying the hurt of my family's not wanting me deep inside. I looked at my plate and knew I wouldn't be able to eat another bite.

The table fell into an awkward silence, broken only by the clink of silverware. I glanced at Alice and Maddie, who both gave me supportive smiles.

"Anyway," Birdie said after a moment, her voice taking on a lighter, more performative tone as she turned to Caroline. "Josie called me this afternoon. She and Rhett are thinking about having their wedding at the Historic Savannah Club. Such a lovely venue."

"You know Josie, she has such an eye for these things. She was responsible for the last Garden Committee event, and it was beautiful," Caroline agreed, her smile saccharine. "Rhett is lucky to have her."

I felt a knot form in my stomach. It wasn't jealousy—not

of Josie, not of Rhett, not even of their engagement—it was exhaustion. I was tired of never measuring up to whatever impossible and unknown standard my family had set. I'd felt it my entire life, first in the way they talked about my weight and now in the way they dismissed my choices, my independence, my career.

"What do you think, Pearl?" Caroline persisted, and I saw malice in her eyes. *Everyone* knew about what happened that summer between Rhett and me. This was her way of reminding me.

"About what?" I asked nonchalantly, not wanting to give Caroline the pleasure of seeing anything resembling my true feelings on my face and in my demeanor.

"You know about what," Caroline retorted. "Now, don't be bitter, Pearl. You'll find someone eventually, maybe once you adjust your attitude."

Alice and Maddie both turned to me, their eyes wide, waiting to see how I'd respond. I smiled at them, a genuine smile this time. "That sounds like a whole lot of work, and right now, I already have a full-time job," I joked, meeting Caroline's gaze head-on.

Cash sighed loudly as if the weight of being the Beaumont patriarch was almost too much to bear. "This is exactly what I mean, Pearl. You're thirty-one years old. Maybe it's time to grow up."

I opened my mouth to respond but then decided it wasn't worth it.

"I think Aunt Pearl is the coolest person I know," Maddie breathed.

"I agree." Alice gripped my hand in hers.

"Girls, this has nothing to do with you," Caroline muttered with fake patience.

"It kinda does, Mama," Maddie continued thoughtfully. "I want to go to college and be an academic. Will you have a problem with me working? It's 2024; we don't expect women to stay home barefoot and pregnant, do we?"

"Darlin', you'll be wearing Jimmy Choos and not be barefoot," Caroline snapped.

Maddy sighed. "That's not what I...." She trailed off and smiled wanly at me.

We fell silent again, and by the time dessert was served—some lemon meringue pie that Birdie insisted was *just divine*—I'd had enough. I bid everyone farewell, but I wasn't lucky because Cash insisted on walking me to my car.

"Pearl, I don't want you to think that I don't appreciate what you did for the family." When Cash and I were alone, our dynamic was different than when he was with the others, demanding I anoint him as patriarch.

"I know, Cash," I said wearily.

"Ah, you know, Lev Steele seems to be in the market for a wife," he continued, "I think that—"

"Lev and I are friendly," I cut him off, "but we're *never* going to date."

"Why not?" Cash tucked into the pockets of his slacks.

"Because I'm not attracted to him." I put a hand on my brother's shoulder. "Cash, I like my life. I don't *ever* feel that I need a man or children in it to feel good about it. It's *already* good. I know you don't understand that, and that's fine, but I need you to stop harping on about it 'cause, if it continues, I'm not going to come over and pretend we're a happy family."

Cash took a deep breath. "I'm a traditionalist, Pearl."

"I respect that and the choices *you* made; you should offer me the same courtesy."

Cash hugged me then, surprising me. "I'll try."

I pulled away and smiled at him. He was nearly seventeen years older than me and had almost been a parent while I was growing up, since our father died when I was so young.

"That's all any of us can do," I said to him.

As I drove home, I wondered if coming to Savannah was a mistake. Then I thought about the people I worked with, I thought of Aunt Hattie, and knew it wasn't. I loved it here. This was my home, and I wouldn't let Rhett, or my family, drive me away.

My mother acted like she was concerned about my single status, but I knew she wasn't. She was disappointed. The fact that I didn't want to get married and wasn't interested in playing the role of some Stepford wife who planned charity galas and lived for compliments about her party-throwing skills wasn't me.

Why was happiness designated as getting married and having kids? The truth was that I didn't want to have children. Still, you couldn't say that because the minute you did, people wanted to know if it was because you couldn't *physiologically* have kids—and if you said that wasn't the case, you were branded as being selfish since you didn't want to propagate the human race.

If I ever met a man who I wanted to be with, I wouldn't get married—I'd love and cherish and live with my partner, but I wouldn't want to wear a white dress, sign marriage documents, or change my last name. And I didn't want to have children. It was a personal choice, but in Savannah, that would be seen as blasphemous.

Aunt Hattie had gone through the ridicule her single status caused when she chose to live the life she did—it hadn't been easy. But now, at the age of fifty-five, she didn't give a flying fuck, as she put it, and she'd live her life the way she wanted, and everyone else *could go stuff their stuffiness where the sun don't shine.*

CHAPTER 9

Rhett

I had agreed to attend the Savannah Lace summer party at Forsyth Park to avoid going to a Vance party. Josie had been disappointed, but when I lied that this was about work and networking, she relented. However, she made sure I understood that these priorities would have to shift after we were married.

Every day with Josie was a trial. She insisted that we move in together, but I held off, wanting to wait until we were married...or maybe *never*.

I looked around at the long stretches of green lawn dotted with picnic tables and tents. The live oaks gave the whole scene a quintessentially Southern feel. A section of the park had been set up for softball, complete with bases marked out in chalk and a small set of bleachers that were already half-filled with laughing Savannah Lace employees, their partners, and families, holding plastic cups of beer, lemonade, and sweet tea. There was a food truck serving tacos parked near the edge of the field and another one doling out ice cream that already had a long line. It was relaxed and easy, tempting even Savannah's elite to loosen their ties and trade their summer linen suits for casual button-ups and sneakers.

I stood near the first baseline, sipping an iced tea and watching the game in progress. My team had just finished a close one—too close for my liking—and I was grateful for a break to catch my breath and observe.

As I'd gotten used to doing in the past months since Pearl came back to Savannah, I sought her out. She was leaning against the outfield fence. Her hair was pulled back into a loose ponytail, and she was wearing shorts and a tank top. She looked good. There had been many changes in Pearl since I used to know her—but hadn't we all grown up since we were teenagers?

Pearl carried herself with more confidence. Was it because she'd lost all that weight? I never had a problem with her curves. I liked them. Even when I was a stupid teenager, I thought she was beautiful. How different would our lives have been if I'd had the courage and conviction to tell the world that Pearl was my girlfriend all those years ago by the pool?

"You know, it's rude to stare," a voice said from behind me, cutting through my thoughts.

I dragged my eyes away from Pearl. I had been caught staring, lingering over her beautiful face, the curve of her generous lips.

I turned to find the owner of the voice. Luna Steele was

taking a sip from her water bottle. I couldn't tell if she was annoyed—her aviator sunglasses, reflecting the park in miniature, hid her eyes and any hint of emotion behind them.

Luna was usually impossible to miss—her biker-babe chic style always stood out, even among Savannah's polished elite. Today, she wore tight black shorts, a fitted tank top that showed off her intricate tattoos and sculpted shoulders, and a pair of well-worn sneakers. She had that kind of effortless cool that drew people in, even though she had no hesitation telling you exactly what she thought, whether you liked it or not.

"I wasn't staring," I defended myself, but the way she grinned told me she didn't believe me for a second. It also told me she wasn't angry with me, just amused.

"Sure, you weren't." She took another long sip of her water before glancing back toward the field.

I shrugged.

"My brother speaks highly of you," she told me.

I nodded, smiling stiffly. I knew Lev Steele well—he was part of Royal's friend circle, and I'd recently started to spend time with Lev, his friend Dominic Calder, and a few others. "I have a lot of respect for Lev."

Lev was a few years older than me, so we didn't interact much in high school and went to different colleges after.

"You know I have no filter, right?" Luna tilted her head as she studied me.

"It may have been mentioned." I was unable to keep a smile from tugging at my lips.

Luna smirked. "Yeah, I'm not much for sugarcoating. But I'll admit, you're a bit of a surprise."

"How?" I was genuinely curious.

She set the water bottle at her feet and stretched her arms over her head. "You're not what I expected."

"What did you expect?"

"An asshole, based on your reputation."

"That was many years ago." I wasn't being defensive but rather explaining where I was coming from. Hadn't we all done things we regretted when we were young and foolish? "I'm not proud of who I was back then."

Luna looked at me speculatively as if trying to gauge the sincerity of my words, just as Nina had done a few weeks ago when I took her to lunch. Finally, she nodded. "Not many of us are."

We stood in silence for a moment, watching the game as one of the players hit a grounder to second base. The crowd cheered, and someone yelled for the runner to slide. My attention drifted to Pearl. She was cheering, too, her voice bright over the crowd's noise. Or maybe I could hear her because I wanted to.

"You're engaged to Josie Vance."

"Yes."

"Then I suggest you stop watching Pearl like she's a tasty morsel and you haven't eaten in a while."

I was too stunned for a moment to say anything.

"I told you, no filter," Luna informed me cheerfully.

I hesitated, unsure how much I wanted to admit to a friend of Pearl's, but then threw caution to the winds. "I regret hurting Pearl. I know there is no way to change the past, and I'm not seeking her forgiveness. What I did was the worst kind of bullying. In any case, it looks like she got over it."

"Does it?" Luna cocked an eyebrow. "How did you figure that out?"

There was heat in her voice, and I wasn't sure what to make of it. "She told me."

"And you believe her?"

I considered her question and then shook my head. "No, I don't. But she wants me to, and what the hell else can I do?"

Luna nodded slowly. "Pearl is strong. Stronger than she realizes, sometimes. But she's also had to deal with a lot of crap from people who were supposed to care about her," she paused, turning to face me fully, "which includes her family *and* you."

"I know," I said quietly.

"You know, I can't reconcile the man you seem to be now with the kid I've heard about."

I gave her a small, humorless smile. "I can't either, honestly."

Luna's lips twitched into a smile. "Well, good luck figuring it out." She picked up her water bottle and drank it empty. She three-pointed it expertly into a trash can. "And Rhett?"

"Yeah?"

"You're engaged to another woman; if you want what I

think you want, you're going to have to go against God and all of Savannah society. You may have changed, grown up and all that, but the fact that you're engaged to that crazy, lunatic bitch tells me you're still more *that* boy than the man you want to be."

With that declaration, she walked away from me.

I watched her for a long moment, contemplating what she'd said before turning my gaze back to Pearl. Luna was right. About several things. First, I was engaged to a crazy, lunatic bitch, and that said more about me than my fiancée. Also, while I was engaged to another woman, I had no business staring at a woman hungrily. I was *not* a cheat.

But is looking cheating? Yes, it is when your intentions are not platonic.

Fuck!

So, I was all but cheating on the fiancée that I didn't want. Could my life be more of a shitshow?

Since I didn't have a solution for where my life was at, I focused on the ball game instead of the woman who had been crowding my dreams, nightmares, and conscious mind for the past months.

The late afternoon sun was relentless as I rolled the softball in my hand, weighing its familiar heft. The game had been surprisingly competitive—Savannah Lace employees didn't mess around. Both teams were hooting, shit-talking, and shouting encouragement from the sidelines as we neared the last inning.

Since I *was* trying hard to avoid looking at her, the

universe decided to throw *me* a curve ball. Pearl was up to bat.

I stood on the makeshift pitcher's mound, gripping the ball, as I watched her step up to the plate. Her hands were wrapped around the bat, and her stance was solid.

My focus, to the detriment of my team, was on her cut-off shorts and those gorgeous legs that went all the way up *and* down. Her sneakers dug slightly into the dirt as she planted her feet. Her ponytail swung slightly as she glanced at me, a teasing smirk pulling at her lips.

"Hey, Vanderbilt, don't mess this up," Diego Perez, one of Savannah Lace's partners and a member of my team, called out.

"Not gonna," I said cockily. "You wanna slow ball since you're...you know, not too experienced playin' ball?" I was going to treat her, I decided, as I had been all the other players. Easy, comfortable, and casual.

"Don't go easy on me, Vanderbilt," Pearl called out, her voice carrying over the chatter of the crowd around us.

I grinned despite myself, shifting my weight. "Wouldn't dream of it, Beaumont."

The outfielders shifted slightly, readying themselves as I wound up. The ball left my hand with a clean arc, spinning toward her just over the plate. Pearl swung, the sound of the crack sharp and satisfying as the ball soared into the air.

"Go, go, go!" Nina shouted.

Pearl dropped the bat and took off like a shot, her sneakers kicking up small puffs of dirt as she sprinted toward first base. The ball arched high into the sky, heading toward left field, where one of my teammates fumbled the catch.

"Run, Pearl!" Luna's voice rang out from the sidelines, followed by cheers and laughter from her team.

Pearl rounded first base and barreled toward second, her ponytail flying behind her as the outfielder scrambled to recover the ball.

"Throw it in!" I yelled, gesturing wildly toward the infield, but the roar of the crowd drowned out my voice.

By the time the ball reached the shortstop, Pearl was already diving into third, a cloud of dust rising around her as she hit the base. I worried she'd hurt herself, but she stood up quickly, her grin wide and triumphant as she glanced toward home plate.

"Go for it, Pearl!" one of her teammates yelled, and the crowd erupted into a frenzy of cheering.

I jogged toward home, bracing myself as the catcher took position behind me. The outfielder was throwing the ball back in now, but Pearl had already taken off, sprinting down the baseline with a determination that made my chest tighten.

"Tag her, Rhett!" someone on my team shouted, but I was frozen, caught somewhere between watching the ball and watching Pearl.

The ball came flying toward me, but Pearl's sneakers hit the plate a fraction of a second before the ball landed in my glove. She skidded to a stop, laughing and breathless, her hands on her knees as her team exploded into cheers behind her.

"*Safe!*" the umpire called, and the crowd roared.

Pearl's teammates rushed the field, surrounding her with high-fives and shouts of celebration.

"That's what I'm talking about!" Luna yelled, pulling Pearl into a playful hug.

I couldn't stop smiling as I jogged back toward the mound, shaking my head. My team groaned good-naturedly, a few of them muttering about needing new outfielders.

Pearl glanced over at me, her cheeks flushed, her eyes bright with the kind of joy that was impossible to fake.

Luna was right about me, I thought, as an epiphany struck me.

Back then, as a teenager, I'd buried how I felt about Pearl beneath layers of cowardice and cruelty, convincing myself that fitting in with my so-called friends mattered more than the truth. They had mocked her, betrayed her, humiliated her—and I'd let their voices drown my feelings, too scared to stand up and admit what was in my heart. It had been easier to join them than to risk being cast out.

Now, standing on this makeshift softball field with the sound of laughter and cheers echoing around me, I knew that I hadn't changed as much as I wanted to believe. I was still a coward, still hiding behind the mask of the man everyone expected me to be. I was engaged to a woman I didn't like, playing the role of someone who had it all together, all the while, the one person I truly wanted—had *always* wanted—stood just twenty feet away, celebrating a victory with a grin so bright it made her eyes sparkle like stars.

As I watched Pearl, laughing and radiant, something inside me unfurled, something I could no longer ignore. I'd spent years running from the truth, and the truth was Pearl. It had *always* been Pearl.

CHAPTER 10

Pearl

S ix months! That's how long it had been since I
returned to Savannah. I'd never thought I'd have
the courage to come back. I never thought I'd want
to. For me, it was a reminder of trauma—but now, as the
days passed, that had changed. I was adapting to my new
reality. Savannah wasn't just a ghost town of memories
anymore. I could now exist without constantly looking over
my shoulder, waiting for the past to ambush me.

But old insecurities clung to me like Spanish moss. Even
now, sometimes, I'd find myself looking at a dress in a shop
window, and I was, once again, the fat girl who hated to buy
clothes because nothing looked good on me—and when I
did find the one thing I could stand to wear, I was made
fun of.

As a teenager, I'd stopped socializing, afraid of being
ridiculed. It was no wonder I preferred reading a book rather
than going to a party.

Now, as I stood under the shade of a tree in Aunt Hattie's garden in a dark blue sundress, my hands were itching to smooth my dress over my hips, my belly, to feel that I had less flesh, there was *less* of me, less of teenage Pearl.

I felt so out of place, but when the party was taking place at my doorstep, I couldn't hide.

Aunt Hattie's estate was old Savannah grandeur at its finest. It was a sprawling plantation-style home with a wide, white-columned porch that wrapped around the house. The well-maintained lawns stretched for acres, dotted with vibrant gardens and a shimmering pond in the distance. That same pond greeted me every morning, its glassy surface visible from the porch and windows of the cottage where I lived.

When I first considered moving to Savannah, I assumed that staying in a cottage in the Odom Estate would be temporary. However, I liked it a lot, and so did Aunt Hattie, so we decided to make it semi-permanent.

We ate dinner several days a week together at *her* place, and her housekeeper, Missy, also took care of my cottage. It was like I *finally* had a family member who loved me unconditionally for who I was, not who I *could* be if I lost weight, became more outgoing, or—

"Some party," Diego Perez broke my reverie.

He worked with Anson Larue, a real estate developer who worked with Savannah Lace and shared office space with us.

Diego, like me, had been born and raised in Savannah and, like me, had left. He'd moved back when his friend

Anson offered him a job. Now, he commuted between Sentinel, where Larue Constructions' headquarters were, and Savannah, where he lived. We'd become friendly as our offices were close to one another.

"Aunt Hattie knows how to throw a party," I agreed.

Harriet Odom never did anything halfway, which is why red, white, and blue bunting draped the verandah rails, enormous floral arrangements spilling over with roses and hydrangeas sat on nearly every surface, and strings of fairy lights zigzagged between the oaks, ready to come alive as soon as the sun set. On the porch, a live jazz band played a slow, sultry tune, their brass notes mingling with the chatter and laughter of the gathered crowd.

The BBQ was what you'd picture when you thought of July Fourth cookouts—luxury edition. There were grills out back, manned by chefs in crisp white aprons, but they were flipping steaks and salmon instead of burgers and hot dogs. Lobster rolls sat next to artfully plated slaw, and a long buffet table covered in white linen held everything from truffle mac and cheese to caviar-topped deviled eggs. Even the iced tea had been fancied up, served in delicate glasses garnished with sprigs of mint and lemon slices cut into perfect stars.

Diego raised his glass of Hattie's special punch, and we toasted.

"What's in this?" he mused after a sip.

"Ninety percent champagne and ten percent...who knows," I told him.

"It should be too sweet for my liking, but I can't stop

drinking the damn thing," Diego complained good-naturedly.

"It's Aunt Hattie's *secret* recipe. I think the mystery ingredient might be honey-soaked bourbon," I stage whispered.

Diego looked at me with narrowed eyes. "So, I'm getting drunk on champagne?"

"Mixed with bourbon, yeah."

Diego was a handsome man, and I had a slight crush on him—well, me and the *entire* female population of Savannah Lace. No matter how we all lusted after him, Diego was very respectful and didn't flirt with anyone, well, except, incongruously, Nina Davenport. Now, *no one* flirted with that woman because she was indomitable, but that didn't seem to deter Diego.

"Are you hiding here?" Diego asked.

I sighed. "Yep! I needed a break from navigating the endless stream of Savannah's elite."

"You and me both, *querida*," he agreed.

I thought I'd be fine, and I had been for the most part, but every time I turned, I felt like I was being assaulted with saccharine politeness that barely masked the sharp edge of people's curiosity—it was becoming exhausting.

"Oh, you're Cash's sister, aren't you?"

"Did you hear about Rhett and Josie's engagement? Are you okay about it?"

"Don't Rhett and Josie look lovely together? Just look at them. So, is it true that you and he were...well...together all those years ago?"

secondefactnst

"Well, women work until they get married, darlin'. So, are you in the market? 'Cause I have a brother/friend/uncle/cousin/someone single and ready to mingle."

"You're so brave to have come back to Savannah. If what happened to you happened to me, I'd never be able to show my face here."

I'd plastered on the polite smile I'd perfected over the years, nodding and responding with noncommittal pleasantries, while mentally calculating the distance between the hub of the party and the pond by my cottage.

"I better get to Nina before her dance card fills up," Diego murmured when the music became louder and people started to dance.

"Good luck." My gaze followed him as he approached Nina. In the blink of an eye, he had wrapped his arms around Nina and gotten her onto the dance floor. He was a smooth operator, I had to give him that.

Speaking of *smooth operators*, I saw Rhett and Josie dancing and smiling at one another. Of course, that didn't mean anything because, in Savannah society, couples kept up appearances. You'd see them together and think, *"Oh, they're in love,"* and a minute later, you'd find out the husband had a mistress ensconced in a house a respectable distance from Savannah.

"Pearl Beaumont," came a voice to my left, almost playful. I turned to see Raphael "Rafe" Rhodes, his smile as disarming as the red, white, and blue bowtie he wore with a linen blazer. Rafe was not what one expected from the Rhodes family. Where his brother Gabe was buttoned-up and serious, Rafe looked like he belonged at an art gallery opening. He had the kind of charm that didn't feel rehearsed, paired with an intelligence that made you want to lean in closer to hear what he'd say next. The fact that he was handsome as sin didn't hurt at all.

I gave Rafe a quick hug. "Enjoying the spectacle?"

Rafe chuckled. He was a tenured professor of quantitative economics at Emory University. He was a few years older than me, so we didn't know each other in high school. However, we had gotten to know one another by accident in LA, where he'd been living for a semester, working on a project at USC. I'd met him through a friend, and as was the case with transplants, we connected over our joint hate for Savannah society.

"Immensely." His grin widened. "It's not every day you get to eat a steak grilled by a Michelin-star chef while listening to a jazz version of the national anthem. It's good to see you here."

"Well, I live here." I tilted my chin toward my cottage.

"I heard," Rafe remarked. "How're you holding up?"

In LA, we'd talked a little about my life in Savannah, and he had the Cliff's Notes version. "It's been going well overall," I said, "but right now, my ecosystem's feeling a little murky, thanks to all the Savannah elitism. And since I've eaten, drunk, and been polite well past my limit, I think it's time I leave and clear the air around me."

Rafe draped an arm around me and kissed my cheek. "You are, darlin' Pearl, as always, a delight."

There was a short time when I'd hoped that I could be

attracted to Rafe. He was straightforward, accessible, hand-some, intelligent...everything a girl could want. *But* we had no chemistry, which was such a pity.

"Well, well," Rafe remarked.

"Well, what?" I looked around to see what he was talking about when my eyes fell on Rhett, who was looking straight at us.

"Yeah, I've heard every variation of *'Aren't Rhett and Josie a great couple?'* and *'Are you doing okay about their engagement?'* Why does everyone assume I'd have a prob-lem?" There was an edge to my voice. Rhett Vanderbilt was rattling me *again*.

"He's not helping by staring at us." Rafe was amused. "The rumor is that he's not happy with Josie."

"Rafe, I'm appalled that you're indulging in gossip." I gently slapped my hand on his chest.

He grabbed the offending hand and kissed my fist. "When in Savannah, you know you must *partake* in the offi-cial sport." He then winked at me. "He's pretty pissed about seeing you with me."

"Is that why you're being so physically affectionate?" I demanded.

"Absolutely," he replied silkily and drew me close to him.

I leaned into Rafe. He smelled of sexy cologne and man. "Why couldn't you and I have clicked?"

"Yeah, a pity that we didn't."

"In any case, you sleep with girls who're way too young, like Leonardo DiCaprio."

"The young women I date are *very* mature," he protested.

"Please, they're *young* and your students," I shot back.

"I usually wait until they're not my students," he corrected.

I watched Rhett as we talked. I couldn't help myself. He stood near the buffet table with Josie at his side. He was the epitome of the Southern golden boy, ready to go yachting in his light-blue button-down, and crisp white slacks.

Josie was everything a Southern Belle should be in her red and blue sundress cinched at the waist with a white belt that screamed effortless elegance *and* Independence Day. She smiled up at Rhett, her hand resting lightly on his arm, while his eyes...they were on me.

His eyes flicked briefly to Rafe and then back to me, his jaw tightening almost imperceptibly. For a moment, the world seemed to narrow, and the chatter and laughter around me faded into the background.

Rafe leaned in slightly, breaking the moment. "Now he wants to rearrange my face. Did something happen between the two of you recently that he's feeling so possessive?"

I shook my head quickly, forcing a laugh. "Don't be ridiculous."

Rafe raised an eyebrow, clearly unconvinced, but thankfully, Luna appeared before he could press the issue.

"Well, aren't you two cozy?" She eyed Rafe, sizing him up with the kind of no-nonsense energy only Luna could pull off. "You hitting on my girl here, Rafe Rhodes?"

"Absolutely not. Scout's honor."

"You were *never* a scout," Luna muttered.

"True." Rafe hugged Luna and then sighed as he looked over her shoulder. "I'm having no luck today."

"What?" Luna murmured, and turned around to see Dominic Calder. "Everywhere I go, he's there."

"And every time I touch a woman, a man is looking at me like he wants to fuck me up," Rafe muttered dryly.

"Hello, Moonbeam." Dom slid an arm around Luna, which she tried to unsuccessfully shrug off. He brushed his lips against her cheek, and she looked part exasperated and well...a little giddy.

I'd been told that whatever was happening between Dom and Luna wasn't a relationship...at least, not yet, but it was brewing, big time.

"You hitting on my girl, Rafe?" Dom asked the same question Luna had a few minutes ago.

Rafe sighed. "I don't know why everyone thinks I'm *hittin'* on anyone. I'm just bein' friendly."

"I'm not your girl." Luna pushed Dom away. "I see Camy Channing is here, and I have it on good authority that she's expectin' a proposal from you by Labor Day."

"Does that bother you, Luna, darlin'?" Dom winked at her.

I fanned myself with my hand. "Rafe, I think I need a cool drink, 'cause the sparks between these two are making me uncomfortably hot," I teased, suddenly feeling alright about being at a party because I was with friends.

But eventually, the introvert in me wanted *me* time. The party continued, but I managed to slip away. No one would notice I was gone. The summer night wrapped around me like a warm, heavy blanket. The air smelled of magnolias, fireworks, and barbecue—a strange combination. The hum and chatter of conversation mingled with the distant hum and chirping of cicadas as I got closer to my cottage.

It had been a strange evening. I had a good time with my *new* friends. My family ignored me. My mother had given me air kisses so that no one would say, *"Did you see how Birdie and Pearl didn't even say hello? I hear there's trouble in paradise."* Caroline had done the same. Since Alice and Maddie were not at the party, I didn't see any reason to hang around my family.

If I'd lived in Savannah my whole life, maybe I'd have more patience and desire to build bridges with my brother and mother, but I'd been gone for so many years and enjoyed my freedom, that being in their presence and experiencing their constant censure was stifling.

I rounded the corner that took me to my cottage and, on impulse, walked up to the gazebo with a view of what I liked to call *my* pond. The gazebo was gorgeous, tucked away near a cluster of hydrangeas that glowed pale blue in the moonlight. It was small but elegant, with white lattice-work and vines of jasmine curling up the posts. I came here to have coffee in the mornings as I checked the news and my emails on my phone. I stepped inside and leaned against one of the wooden railings, letting out a long, unsteady breath.

"Escaping, too?"

I jumped at the sound of Rhett's voice, spinning around

to find him standing just outside the gazebo, his hands in his pockets.

"I live here," I told him.

"Well, *I am* escaping," he announced.

"Good for you." I was about to walk away, but he stepped inside the gazebo, cutting off my access to the stairs that would take me down the garden to my home.

"I run by here most mornings," he told me as he walked to the other end of the gazebo, looking at the little pond dressed up with lotus flowers *and* a few ducks.

For a moment, neither of us spoke. The silence stretched between us, thick and heavy but not entirely uncomfortable. He leaned against the rail, facing me. I could walk away now if I wanted. I didn't have to be here.

He sighed.

I arched an eyebrow. "That sounded profound."

"Did it?"

Go home, Pearl. You don't have to talk to this asshole.

"Yeah, like you're carrying the weight of the world on your shoulders."

He seemed more reflective in the moonlight. He didn't have the polished, Savannah-golden-boy façade. He looked tired. Not physically, but definitely emotionally. I knew how that felt; I could recognize it.

"I sometimes feel like I am." He looked past me at the garden behind me. "I needed a break."

"From what?" I challenged, folding my arms, my posture defensive.

He didn't respond right away, he just watched me with a quiet intensity. "From pretending," he said at last.

I stiffened. "Pretending to be what?"

His jaw tightened. "A Vanderbilt."

I let out a sharp, bitter laugh. "Are you having a case of the poor, little rich boy blues?"

He smiled sadly. "Can't blame you for thinkin' that, Pearl."

It unsettled me. When we were teenagers, he'd have responded barb for barb.

"Well, I'll leave you to—"

"I'm sorry," he blurted out.

I stared at him.

"What I did was cruel, horrible, and...I'm sorry. I'm so very sorry. It haunts me, Pearl."

How dare he make this about how it affects him?

"Me too," I threw back at him.

His eyes lowered. "I can only imagine. I am sorry."

"You behave like you slipped up and, oops, made a mistake." I felt the need to purge my thoughts so intensely, I couldn't stop myself from letting him see what was inside of me: the pain, the struggle, the heartbreak. "You *chose* to hurt me, Rhett. You made a bet, you slept with me, and then you let everyone in Savannah rip me to shreds because of it."

"I know."

"And you think your measly apology makes up for it?"

"Nothing can make up for it, Pearl. Do you think I don't know that? I hurt you. I—"

"We were friends, Rhett," I accused him, my eyes filling

with tears I didn't want to ever shed in front of him. "Well, I *thought* we were. I didn't think you were capable of saying the things you did about me."

"I know," he said tenderly. "I had a rot inside of me, one that made me want to *fit* in, live up to my reputation of being an asshole."

"You were my first, and you made it ugly with your words. Do you know how hard a climb it has been for me?"

The words hung in the air between us, raw and jagged. His face twisted with shame, regret, and pain—but he didn't look away.

"You are one of the bravest people I know," he told me sincerely. "Believe me when I tell you, Pearl, that I've hated myself for it every day since."

"No more than I have," I cried out.

I saw him take a step toward me, but I held my hand up so he would stay put. "Why did you do it? Why did you hurt me? I'd never done anything to you."

"Because I was a coward." His voice was barely above a whisper.

I blinked, caught off guard by the rawness in his voice.

"Because I wanted to show everyone what a big deal I was. I fucked Pearl Beaumont over a bet. I didn't realize how that demeaned me and showed everyone how low I was."

The honesty in his words overwhelmed me, and before I could stop myself, the tears came. Hot and fast, they blurred my vision, and I turned away, trying to hide them. But Rhett didn't move, didn't look away.

"I'm so sorry for hurting you," he continued, his eyes shining with emotion.

That made me only angrier. "You don't get to cry about this." My voice broke. "You don't get to feel bad about this. You don't get to take that away from me."

He stepped closer, his voice thick with emotion. "Pearl, I—"

"Don't," I snapped, cutting him off. "Don't apologize. Don't say it was a mistake. I don't want to hear it."

"Okay." The gentleness in his tone made me hate him a little more because it made me like him *again*. One apology, and I was already swaying.

"I need to go." I didn't know what to say to him. My emotions were a tangled mess of anger and confusion.

"Pearl," he started, but I shook my head.

"No. I can't do this. I *won't*."

I left him standing in the gazebo and retreated to the quiet solace of my little cottage, where I cried until the stillness of the early morning.

I wasn't over what happened to me, I realized. I needed to heal if I wanted to move forward. I set up an emergency appointment with my therapist on his online portal and fell into an exhausted sleep.

CHAPTER 11
Rhett

scape! Somehow, at the age of thirty-two, my main goal in life had become to get away from my mother, my fiancée, her mother, my sister, and my father, and in that order.

They were talking about the wedding all day, every day. It was now only twelve months away. That was a whole fucking year, but if you heard Josie, you'd feel like we had minutes to go before tying the knot, and *what the fuck* about the fucking flowers!

According to my friend Royal, I was behaving like a man who didn't want to get married. Royal had recently married the love of his life, and I knew he was happier than almost any other husband I knew.

"Why do we get married?" I wondered when I met him for a drink at The Alley Cat Lounge, a dimly lit speakeasy tucked into an unassuming brick alleyway downtown.

As was the norm with such establishments, the entrance

was marked only by a small, engraved plaque next to a nondescript black door. You had to know where it was to find it.

Inside, the bar was a cozy labyrinth of low ceilings, exposed brick walls, and vintage lighting. Edison bulbs added to the vintage theme, their warm glow reflecting off the polished brass bar top and the rows of glass shelves stocked with rare spirits.

All the furniture at the speakeasy, including the tables and chairs, were from the twenties and thirties. The mismatched but beautifully restored furniture added to the place's appeal.

Royal rested against his leather armchair with an Old Fashioned in hand. I had my elbows on the antique table as I stared down at my glass of Johnny Walker Blue.

I took a sip and then loosened my tie. I'd already removed my suit jacket before I sat down. The weight of the day felt like it was peeling off me, layer by layer, in the sanctuary of this dark, quiet bar.

"Different people get married for different reasons." A smirk tugged at Royal's mouth. "I married for love."

"I don't love Josie."

"No," Royal agreed.

When I rolled up the sleeves of my white dress shirt, Royal sighed. "What? Wedding planning becoming too much for the Vanderbilt heir?"

I groaned, rubbing a hand over my face. "You have no idea. If I hear one more conversation about hydrangeas versus peonies, I swear to God, I'm going to lose it."

Royal took a slow sip of his drink. "Classic avoidance behavior."

"How did you...how did you walk away?" I asked. It was well-known in Savannah that Royal had broken ties with the Legere family. There were a few others I knew who'd done that, but the majority of us just put one foot in front of the other.

"I'm assuming you're asking about how I did it emotionally rather than financially?"

"Financially, I think my father has more to lose breaking off with me than the other way around." I managed the Vanderbilt wealth and did it profitably.

"Let me ask you a question." Royal set his glass down. "How do you feel *after* you speak to...say, your father?"

"Speak about what?"

"Anything. Just when you talk to him or are in his presence. How do you feel?

"Like I want to ram my fist into a wall," I replied.

"Is that because you argue?"

"No one argues with George Vanderbilt."

Royal nodded. "You want his approval."

"Yes." I ran a hand through my hair. "He's my father. I don't want to disappoint him."

"Every encounter I had with *any* member of my family, except for my grandmother, left me feeling like you do after you talk to your father," Royal explained. "What I realized was that, at its core, my family and I didn't share the same values. Once I internalized *that*, it made no sense to continue the farce of having a relationship. Then

Grandma died, and she was the last Legere I gave a fuck about."

"I've been raised to care for the Vanderbilt name. You know how that goes?"

"I do! Take Gabe Rhodes. He took over the Rhodes hotel business. His brother Rafe, on the other hand, wanted to get into academia, and the family was fine with it. Gabe wanted to marry Aurora, his parents supported him. They share the same values. Can you see the difference between your situation and his?"

"I don't have any brothers like you do," I pointed out.

"It doesn't matter, Rhett," Royal explained patiently. "What you need to think about is that this is your *only* life. This is not a drill. You marry Josie, who you obviously don't like no matter the show you put on for everyone else—you'll be unhappy for the rest of your *only* life."

I stared at my drink, the amber liquid catching the light, swirling slightly as I tilted the glass.

Royal arched an eyebrow. "Why are you getting married, Rhett?"

"Because I knocked her up, and now, even though there is no baby, I'm expected to."

He shrugged. "I got married because I found someone I can't imagine living without. Someone who makes me better. Someone who feels like home."

I let out a bitter laugh. "Josie feels more like a real estate deal. Great on paper, looks good to the outside world, but inside...." I trailed off.

"Then why would you do this?" he asked exasperated.

I hesitated, swirling my drink again. "Because it's easier to keep moving forward than to stop and ask yourself if you're going the wrong way."

Royal leaned forward and rested his elbows on the table. "That's not a reason, man. That's inertia."

That was the word, I thought, *inertia*, that made the world put one foot after the other. We didn't want to fuck with the status quo, so we kept making the same mistakes over and over again.

"I know," I confessed. "But if I *internalize* that, I'll be stepping into a free fall that I'm not sure I'll survive."

My friend Sage joined us then. "Sorry, I'm late."

She gave Royal a quick hug and did the same with me before taking a seat. She looked from Royal to me and raised her eyebrows. "Who died?"

"I think he's reevaluating his social life," Royal mocked.

Sage's eyes widened. "Tell me you're going to dump that bitch."

"Told ya." Royal raised his glass smugly.

A server came by, and Sage ordered a Sazerac before focusing on me again. "You can't stand her."

"How will it look, Sage?"

"Like you can't stand her," she offered and then shook her head as if disgusted with me. "Why the hell are you so afraid of your father?"

"I'm not afraid of him," I snapped. "I respect him."

"Why?" Sage asked, bewildered. "The man is so conservative he thinks women who wear pantsuits are lesbian and should be put to death."

Alas, that was only a *slight* exaggeration. "I'll lose my family if I do this." I had been raised to respect my elders, take care of my family, and be the man I was supposed to be.

"Maybe they aren't worth keeping." Sage put a comforting hand on my shoulder.

"You should talk," I shot back. When you have no defense for yourself, you go on offense.

"I should." She smiled. "I know what it feels like to sacrifice your happiness for doing right by the family. I paid for it...I'm *still* paying for it."

My friends' words stayed with me as I escaped once again, this time leaving Savannah for a conference in Newport Beach. I was relieved because that would give me a break from the incessant familial nagging, *and* I was excited because Pearl was going to be at the same conference.

The conference was being held at the opulent Resort at Pelican Hill, perched on the bluffs above Newport Beach, with sweeping ocean views that seemed almost unreal. The place was straight out of a luxury travel magazine, all Italian-inspired architecture—terracotta roofs, colonnades, and lush green courtyards dotted with fountains. Even the air smelled expensive—of salt from the ocean breeze and a scent that was faintly citrusy, probably pumped in through hidden vents.

A few people from Savannah Lace and my company attended the conference, which focused on the architecture and construction business.

Our small contingent from Savannah met for dinner after a long day of lectures and workshops. After our meal at one of the resort's restaurants, we gathered around a fire pit, the flames crackling against the cool evening air. Overhead, strings of lights hung in lazy loops, casting a golden glow over the patio. Beyond us, the ocean stretched into the horizon, dark and endless, with the occasional glimmer of moonlight reflecting off the waves.

I sipped my bourbon, letting the warmth of it settle in my chest as I listened to the conversation flow around me. Layla Warren, Savannah Lace's CFO, was deep in discussion with one of Pearl's colleagues about supply chain strategies. A few of my team members were chatting about an upcoming client pitch, their voices low and serious despite the relaxed setting.

I had managed to sit next to Pearl—I had not been able to help myself. I felt drawn to her—I probably always had been. When I looked back at our teenage years, I remembered her as this elusive and charming person people made fun of.

I had approached her because of the bet, but I stayed because of *her*. She was the only authentic person I knew in my young life. She was open and honest—naïve and affectionate. There was no calculation. *That* young girl was no more. The woman sitting next to me had her walls up. She wasn't the innocent girl any longer. She had lived her life—and from what I could see, what happened *then* had not changed just me but also her. The consequences of that one thoughtless, heartless act had forced me to look at myself and strive to become a better person—but what had it done to Pearl?

She looked relaxed, one leg crossed over the other, a sparkling drink in her hand that she barely drank. She wasn't particularly seeking out conversation; she was comfortable in herself and the silence. She didn't seek attention, but she didn't fade into the background, either—she never had. She had an effortless presence. Why had this made so many of us insecure when we were young?

"...and that's when I told him, '*If you're going to try to micromanage a spreadsheet, at least learn how to use Excel first,*'" Layla was telling a story about a previous consultant, her tone half exasperated, half amused. Everyone burst into laughter.

"You actually said that?" someone asked.

"Of course, she did," Pearl interjected, her grin mischievous. "I mean, he was color-coding cells like it was an art project. Someone had to stop him before he hurt himself."

I couldn't help but smile. Pearl had a way of being sharp without being unkind, confident without being mean.

As the conversation shifted to market trends, I found myself watching her more than listening. I noticed how expressive her hands were as she spoke, how she leaned forward slightly when making a point, and how her clear and steady voice got respect without her ever demanding it.

She wasn't gossiping, wasn't talking about who was dating who, or what scandal was brewing in Savannah's social circles. She was talking about ideas, challenges, and solutions, and she did it with a kind of ease that made everyone at the table want to hear what she had to say.

And I realized, with a suddenness that made my chest

tighten, that I was falling for her. I wasn't just physically attracted to her—though God knew I was that, too—but actually *falling* for her for the way she thought, the way she carried herself, her easy charm—*everything*.

I was sucker punched.

I recognized that this wasn't just some passing interest, wasn't some fleeting curiosity about a woman I'd once wronged. This was deeper, messier, and far more dangerous. Because as much as I wanted her, I couldn't have her. Not the way I wanted, not while Josie was still wearing my ring, and my life was tied up in knots I hadn't figured out how to untangle.

"Rhett, you with us?" Layla's voice pulled me out of my thoughts.

"Sorry." I set my glass down. "I was a million miles away."

Pearl watched me with curiosity. "Layla asked if you thought the industry was ready for more aggressive fin-tech integration," she supplied, tilting her head slightly. "Or do you think we're all still a little too afraid of change?"

I cleared my throat, shifting in my seat. "I think there's always resistance to change." I forced myself to focus and be social like I'd been taught and trained. "But the ones who embrace the right kind of change early tend to be the ones who come out ahead. It's just a matter of convincing people that the short-term disruption is worth the long-term gains."

"Spoken like a true consultant," Pearl remarked, her tone teasing but not unkind.

"Guilty as charged," I said graciously, thrilled that she was talking to me.

Since our conversation by her pond, the antagonism between us had diminished. We could *talk* to one another without constantly bringing up the past, without me apologizing, and her telling me to go fuck myself.

The conversation moved on, but my attention stayed with Pearl.

"How has the conference been for you?" I wanted to talk to her and get to know her better. I respected and admired her. All things I was fully aware I didn't feel for my fiancée.

"Good." She let out a deep breath. "As exhilarating as these conferences are, they leave me exhausted. The time zone shift *and* constantly being *on*, it takes a lot out of you."

The *staying-on* part was a problem for me as well, and it was probably a bigger one for Pearl, who was an introvert.

"Do you feel like going for a walk?" I asked impulsively.

She stared at me, and I waited to hear her verdict of how she saw the man I'd become because I wanted to be the kind of man Pearl respected.

"Yes," she agreed.

We left the others and went to the beach. Pearl walked barefoot, her sandals dangling from one hand. The hem of her ankle-length dress swayed in the breeze, and her ponytail had loosened into soft strands that framed her face. She looked beautiful. She was so damned gorgeous and it broke my heart to think I'd ever made her feel *less* over something as trivial as her body weight.

"Tell me something true," I asked, desperate for her to open up to me.

She stopped and turned to look at me. "What do you want to know?"

I licked my lips. *Everything* I wanted to say, but how could I when I had a fiancée waiting for me at home?

"How...how...." I closed my eyes and waited for the storm to pass. "Tell me how I hurt you."

Her eyes went wide, both with, I thought, shock *and* emotion. "What?"

This was not the time for this conversation, but I desperately wanted to make amends, and the only way to do that was to understand the damage I had done.

"You're a different person than you used to be," I explained. "So am I. That day changed me, too, Pearl."

"How?" she demanded, challenge flickering in her eyes.

The crash of the waves against the sand merged with the roar of my guilt as I confessed the truth. "It made me realize that I had no integrity. I was the kind of person who could hurt another human being simply because...*I could*. I felt a lot of shame. But not enough, Pearl. Not nearly enough."

She folded her arms, her sandals still dangling absently from her fingers, as if she needed to comfort herself.

"When I saw you a few years later, I pounced at the opportunity to absolve myself. I thought if I said I was sorry, you'd accept, and it would be over, this cycle of shame and self-loathing." I smirked in self-deprecation. "I was such a fool. I didn't understand then that a mere *apology* was worthless. I was even annoyed that you wouldn't accept my generous confession of remorse."

"My mother and Cash were quite upset with me for being rude to you." I could feel her disdain for them *and* me in her tone. "I didn't come back to Savannah for several years after that."

"I know." I gave her a weak smile. "I waited, you see, for you to come so I could...do better."

She cocked an eyebrow. "Really?"

"But, I realized too late, actually, only recently, that a man who was not a coward would have followed you to California and made his point." It was not easy to lay myself open to her, especially since I didn't know if she'd kick me in the ribs while I was down. But if she did, it was no less than I deserved.

She turned and began walking again. I kept pace with her. We were silent for a while. When she finally spoke, her voice was low, almost drowned out by the sound of the waves.

"It messed me up...big time," she began, and I immediately felt my stomach tighten because I knew whatever she was going to tell me was not going to be pleasant. But if she'd lived it, I had to have the balls to hear her out.

"It was my first time," her voice was small.

"Yes." I could barely get the word out.

She walked straight, looking ahead, while I looked at her, watching her face, waiting for her to explain the devastation I'd brought upon her.

"It took me a while to have sex...I did...I mean, I do. But

I tend to go for short relationships, one-night stands. Sex is complicated when you...." She trailed off.

"When you went through what you did?" I finished softly.

She shook her head. "When you look at your body and you hate everything about it."

Fuck!

"Pearl, I thought you were beautiful then, and I think you're beautiful now. It has nothing to do with how you look—though you are gorgeous, it was always about who you are."

She stopped walking and turned to face me.

"You said that my being a virgin made up for how I looked."

She remembered what I'd said, just as I did. You never forgot the time you dropped the lowest you ever could as a human.

"I didn't want them to know that I was attracted to you. That sex with you had been...amazing."

She swallowed.

"You called me Bumblebee."

I closed my eyes because I could feel emotions well up, and it wasn't fair for me to show her my tears and make this conversation about me when it was about her.

"I'm sorry." What else was there to say?

She smiled wanly. "Do you know what my Tinder handle is?"

I shook my head.

"Bumblebee1703."

March seventeenth was her birthday.

"I owned that name," she said proudly. "I had to work through a lot. I was never the best for *anyone*. My parents always thought Cash was better, and Birdie wished Josie was her daughter. I was too fat, too dull, too ugly. You...well... let's not belabor *that* point. You know what happens to a young person who only hears about themselves in reference to their body?"

I could guess, but I didn't reply to her rhetorical question and waited for her to reveal her truth.

CHAPTER 12

Pearl

"I'll tell you what happens." My chest tightened, ready to eject all my unpleasant thoughts and self-loathing. "You start to believe that's all you are. A body. An ugly one. You become a collection of flaws for people to critique, to judge, to laugh at. You start to think, *If I can just fix myself, if I can somehow become smaller, prettier, better, then maybe...maybe I'll finally be enough.'*"

We stopped walking and stood on the beach, with the endless expanse of the Pacific Ocean in front of us.

"It started small. Skipping meals. Eating just enough to get by but never enough to feel full. I told myself that I needed to be more disciplined. I ate too much, ate the wrong things, ate at all—that was the problem. Not eating started to feel like I had control."

Rhett's brow furrowed. He put a hand on my cheek as if he was unable to temper his need to touch me.

"Soon, I was terrified of food. I checked my weight

relentlessly. Even if I gained half a pound, I saw it as a personal failure."

I stepped away from him because his touch *was* comforting, and I didn't want to draw relief from *him*. I couldn't. He was engaged to another woman, and no matter how much I'd loved him as a teenager and still wanted him now, the truth was that he wasn't mine. He had *never* been, even if my sixteen-year-old heart had fleetingly dreamed that.

He let me go.

"I was diagnosed with anorexia," I said the word with fear as if it would break me *again* as it had in the past. "What do you know about anorexia?" I kept my voice casual as I started to walk again, feeling the sand under my feet. Even though it was summer, the evenings in southern California tended to be cooler because of the sea air. After the Savannah heat, it was delicious.

"I know that it's an eating disorder," he stated, his voice so low that I could barely hear him.

"I had...have anorexia nervosa. It's not about food but about control. It's about fear. And yes, depression and anxiety are a big part of it. They're like background noise you can never turn off. The depression tells you you're not good enough, and the anxiety makes you believe you have to keep proving yourself, over and over, even when it's killing you."

I glanced at him, gauging his reaction. His jaw was tight, his hands fisted at his sides, but his eyes were soft and full of sorrow and anger—not at me but at himself.

129

"Did you throw up your food and all that?" he asked tightly.

I shook my head. "I don't have bulimia. I never purged. But I restricted my food to the point where it wasn't just unhealthy—it was dangerous. And the worst part?" I chortled bitterly. "People praised me for it. *You look so good, Pearl! Have you lost weight? What's your secret?'* My secret was that I was starving myself, but no one cared as long as I was thinner."

"Jesus," Rhett whispered, running a hand over his face. "I...I never would've thought...."

"Of course, not," I snapped, a sharp edge creeping into my tone. "Why would you? People like you—the ones who always fit, who always belong—you never have to think about what it's like to have your worth reduced to your reflection in a mirror."

I knew it wasn't fair to lash out at him, but I was opening old and new wounds so he could see me bleed. He was here, wasn't he? He was the only person I could express my anger at. The fact that he didn't respond with rage or defensiveness, just understanding, made me feel small.

"I...." He trailed off, shaking his head as if searching for the right words. "I can't...I can't imagine what that was like."

I nodded, acknowledging the truth in his words. "You can't truly understand it unless you've lived it. But I'll tell you this—anorexia isn't *merely* an eating disorder. It's a mental illness. It's a disease that worms its way into your brain and convinces you that thinner is better, that food is the enemy, and that your value is measured in numbers:

pounds, inches, calories. It's not rational. It doesn't make sense. But it's so loud, Rhett. It drowns out everything else until it's all you can hear."

He drew me to him and held me. I didn't resist. I needed his strength, and I drew on it. I leaned my forehead against his chest, took a deep breath, and filled my lungs with salty air.

Rhett pulled away, even though he kept me in the circle of his arms. His looked raw, unguarded. He was in pain. He felt *my* pain. I'd never felt more seen than right now. "Are you...are you okay now?"

I gave him a small, assuring smile. "I'm okay. I eat. I do therapy. I work hard to keep myself in a good place. But some days are harder than others. Some days, I look in the mirror, and all I see is the girl I used to be—the one who wasn't enough. The one who thought the only way to matter was to disappear."

"Being in Savannah doesn't help, does it?" he intuited.

"My therapist warned me that there would be triggers. *And* there are. *But* so far...it's been manageable."

He kissed my forehead gently. "That girl you sometimes still see in the mirror was incredible. The woman you've become is also incredible. I hate that I've played such a big part in making you feel less, and have done nothing to make you see who you are."

His words were heavy with regret.

"It's not just about you, Rhett." I pulled away from him. As tempting as it was to dump all my problems on Rhett, it wasn't true. I wanted to be fair to him but also myself. "This is also about how I let myself believe the lies people told me. About how I hurt myself because I thought I wasn't good enough. You were a part of it, yes, but you weren't the whole story. I had to learn to love myself."

Even though he wasn't holding me, his entire attention was on me, and it felt damn good. "When did you start getting help?"

I was about to answer when it hit me just how easy it was to talk to Rhett. No one else in my life, besides Aunt Hattie, knew what had happened to me, what I'd done to myself. And yet, here I was, sharing my deepest, darkest secrets with the very man who had betrayed me, who had once shattered my trust.

What surprised me even more was how right it felt. It was as if this was exactly what I needed to do to restore some order to my universe.

I walked to the waves, letting the cool water lap at my ankles. "It took a while."

"So, leaving Savannah didn't make it better?"

"That's just geography." I kicked at the same waves, making little splashes.

"I understand," he murmured.

Surprisingly, I knew that he did. The boy I remembered had always carried the potential for the man he'd become, but back then, he'd been too consumed with fitting in, too desperate to be liked. He'd seen vulnerability as a weakness, and compassion as something that could cost him his place in the crowd.

I took a deep breath and let the walls fall. "It happened

in the college library. I was sitting at a table, staring at this textbook, but I couldn't focus. I hadn't eaten anything that day or the day before. I'd had plenty of coffee, though."

I saw Rhett's jaw tighten, but he remained silent, letting me talk.

"I started to feel lightheaded, like the room was tilting. My vision got blurry, and I remember thinking, *'Just sit still. Just stay calm.'*" My laugh was bitter and harsh in my throat. "As if sitting still would fix the fact that I was starving myself to death."

I could feel the tears building behind my eyes, but I didn't stop. There was an urgency, a need to let it out—to finally let it go—and to say it to Rhett. For so long, I'd carried the weight of blaming him for what happened to me, and now, this moment was both agony and release. To tell him my truth and his part in shaping it felt like ripping open an old wound and stitching it shut at the same time.

"The next thing I knew, I'd blacked out. Everything just...faded."

I wrapped my arms around myself, feeling exposed. "When I woke up, I was in a hospital bed. There were tubes in my arms and an oxygen mask on my face. A nurse told me I was lucky. My potassium levels had dropped so low that my heart had gone into arrhythmia."

"Arrhythmia?" Rhett repeated, his voice dry, fear lacing it.

"I went into cardiac arrest. My heart stopped."

Rhett looked horrified; his lips parted like he wanted to speak but couldn't find the words. His hands had come out of his pockets, clenched at his sides. For once, the ever-composed Rhett Vanderbilt looked utterly undone.

"How long?" he asked, his voice thick. "How long were you...?"

"Dead?"

CHAPTER 13
Rhett

"Yes," I managed to get that one word out. My legs felt shaky. My hands were clammy. I was having a version of a panic attack.

My heart hammered as I waited for her response. Of all the things I'd imagined she'd tell me, this had not been one of them.

"About a hundred and twenty-three seconds," she admitted. "Long enough that I shouldn't have made it."

I took a shaky breath. "Jesus, Pearl."

Bile threatened to choke me. Pearl could've *died*... because of what I did to her. I had destroyed this remarkable woman. And for what? So, I could look *cool* in front of my friends?

I couldn't imagine how awful she must have felt with everyone telling her how great she looked and how thin she was, when the cost of it had nearly been her life.

She looked down at the wet sand beneath her feet,

curling her toes in. "It was a wake-up call. I got help. I got talk therapy. I got anti-depressants. I got tools."

"Such as?"

"I have tools to recognize *my* patterns. The lies my brain tells me. I learned how to catch the spiral before it gets too far. To remind myself that food isn't the enemy and that my worth isn't tied to my weight or my reflection. My therapist has taught me grounding techniques—ways to stay in the present when my anxiety is clawing at me."

I soaked up her words. I wanted to be there for her in the present and the future in any way she'd allow me, and that meant I needed to know how to help her.

"What else?" I persisted.

She shrugged. "I used to keep a journal. Not the *dear diary* kind, but a place to write out the noise in my head. Sometimes, putting it down on paper makes it feel less powerful. Less like it's consuming me."

"But not now?"

She shook her head. "It doesn't help me any longer."

I nodded, my gaze steady on hers. "And the antidepressants? Do they help?"

"They do." She looked more relaxed now, as if telling me the horrible thing that happened to her made her lighter. I could only hope. "They don't fix everything, but that and talk therapy keep me healthy and functional."

I couldn't help it—I wanted...I *needed,* to touch her. "May I hug you?" I asked for permission this time, unlike before.

She smiled at me. "I'd like that."

I walked slowly toward her and opened my arms, letting her make her choice. She stepped in. It was a reprieve, and I embraced not only her but also my guilt. I was aware now that it didn't help Pearl. I was going to live in the present and be there for her as a better man.

"I know about depression," I told her, my chin nuzzling her hair, taking her scent in. "I know that it's not a disease you overcome but one you manage. Pearl, I know I don't deserve it, but will you let me be your friend? Will you let me be there for you?"

"Why?" she asked.

Here it was—the moment of truth. I had to tell her, even if it meant she might turn away from me forever. I gently tilted her face so she could see me, so she could see the sincerity in my eyes.

"Part of it is because I need redemption," I began, my voice steady despite the knot tightening in my chest. "But the other reason is...I like you, Pearl. I know you probably won't believe this, but I've always liked you."

I paused, feeling the vulnerability of my words hanging between us. I felt like a high school boy again, clumsily opening his heart to his first crush, yet I'd never felt the rightness of a moment so profoundly before.

"Do you know," I added, my voice softening, "I fell in love with books because of you?"

She licked her lips and shook her head.

"I was an asshole teenager. I promise you that's not who I am anymore."

She chuckled.

"Even though I'm engaged to Josie." I was only half joking. "Why didn't you tell anyone about your heart?"

"It's not exactly dinner table conversation, and I didn't... *don't* want anyone to know. I couldn't stand it if people looked at me with pity."

"Hey. You can trust me." I forced her to look at me. "I'll *never* betray your trust ever again. Please believe that. I am honored that you told me your truth, and I'll treasure it as I will your presence in my life."

Please let me in, Pearl. Please.

"Okay," she said sweetly, and with that one word, she let me in.

My heart swelled, so full it felt like it might burst. And that's when I knew—I wasn't just attracted to Pearl. I was in love with her. I realized I'd probably half fallen in love with the memory of her, the girl I'd wronged so many years ago. But the reality of who she was now, the strength, the wit, the quiet resilience—that had stunned me. And in these past few months, I fell all the way for her.

CHAPTER 14

Pearl

Since we had several hours to spare before our flight out of LAX, I decided to visit downtown LA and check out a few of my old haunts. Rhett asked to come along, which excited me.

Our walk that night on the beach had cemented a bond between us, which I suspected was friendship, even though I was uncomfortable calling it that. After spending half my life thinking of him as my nemesis and cause of destruction, it was discombobulating to have him as an ally.

"Did you like living in LA?" Rhett asked as we walked down Broadway.

"I lived in downtown and loved it. I don't think I'd like living in West Hollywood or the hills or whatever," I replied. "DTLA is diverse and alive."

"Where did you live?" he asked, looking around the buildings in the historic district.

"Eighth and Grand." I pointed behind us. "If we have time, we can walk by there."

The Last Bookstore was one of my favorite places to spend a couple of hours. Part bookstore, part art installation, part labyrinth, the massive two-story space was a shrine to books old and new. Its high ceilings were crisscrossed with exposed beams and string lights, and its walls were stacked with books in colors, sizes, and ages that seemed endless. Shelves curved into arches, creating tunnels you could walk through, while others spiraled in dizzying, artful displays.

"This is amazing," Rhett confessed as I took him around the store.

The air smelled faintly of paper, ink, and time, a blend of old and new. Through the tall windows, a view of Los Angeles street life bled in. It was vibrant, chaotic, and *very* DTLA.

I picked up an old Raymond Chandler book and read the back cover. "They have so many old books here. They even have a room with antique books."

We wandered through the aisles in silence for a while, the noise of the city fading as we stepped deeper into the store. I ran my fingers along the spines of books, some new, some so old their titles had faded.

From one of the classic book aisles, Rhett picked out a book and held it for me to see: *The Grapes of Wrath*. My hand froze on the spine of the book I was going to pick up, and I felt a pang deep in my chest.

"I *never* read it," he whispered.

"I haven't read it since," I admitted. "I couldn't. I threw my copy away."

His jaw tightened slightly, and he nodded again as if he'd expected that answer. "You were bringing this book to me that day." He sounded sad.

"Yes."

He took a deep breath. "I have nightmares about that day—over and over again."

I raised my eyebrows in surprise. "Me too."

Pain swarmed his eyes. He put a hand on my cheek. "I'm so sorry, Pearl. What I did was unforgivable."

"Yes," I agreed, my voice low.

My therapist had said that I didn't have to forgive anyone or forget anything—I had to accept it happened, and that it wasn't my fault or responsibility and, therefore, not my burden to carry.

"Look, I know you want redemption, but *I* don't want to keep remembering." I tried to keep the edge out of my voice but couldn't.

He dropped his hand from my cheek. I looked down, my eyes tracing the intricate patterns of the hardwood beneath our feet.

"I am"—he laughed mirthlessly—"*sorry*. It appears I keep apologizing to you."

"Can we move past the apologies and the past?" I wondered, looking up at him. "I'd like to."

"Yeah?"

"Just don't ask me to forgive or forget."

"I won't do that," he promised. "I understand what I did to you; what it led to can never be made okay."

"But we can move forward, can't we?" I wondered if we could, but I hoped he might.

"Do you think...." His voice broke the stillness, tentative. "Do you think we could try again? Read *The Grapes of Wrath* together. Make peace with it."

I lifted my head, studying him. There was no smirk, no cocky façade. Just Rhett, looking at me with guilt *and* hope. I thought about it. About the years I'd spent avoiding not just the book but everything it represented.

Burying issues and challenges didn't make them disappear. I'd had enough therapy to know that. It was time to lift myself out of what happened to live in the present and in anticipation of a brighter future.

"Yes. I'd like to catch up with the Joads. To see Ma's strength again, to watch how she holds everyone together while—"

"Hey, no spoilers," he protested, and just like that, the mood between us was lighter.

"*Fine.*" I rolled my eyes.

A small smile tugged at the corner of his mouth as he pulled out two copies of the Steinbeck classic.

There was always a long line to get the cash register downstairs, and as we waited for our turn, Rhett revealed a little more about himself to me. "You're the reason I started reading."

"You were reading before we met," I objected.

"Well, yeah, but it started because of you." He looked

almost sheepish. "You always had a book with you. I remember seeing you with *Moon Palace* once. I wanted to ask you about it, but I didn't want to sound like an idiot, so I looked it up. When we...you know, started to hang out, you told me Paul Auster wrote for people who liked to think in circles. So, I read him so I could understand what you meant."

I wanted to rage at the term "hang out" because what he had been doing was seducing me for a bet, but hadn't I just decided to live in the present? So, I let it go and laughed, shaking my head. "And did you find out?"

"I didn't get it at the time," he admitted. "But I re-read the book later when I was a little more mature, and that's when I got it. You were the only person I knew who made books seem cool then."

"I wasn't cool," I said, smiling despite myself.

"You were to me." He was so sincere that I had no choice but to believe him.

As we waited, we talked about the books we'd read since. Obviously, we circled Southern literature. After all, we were from Georgia. Dorothy Allison came up, and we bonded over our shared love for *Bastard Out of Carolina*. Then, James Baldwin, whose words had shaped so much of how I viewed the world. We talked about *Another Country* and how it gutted us in the best way.

Rhett paid for our books, and after, we walked toward our next stop, my favorite wine bar downtown, Garçon de Café, for lunch.

"I've always believed that books burrow into your soul

and stay there, shaping how we see ourselves, how we see others." I hitched my purse on my shoulder as we walked down Spring Street to the Spring Arcade building, where the wine bar was.

"I agree." He tucked one hand into the pocket of his linen pants while the other held a paper bag with our books. I usually saw him in a suit, but he was in travel wear: pants, a T-shirt, and sneakers. He fit right into the easy SoCal sartorial culture.

The boy had become a man, and I found myself just as drawn to him now as I had been all those years ago. But what made this grown-up version of Rhett even more appealing wasn't just how he looked—it was his self-awareness, his maturity, and the humility he'd cultivated along the way.

"I'm really glad we're doing this, Pearl," he told me when we stood outside the wine bar. "Not just talking openly and reading *The Grapes of Wrath* together...but all of it."

I glanced at him, his face open and honest.

"Me too," I admitted.

CHAPTER 15
Rhett

Since Pearl had lived in Downtown LA for many years, I wasn't surprised that she knew all the *cool* places. The wine bar she took us to was a not-so-hidden gem.

Garçon de Café made me feel like I'd stumbled onto a Parisian side street.

Inside was an understated yet elegant bar with a long, polished counter. Bistro tables scattered across the room, their surfaces catching flickers of light from the votive candles. Soft jazz floated through the air, and in the corner, a sleek black piano stood waiting, promising live music later in the evening.

Behind the bar, the bartender looked like he'd stepped straight out of central casting—effortlessly suave, with a neatly trimmed beard, and a crisp white shirt rolled at the sleeves.

As soon as he saw Pearl, he hugged her, and they chatted in *French*. Sure, we'd all taken French in high school, but I could barely say more than *oui* and *merde*. Pearl sounded fluent.

"This is my friend, Rhett," Pearl introduced me, and I shook hands with Mathieu, who owned Garçon de Café and had known Pearl for many years. Stupid jealousy reared its head.

Mathieu handed us menus and poured water into crystal-clear glasses before stepping back to let us browse.

The wine list was as eclectic as the bar itself. Alongside the expected French selections, there were bottles from lesser-known regions like Jura, along with an intriguing mix of natural wines from Portugal and Spain, made with grapes I'd never even heard of. Scattered among the offerings were California wines from small, independent vineyards, the kind you rarely found on standard menus. It wasn't a list designed to impress—it was curated to invite exploration, to make you want to linger over every sip.

I'd never been a wine guy—not like my father, who pretended he could taste notes of leather and tobacco in every glass—but this place made me want to lean into the aesthetic. When I told Pearl, she giggled.

"Mathieu, here, has enhanced my wine education," she told me.

"She has specific tastes, so serving her the wine she likes is always a challenge," Mathieu explained in a French accent.

We sat at the bar, and I watched Pearl and Mathieu chat about people they knew. Sara, the bartender who was doing a PhD in psychoanalysis, someone called Patti, who was a singer, and others.

"Well, what would you like?" Mathieu asked both of us.

"Ah...." I perused the menu.

"Don't tell me you're the kind of guy who orders Chardonnay just because it's the only thing you recognize," Pearl teased.

I smirked. "Do I look that uncultured?"

Mathieu raised a hand as if swearing in. "I have some excellent Chardonnays from Burgundy by the glass. Would you like to try?"

"Absolutely." I set the menu away. As the bartender went to get our glasses and wine, I sighed. "I told you, my father is the wine aficionado in the family."

"Your father is a wine snob," she exclaimed. "Trust me, I've met the kind who think that because a bottle is expensive, it's good."

"I thought that was sort of the rule."

Her eyebrows lifted. "Absolutely not! I have found some amazing wines under fifty dollars. I'm assuming that's not the kind of thing George Vanderbilt ever indulges in."

There was strength in her voice when she spoke—a quiet confidence that was unmistakable. This was the new Pearl, the grown-up version. Since moving to Savannah, she'd kept her distance, only interacting with me when work required it. But now, for the first time, we were having a real conversation. She didn't mince her words, and I could tell she had no intention of tiptoeing around anything to spare my feelings.

It was such a stark contrast to most of Savannah's social

circle, where conversations were full of polite half-truths and carefully veiled intentions. Pearl spoke her mind, plain and simple, and I liked that about her—I liked it a whole lot.

"I'll have you know, I once shared a bottle of Châteauneuf-du-Pape with my father and his equally insufferable friends. I'm not saying I enjoyed it, but I survived."

"That could be harrowing, depending on the vintage," Pearl mocked.

"Now, who's sounding like a wine snob?" I teased.

Pearl tilted her head and shrugged. "What can I say, it's just who I am," she said in a very bad French accent.

Mathieu guided us through a tasting of the wines he had by the glass. Pearl eventually settled on a Sancerre—crisp, refreshing, and apparently, exactly what she wanted. I chose a Pinot Noir from Oregon, which, according to Mathieu, was light enough for a sunny LA afternoon but carried enough depth and complexity to keep it interesting.

"See, I didn't get a Chardonnay," I showed off to Pearl.

We ordered a charcuterie board to share—prosciutto, brie, olives, the works—and I watched as she leaned back in her barstool, her fingers tracing the stem of her glass after Mathieu delivered our drinks.

It was easy with her, easier (and more fun) than it had been in a long time with any woman. The silences were simple without the need to be filled up with small talk.

Is this what life could have been for me if I'd had the courage to be in a relationship with Pearl or even be her friend? Instead of the constant chatter and gossip about *others,* would I find myself *learning* new things, like how an

Oregon Pinot Noir could, apparently, be as good as one from Burgundy?

"You know a lot about wine. How did that come about?"

She shrugged. "I didn't drink wine for the longest time. Just a few years ago, I slowly started...." She hesitated for a moment. "It's not easy for me to try new things, so...it's been a process."

I loved that she was being open with me and hated that I was the cause of her having a fucking eating disorder. She could say it was her family, her mother, her friends...but the truth was, I'd been the one who had seen her naked for the first time in her life, had sex with her, and then called her repulsive. If only I'd known, then, the weight of my heartlessness, the price Pearl would have to pay for my cruelty.

But would that have changed anything? I asked myself.

I liked to think so. I wasn't a monster. But when I remembered how I talked about her that afternoon by the pool, I did feel like one, the worst kind, with no integrity, who preyed on the unsuspecting and the innocent.

"But," she continued, her tone brightening with cheer, "I've learned how to enjoy food and drink—obviously in a balanced way. I love wine. Places like Garçon de Café, and there's another wine bar on Olive called Good Clean Fun, have helped me figure out what I like and why."

We talked for a while about several things, and I finally asked the question that was burning inside me. "Have you had any long-term relationships?"

She shook her head. "Mostly, I used to Tinder to...you know...have some fun."

"And was it fun?"

She shrugged. "Sometimes. It's like when you pick up a book, you don't know if you'll love it until you read it."

I grinned. "Are you equating sex to reading?"

She chuckled. "No, a booty call to a book."

I snorted. "Speaking of books." I took a sip of my wine, and it was good, earthy, and not heavy at all. "What was the verdict on *The Grapes of Wrath*? Was it worth it? Before...well, you know."

She swirled her wine in her glass thoughtfully, watching the light catch in its pale, golden depths. "It was. I mean, at the time, I loved it. It's this big, sweeping story about injustice and survival. But afterward...." She trailed off, shrugging. "The day at the pool ruined it for me."

I winced, setting my glass down. "Fuck, Pearl. I—"

"Please don't apologize," she pleaded. "And don't sound so wounded; after all, we're going to reclaim it when we read it together, aren't we?"

I wanted to rage at myself, but that wouldn't help Pearl, even if it made me feel better. Maybe I needed to think about *her* for a change, not just myself.

"Yeah, yeah. Redemption through Steinbeck." I kept it light, wanting to move forward and not keep looking back.

"Steinbeck would approve," she offered.

I took another sip of wine, glancing around the café. "What was the least favorite book you had to read in school?"

"Oh, that's easy. *The Scarlet Letter*." She made a face, leaning forward as she dropped her chin into her hand. "I hated every single person in that book."

"Even Hester Prynne?"

"*Especially* Hester Prynne. I mean, I get it, poor woman and all, but let's be honest—she could've just told everyone to shove it, and moved on with her life. I have no patience for martyrdom. What was your worst read?"

"*Great Expectations*." I leaned back in my chair, grimacing at the memory. "Pip's the most annoying character ever written. He spends the entire book pining after someone who clearly hates him. I wanted to shake him *hard*."

Pearl laughed, a warm, genuine sound that made the corners of her eyes crinkle. "You hated Pip? I didn't even think that was possible. He's so...." She paused, searching for the word.

"Pathetic?" I offered.

She made a face. "Not exactly," she said, and then, with a twinkle, added, "In British English, they'd say *wretched*."

"Exactly." I pointed at her with my wine glass. "You get it."

"He isn't my favorite, but *hate* might be too strong a word." She raised her glass in a mock toast. "To being mildly irritated with Pip."

"That's too coy. I'm going to go strong with hating Pip." I clinked my glass lightly against hers.

Mathieu returned with our charcuterie board, setting it down between us. For a moment, the colorful arrangement of cheeses, cured meats, and fruits became the center of attention—until she began to eat. I found myself watching her closely, curious if her anorexia might reveal itself in the way she handled her food. There was no such sign, but then again, what did I know? I wasn't exactly an expert on the disease, was I? Still, I resolved to learn more—something a good friend would do—and to stay vigilant for her sake.

Yeah, your fiancée is going to really appreciate that, Rhett?

Fuck! Being with Pearl made me forget Josie, forget that I was trapped in a relationship I didn't want. Could I break free? It would be a shitshow, but then wouldn't divorce later be a bigger one? My *real* friends knew this was a bad relationship for me, I just needed to find my balls and do the right thing.

Pearl and I fell into an easy rhythm of conversation, picking at slices of prosciutto and soft brie as we talked about everything and nothing. Books, mostly old favorites, recent discoveries, authors we'd loved and hated. But there were other things, too. Small glimpses of the people we'd become, the lives we'd lived outside of Savannah.

I learned that she'd been to Paris once, which she'd always wanted to do, and had spent an entire afternoon wandering through Shakespeare & Company, the iconic English-language bookstore on the Left Bank, just across the Seine from Notre Dame. She said it felt like stepping into a dream.

"Do you have someplace you've always wanted to visit?" she asked.

"I'd like to go to Patagonia someday," I confessed.

"Really?"

"It's like the end of the world, isn't it?" I pondered wistfully. "Someplace untouched, wild. Like you could stand there and feel...small, but in a good way. Like all the noise and expectations would finally be far enough away to let you just exist."

She tilted her head as if studying me. "By expectations, I assume you're talking about your family?"

I nodded. "The truth is that sometimes I feel like I've spent my whole life living for other people—doing what's expected, being who I'm *supposed* to be."

"And Patagonia?"

"It feels like it would be the kind of place where none of those things would matter. Just the mountains, the glaciers, the sky. I'd be *free*."

Her fingers grazed the rim of her glass. "So, what's stopping you?"

I smiled self-deprecatingly. "Everything. Work. Family. Expectations. You know how it is."

"Maybe you should say '*to hell with everything*' and go see the glaciers."

I wanted to ask her if she'd come with me. I wanted her holding my hand when I looked up at blue skies, breathing in my freedom.

"Patagonia will have to wait," I replied quietly.

We both knew I wasn't talking about taking off to the southernmost tip of South America.

"Leaving Savannah showed me there was more to life than...well, whatever it was Birdie was always chasing." She put her hand on mine in a comforting gesture. Her compassion bowled me over. I was the asshole, the villain in her story, and yet, she was being kind to me. But what was even more surprising was how easy it was to open myself up to Pearl, to show her the cracks I'd been hiding, the weight of expectations I wasn't sure I could carry any more.

CHAPTER 16

Pearl

There was a skip in my step. No, seriously—I'd never skipped before in my life, but there it was. For a woman who had always felt heavy, no matter what the scale said, this was a banner day.

I'd talked to my therapist the day after I returned from Newport Beach, and he'd been happy to hear that I'd not forgiven or forgotten what happened with Rhett but that I had made my peace.

"Why the hell didn't I do this before?" I wondered, *annoyed with myself for holding my bitterness and anger, my fear so close to me that it had almost killed me.*

"You weren't ready," my therapist informed me. *"You'd never have believed his sincerity earlier."*

"Am I a fool to believe it now?"

"That's fear, Pearl."

"Yeah, tell me about it; I feel it all the fucking time."

"Okay, say he's pretending to be sorry. What's the worst thing that could happen?"

I pondered that question for a while. He and I often did an exercise in which we unraveled a situation to the worst possible result, and then I had to find my way back to the plausible present.

"He'd find a way to make everyone laugh at me, ridicule me."

"Okay. How would that look like?"

I licked my lips, humiliation coursing through me as memories of the past assaulted me.

"He'd tell everyone that I was still interested in him, but he isn't interested in me because I'm fat and ugly—and he's engaged. He'd tell everyone that I'm a horny slut who wanted to fuck him, even though he found me disgusting."

It wasn't until I felt my cheeks become wet that I realized I was crying.

My therapist gave me a somber look from across my computer screen. "What brought up those tears for you?"

"I remembered how I felt after all that happened." I felt weighed down suddenly, like I was, once again, a gazillion pounds. "I was feeling fine, but now...I...."

"Pearl, did you throw yourself at him?"

I shook my head.

"Did he indicate in any way at all that he'd make fun of you?"

I shook my head again.

"What is the likelihood of this scenario ever happening?"

I shrugged. "I don't know." I felt pathetic.

"Pearl, let's say all of Savannah laughs at you. Do you really care what they think?"

"I do care." My voice was small, I felt small.

"Do you care what your mother thinks?"

I paused. "No." I really didn't.

"Cash?"

I snorted.

"Would Nina Davenport believe these rumors?"

"No. And even if she did, it wouldn't change how she felt about me. She'd continue to mentor me, respect me." I was confident of this.

"Aunt Hattie?"

I smiled. "She'd tell me I could do better than her nephew."

"So, the people you respect would not let you down."

"Yeah, you're right."

Once I internalized that, I started to feel a lot better. But what also helped was Rhett texting me. They were innocuous messages similar to ones I received from Luna, Aurora, and even Aunt Hattie. He and I were friends, and sure, I had the hots for him, but he didn't know that. In any case, he was engaged, so it wasn't like we'd ever go there.

Why the hell was he with Josie? A man who appreciated Paul Auster and hated Pip would not be happy with someone like her.

Stop it, Pearl. You don't want to be one of those people who wants the lives of others.

"Someone looks like they either got up on the right side

157

of the bed or from the *right* bed," Nova, our office manager, grinned appreciatively when she saw me stroll into work.

My clothing choices tended to go from black to gray to beige. But when I woke up that morning, fueled by a good conversation with my therapist and a funny "good morning" meme from Rhett, I hadn't wanted to slip into my usual boring suits. Instead, I put on a peach-colored dress.

Yep!

A bright peach sheath dress with a matching suit jacket. I wore my bumblebee necklace and daisy earrings to go with it.

Owning the name Bumblebee had been an idea I'd gotten from reading a book where a woman who'd been bullied did the same. I felt empowered when I created my Tinder account and started to expel the old feelings I experienced when I thought about the cruel way I was treated.

"I always am in the right bed: *mine*," I scoffed with good humor.

I felt remarkably light, as if telling Rhett the ugly truths had somehow helped me shed them. I had told the man who'd hurt me how much he'd fucked up my life, and he'd been penitent; he'd validated what I felt and what happened to me—he hadn't made fun of me or made excuses, as I feared he would.

The weight I'd been carrying for so long was not exactly gone, but it had shifted, so it wasn't pressing down on me quite so heavily anymore.

As I walked to my office, the usual clatter of keyboards and muted phone calls were like background music. When I passed through the finance department, people gave me curious looks, most probably because of how I was dressed. Usually, I avoided eye contact, keeping my head straight and my steps brisk. Today, I smiled back and cheerfully said *good morning*. It was strange how small things like that felt so monumental.

"Good morning, Pearl," Layla called as I passed her office door, waving me in.

"It's *absolutely* a good morning." I stepped inside.

Layla set her phone down on her desk and leaned casually against the edge, crossing her arms as she studied me with a raised eyebrow. "Alright," she teased, her lips curving into a sly smile, "you've either had a life-changing epiphany or someone spiked your coffee with something strong. Spill it—what's going on?"

"What? Can't a girl wear some color without everyone wondering what's going on?"

"Absolutely not," Layla stated.

I chuckled, shaking my head. "I feel good today."

"Really?" She raised an eyebrow. "Usually, you're rushing to start up a call or a meeting, and what you say is you're *busy*, never *good*. Should we alert the press?"

I rolled my eyes, but I couldn't stop the smile tugging at my lips. "I don't know what to tell you, Layla."

She gave me a knowing look. "You don't have to tell me a thing, Pearl. It's good to see you so bright and cheerful."

I nodded, my fingers brushing over my dress. "I am, however, still as busy as they come."

"Of course, you are." Layla smirked. "Well, whatever it is

that's happening, keep it up. You've got a glow about you, Pearl. Don't let anyone dim it."

A glow? I didn't know if I believed that, but as I sat down at my desk and opened my email, my phone buzzed with a text, and I couldn't help but smile when I saw Rhett's name on the screen.

Rhett: *Okay, I'll admit it. Steinbeck's description of the Dust Bowl is...kind of brilliant.*

Me: *Kind of brilliant? The way he makes you feel the suffocation is completely brilliant!*

Rhett: *Fine, completely brilliant, but still depressing as hell.*

Me: *True, but also profound and life-changing.*

Rhett: *Want to place bets on how many chapters it'll take before I'm completely emotionally wrecked?*

Me: *Three. Tops.*

Rhett: *If you lose, I pick the next book we read together.*

Me: *Deal! P.S. I started last night and my heart hurts already. I forgot how this book wrecked me in the best ways possible.*

Rhett: *I'm going to hang in there and show you I'm made of sterner stuff.*

I set my phone down, still smiling as I turned to my spreadsheets. Maybe Layla was right. Perhaps I *did* have a glow about me.

By the end of the day, I was buzzing with energy. Halfway home, an idea hit me: *I should cook dinner tonight.*

It was such a simple thought, but it stopped me in my tracks. Cooking had never been my thing. Food, for so many years, had been nothing but an enemy, a constant battlefield. But lately, the idea of food—real food, prepared with care—felt palatable.

I stopped at the market and bought some fresh vegetables, chicken, a loaf of crusty bread, and a bottle of Chardonnay.

When I got back to the cottage, I called Aunt Hattie.

"Dinner?" she repeated, her tone laced with mock suspicion. "You're cooking?"

Aunt Hattie and I often ate together, usually at her place. She had a cook, and she knew I wasn't proficient in the kitchen, so I understood that she was surprised *and* suspicious.

"Yes, Aunt Hattie," I said with a laugh. "I promise it'll be edible." *Fingers crossed!*

"Alright, alright," she asserted. "What time should I be there?"

"Seven, and it's nothing fancy," I warned her, suddenly feeling chagrined that I'd fuck up the meal, as I hadn't cooked in a long while.

"Darlin', even if you made grilled cheese, it'd be fancy 'cause *you* made it."

I changed into shorts and a tank top, put on Brazilian jazz, and, as I hummed to "Girl from Ipanema," I put together a meal thanks to Jamie Oliver's step-by-step video instructions.

By the time Aunt Hattie arrived, my cottage smelled like garlic and thyme. The chicken, along with carrots, potatoes, and Brussels sprouts, was roasting in the oven, and the blanched green beans were ready to sauté as soon as I set the chicken to rest.

"Oh my," Hattie announced as she stepped in with a bottle of Malbec and she saw I'd set the table with simple white plates, silverware, and white cloth napkins.

"Pearl Beaumont." Hattie surveyed the scene. "I didn't think I'd live to see the day."

"Very funny." I waved her toward the table.

We sat down, and for the first time in forever, I felt relaxed as I ate.

The chicken was a little overdone, and the green beans weren't as crisp as I'd hoped, but Hattie didn't seem to mind. She sipped her wine, laughing as we talked about everything and nothing.

"What brought this about, darlin'?" Hattie asked when I was clearing the plates.

"I feel good," I told her, and then, because she deserved to know why, I added, "Rhett and I talked in Newport Beach."

Aunt Hattie cocked an eyebrow.

I grinned and told her *everything* except how I was attracted to Rhett. Partly, because he was engaged, and partly because it made me feel like a fool to be even remotely interested in a man who had done to me what Rhett had, albeit, back then, he hadn't been a man but a boy.

"He finally got his head out of his ass," Hattie mused. "I'm *very* pleased to hear that. Now, if only he'd get rid of Josie, he could *finally* be happy."

"You don't think he's happy with Josie?" It seemed like

the proper follow-up question, so I asked it, not because I wanted to know.

Right!

"I told you she trapped him by pretending to get knocked up."

"Aunt Hattie, no one does that anymore," I protested as I closed the dishwasher. "Not even Josie."

She snorted.

I returned to my seat next to her at the dining table.

My cottage had an open-plan kitchen-dining-living space, and two bedrooms—one of which I'd converted into an office. It also had a gorgeous porch with a path to the pond. The porch was surrounded by Aunt Hattie's beautiful garden, which included magnolia, live oak, and fruit trees, as well as manicured rows of flowers. I loved living here, and having Aunt Hattie so close was a bonus.

"Rhett is so busy being a Vanderbilt that he's forgotten to just be himself. Actually, I don't think he even knows who he is. But I know he's trying to find out. The fact that he opened up to you and apologized makes me proud." Aunt Hattie took my hand in hers. "And I'm proud of you for moving past the past, my darlin', 'cause you deserve all the happiness this world has to offer."

That night, as I brushed my teeth, I felt like I climbed Mount Everest in my shorts. I'd made a meal. I'd shared it. I hadn't thought once about how much food was on my plate or how much I was eating. And the best part? I enjoyed all of it.

By the time I climbed into bed, I was pleasantly tired.

I was just about to turn off my lamp when my phone buzzed with a call on the nightstand. I picked it up, and Rhett's name flashed on the screen.

I answered immediately. "Hey."

"Hey," he said, his voice low and warm. "I hope I'm not calling too late."

"No, it's fine." I settled back against my pillows. "What's up besides you and me, that is?"

Was Josie not with him? I knew from the grapevine that they weren't living together. Josie was still at her parents' place, since she'd sold her place after Rhett proposed to her. The rumor was that she'd been ready to move into his house, but he'd told her he wanted to wait until they were married. The other rumor was that Josie wanted the whole house overhauled, renovated, and updated, which was why she hadn't moved in.

"I just finished chapter three." I could hear the faint smile in his voice. "You were right. I'm wrecked."

I giggled. "I warned you. Steinbeck doesn't hold back."

"So, you're going to have to pick the next book for us to read when we're done with *The Grapes of Wrath*."

Given how I felt about him, I shouldn't have encouraged this friendship. But...there was nothing wrong with being friends with an engaged man—as long as we kept it platonic, right?

"Have you read *Catch-22*?"

"Major Major?"

"You have!"

"A long time ago. I don't mind rereading it if you don't. I've forgotten so much."

"How could you forget Doc Daneeka telling Yossarian that there was a catch?" I teased.

"Words to the effect," he stopped as if recollecting. "*If you're sane enough to not want to fly, you must. If you're crazy enough to want to, you can't.*"

"Ah, so you do remember."

"You know what I *really* remember? How reading the book made me feel. I was laughing a lot at the beginning, but then I started to realize how messed up everything was. By the end, it hit me—none of it was funny. Not Nately's whore, not Yossarian standing in the lineup naked—none of it."

I was surprised that he not only had read *Catch-22* but he had also reflected upon it. "I think it'll be good to read that book with you."

Stop this, Pearl. You're falling for this guy again. Nothing good is going to come out of it.

For a while, we talked about Joseph Heller's only great book—Rhett's thoughts on the characters, and my memories of reading it for the first time. But the conversation drifted, as it always seemed to with Rhett, to other things.

He told me about a client he'd met that day, someone who reminded him of one of Steinbeck's Joads, and I told him about dinner with Aunt Hattie.

"What did you make?" He didn't make a big deal out of me cooking, just asked a natural question.

I told him, and added, "It wasn't anything fancy, but it felt...good."

"It sounds good," he said, his voice soft.

For a moment, there was silence, the kind that felt heavy with things unsaid.

"Pearl," he said finally, his voice quieter now, almost hesitant. "I...I'm happy we're talking again. That we're friends."

"Me too," I said, my chest tightening.

But as the call ended and I set the phone down, I couldn't ignore the way my heart ached. Because no matter how much I tried to tell myself we were *just friends*, the truth was I wanted more.

And he wasn't mine to want.

CHAPTER 17

Rhett

I was done.

I probably had been for a while, but until I spent time with Pearl, I didn't realize how far I had fallen from who I had hoped to become. I admired her. She'd overcome unfathomable pain to live her life on her terms. The irony of being inspired by Pearl to live better when I'd been so clueless as a teenager wasn't lost on me.

I *had* wanted to talk to Josie privately at my place, but she insisted that we go to Elizabeth's on 37th for dinner. It wasn't ideal, but it would have to do.

I had decided to end our engagement.

I didn't love Josie—and I'd *never* love someone like her. Getting married for the sake of reputation and status was making less and less sense to me. It wasn't going to be easy. Hell no! Josie would fight this. My parents would be absolutely against it. But as Royal put it, George Vanderbilt didn't have to marry and live with Josie; I did, and I didn't want to. It was as simple as that, and would be complicated as fuck to navigate. In our world, we didn't do things or *not* do them because of the heart's desire. We followed a path put in front of us by society because we *were*, after all, society. If the elite didn't follow the dictates, the world order would fall apart. I guess I was about to topple said order.

Bring out the gallows!

"I've been dying to eat here for ages," Josie exclaimed as we sat at the bar, waiting for our table to be ready.

I appreciated a good restaurant as much as the next person, and this one was impeccable—crisp white tablecloths, candlelight flickering in crystal holders, and a polite hum of conversation spoken in low tones.

I doubted I could laugh too loudly without earning a judgmental glance—probably from someone who knew my family or me. There had already been several nods and murmured acknowledgments. Josie, of course, fit in effortlessly. Her cream-colored dress was tailored to perfection, her blonde hair swept into a chignon that had likely taken her stylist an hour to create.

She was as fake as the elegance of this place and I could almost hear my father say, *"Josie Vance will make an excellent Vanderbilt bride."*

I was regretting this setting more and more as I saw one familiar face after the other. I should've thought this through—but honestly, I didn't need another argument with Josie when we were about to have the mother of all fights when I told her she could keep the ring but not the man.

"Rhett, Josie! We haven't seen you since the engagement party," chirped Clementine Chamberlain, one of Savannah's many professional gossips. Her husband Robert stood at her side, nodding amiably while his eyes darted toward the bar. He was a known alcoholic.

"Clementine, darlin', you look lovely." Josie's smile was so polished it practically gleamed. "It's been a whirlwind. Between wedding planning and Rhett's busy schedule, we haven't had a moment to breathe."

"I can imagine." Clementine shot me a sly smile. "You're a lucky man, Rhett. Josie's quite the catch."

I nodded politely, noncommittally, before glancing at Josie, who now looked irritated. She noticed the lack of enthusiasm in my demeanor, I could tell. She always noticed when I was pulling away, and I knew that she knew that the conversation I wanted to have wasn't about what fucking flowers I wanted for our wedding. It was probably why she insisted we eat out. Damn the woman! Did she really think she could put this off?

After a few more strained pleasantries with Clementine and Robert, we were finally taken to our table with our drinks.

Once we were seated, Josie took a sip of her wine. I could see the tension in her shoulders. The way her fingers gripped the stem of the glass tightly made me wonder if she knew what was coming.

She talked about this, that, and the other with gusto, aware that people looking at us should always see us as a happy couple, so in love with each other.

No matter what people looking into our relationship saw or thought, she knew that we weren't in a good place. I barely talked to her. I didn't fuck her. I all but checked out when she spoke of the wedding.

I wish I'd had the emotional wherewithal not to have proposed to her, regardless of how knocked up she was. I should've said we'd co-parent, that I'd be there for her, but I wouldn't marry her. Sure, that would have pissed our families off, but it wasn't like I could avoid it now. Actually, I'd made it worse. Breaking up after that farce of an engagement party was going to cause endless chatter.

She kept talking, but I was barely paying attention, trying to figure out how best to tell her in a fucking *public* setting that the engagement was over; the wedding was off. And, yeah, I'd cover any costs that came from canceling whatever the hell had already been booked a year in advance.

She set her glass down with deliberate precision. "I thought you wanted to talk, but now getting you to say anything is like pulling teeth."

I looked down at my bourbon, the amber liquid swirling as I turned the glass in my hand.

Damn it, this wasn't how I wanted to do it. Not here, not like this. But there was never going to be a good moment for this conversation, was there?

"I'd have preferred to do this in privacy."

"Do what?" Her lower lip trembled.

"I've been thinking a lot about *us*, Josie. I don't believe we're suited for one another. You're lovely, and you'll make—"

"Shut up," she hissed.

Christ! The dramatics had already begun.

"I'm happy to do so," I drawled, "but it's not going to change the facts."

"Which are?" she demanded angrily, and then, just like that, she smiled because our server had come to the table.

Yeah, she was as genuine as a three-dollar bill at a church bake sale.

"Darlin', why don't you order first? I'm still making up my mind." She even fluttered her eyelashes.

The poor server was speechless. Josie was beautiful. If only he could see what was inside.

I ordered the pepper-crusted beef tenderloin with buttermilk mashed potatoes, asparagus, and Madeira cream sauce.

I told the waiter *no*, I wouldn't be ordering an appetizer. I didn't think I could stand eating a three-course meal with Josie.

Josie wasn't in on my dinner and dash plan, so after much dawdling, she ended up ordering the sea scallops without the lemon butter. However, she obviously wanted a side salad.

"It's too greasy with the butter, and I need to, you know, lose some weight before the wedding." Josie handed her menu to the server, who flushed.

"Isn't the whole point of scallops the brown butter?" I couldn't resist throwing at Josie.

She scoffed and rolled her eyes. The server was gone; the *real* Josie was back.

"And you should eat the butter if you want to, Josie, because there isn't going to be a wedding," I added.

Her face tightened. "What's that supposed to mean?" she asked, her tone sharp.

"Jesus, Josie, exactly what I said. I don't want to marry you." Okay, so I didn't want to say it like this, but she was shredding my patience.

Her eyes narrowed, and for a moment, she said nothing. Then she leaned forward, her voice low and laced with disbelief. "Rhett, we've been engaged for six months. We're getting married in a year. The venue has been booked. I'm getting ready to buy my dress. Now is not the time to get cold feet."

I shook my head. This woman was unbelievable. "Josie, I don't have cold feet. I'm ending our engagement and calling off the wedding. I'm telling you I don't want to marry you."

Was that fuckin' explicit enough for her?

"Please." She picked up her glass of wine and sipped. "Your mother warned me that you'd want to pull a rabbit."

I almost laughed at that. Did Josie really think insulting me was going to help her case?

"Darlin', I ain't rabbiting on you; I'm telling you that we're not getting married."

I had wanted to be subtle and careful, but the hell with it. If she couldn't treat me with respect, I wasn't going to afford her the same courtesy. Just because I was polite didn't mean I didn't have an asshole streak. She, of all people, should know that.

"How do you think your father is going to feel about this?" she sneered.

"My father isn't marrying you, Josie."

The server returned with bread for our table, and Josie all but snarled at him, "I just told you I'm getting married, so please take that away."

"Please forgive my companion; she hasn't eaten much all day, so she's hangry." I smiled at the server. "And do leave the bread. I love your focaccia."

The server, not sure what was up, left the breadbasket, and all but ran from our table.

I picked up a slice of warm, freshly baked roll and cut it open. I spread butter over it while Josie seethed.

"What do you think you're doing?" she demanded.

"Eating carbs." I bit into the bread with relish.

She flinched. "What's gotten into you, Rhett?"

"I was hoping we'd have a conversation, Josie. Instead, you decided to just ignore what I was saying." I took another bite and chewed thoughtfully. "So, are we going to talk now, or are you going to pretend I didn't say what I just did?"

She flinched. "What's gotten into you?"

"This is who I am," I said bluntly, locking eyes with her. "I like getting my way, Josie, and I know you do, too. But this time, you're not getting yours. I'm not going to marry you. I'm sorry to put it like this, but if you've been paying attention—and I know you have—you saw this coming."

"What's that supposed to mean?" Her face was all but crumpling, and I was afraid she was going to cry. I would not hear the end of it if she did at this restaurant with at least fifty sets of familiar eyes on us.

Despite how much of a bitch she could be, what I was doing to her was a terrible thing. This would be a second engagement that was ending for Josie, and even though she'd be more devastated about how that looked rather than the fact that we'd not be together, she didn't deserve this.

"I am sorry," I said sincerely. "I should've discussed this with you much earlier. In fact, we should never have gotten engaged just because you were pregnant."

"Is this because I lost the baby?"

I was horrified that she'd suggest that, but I understood why she went there. Losing a baby was hard. I hadn't even been physically pregnant, and I'd felt the loss. She had been connected to our child, so I could only imagine her pain and guilt. And wasn't that why I'd succumbed to the pressure to marry her in the first place?

"No, Josie, I would have ended it right then, if that was the case." I took a deep breath and tamped down my anger. I didn't want to become the Rhett who said hurtful things. I had done that way too many times, and now I knew what the consequence of that was for at least one person. "The truth is that I don't love you."

"What's that got to do with us getting married?"

She couldn't be that jaded, could she?

"You've told me several times that you love me. Do you?"

"Yes."

I didn't believe her. Josie was one of *those* people, I had learned, who only loved herself and didn't know how to care for others, not genuinely. This was why she was unable to listen to what I was saying about not wanting to marry her. In her mind, she wanted to marry me, and that was that.

"*I* don't love you," I said flatly.

Before she could respond, the server returned with our food.

Josie barely touched her meal, and I felt tremendously guilty for letting my mouth run off. I should've been careful with her, been kinder.

"Your father isn't going to let you back out." Her eyes were blazing with anger.

"Like I said, my father isn't the one getting married."

"Does he even know what you're saying to me right now? He finds out, and he's going to...."

"To what, Josie?" This was why it was hard to be compassionate when it came to my soon-to-be former fiancée. She went from sad to snake in seconds. "I'm not financially dependent on him—though the Vanderbilt wealth is on me."

She looked surprised, and I knew why. Not many knew, or rather, my father had made sure that it wasn't common knowledge, that I managed the Vanderbilt estate and trust. I was the reason that our family was doing so well financially.

"You're going to destroy the Vanderbilt name," she shot back.

"Not when I'm making as much money as I am." I

decided to enjoy my meal because one thing was clear: Josie
didn't warrant my sympathy or compassion. She was actually
threatening me to continue this engagement.

"After all that I've done, you're going to just end us?"
There were tears in her voice, but for once, I wasn't sure if
they were genuine or if she was putting them on; she was
capable of doing so.

"Come on, Josie, what have you done?" I asked, exasperated.

"So, if I'd had the baby, you'd marry me?"

It was like talking to a wall, I thought. "No, Josie, then
we'd co-parent, but we wouldn't—"

"Like I'd let you come near my child after you break our
engagement."

I sighed. "Josie, there is no child." *And I'm so fucking
glad because you, as a mother, would ruin any kid.*

"I can't believe you're doing this. I mean…did something
happen in California?"

"What do you think would happen?" I challenged.

Her eyes went from sad to horrified to malicious. "Oh
my God! This is about Pearl, isn't it?"

"What the fuck is wrong with you?" I demanded, now
nearly entirely out of patience. "This is about *us*. About the
fact that I don't think I'm the man you need, and you're not
the kind of woman I want. We can't give each other the lives
we want."

"That's bullshit," she snapped, her voice rising enough
to earn a few curious glances from nearby tables.

"Keep your voice down," I muttered.

She leaned in closer, her eyes blazing. "You're scared. That's all this is. You're scared of settling down. But I love you, Rhett. I've loved you since the day we met. And I know you love me, too."

I didn't say anything because we were going in circles. There was no point. I would talk to her parents—I'd have to —and mine, and close this down.

Her voice trembled with desperation. "Please, Rhett. Don't do this. Don't throw away everything we've built. We're good together. We're perfect for each other."

This woman was remarkably clueless, but I wasn't any better. I had actually thought I could marry her, build a life with her, and have children with her, which would've been the ultimate travesty.

"I'm sorry. I wish I could feel the way you do, but I don't. You should marry someone who loves you as much as you love them, Josie."

Tears welled in her eyes, and she blinked them back furiously, refusing to let them fall. "I can't believe you're doing this at a restaurant, of all places."

"For Christ's sake, Josie, *you* insisted we come here."

"I didn't know you were going to do this."

I sighed. There was no point repeating that I wanted to have a private conversation. I had told her, but she'd....

"We can fix this," she pleaded.

I wanted to tell her that there was nothing to fix. *That* was the problem. This wasn't a fight or a misunderstanding.

It was a truth I'd been running from for months, and now that I'd finally spoken it, I couldn't take it back. Hell, I didn't want to.

"I'm sorry," I said again. "But I can't do this."

"We'll see," she threw back at me, and pierced a butterless scallop and chewed on it.

CHAPTER 18
Pearl

Aunt Hattie and I were sitting in her garden room, which was blissfully air-conditioned. It was *hot* in Savannah. Summer was here with a vengeance, and anyone who ever thought that climate change was a myth could rethink that notion because we were having record-high temperatures.

Missy, Aunt Hattie's housekeeper and majordomo, set out iced tea for us and joined us. Missy had been with Aunt Hattie for nearly two decades. She was younger than her employer by a decade or so, but no one was really sure. There were rumors that Missy and Aunt Hattie were lovers, but I hadn't seen any indication of that, but if they were, more power to them.

Missy was African American and carried herself with immense grace. Her presence commanded respect, whether she was managing Hattie's household or calmly stepping into one of Savannah's more contentious charity meetings to restore order. She always dressed impeccably in crisp linen blouses and tailored skirts; her hair swept back into a low bun that gave her an air of effortless elegance.

Aunt Hattie shuffled through a folder filled with papers. "Pearl, darlin', I know you hate this stuff, but we need to talk about the gala," she said, her Southern accent curling around the words like ribbons of honey.

I groaned.

"None of that, young lady. It's going to be the event of the season, and I'm counting on you to charm some of those deep pockets into opening up their wallets."

I shook my head, amused. "You know I'm better with numbers than people, Aunt Hattie."

"Don't sell yourself short, sweetheart," she admonished. "You've got that Beaumont charm—when you choose to use it, that is."

"Beaumont charm sounds like an oxymoron." I held up my iced tea with a toast.

Missy chuckled. "Now, Miss Pearl, you know Hattie's got a knack for 'voluntelling' people to do things. If she says you're going to charm them, you better believe it."

Hattie gave a mock gasp, clutching at her pearls. "Missy, you wound me. I merely guide people toward their *true* potential."

"Guided me right into a whole lot of trouble over the years," Missy reproached.

I smiled, watching the easy banter between the two of them. Missy had a way of making Hattie seem less like the Grande Dame of Savannah and more like...well, herself.

"What's the focus this year?" I asked, steering the conversation back to the event.

"Women's healthcare," Hattie said, her tone growing serious. "We're partnering with the Savannah Women's Health Initiative to raise money for free mammograms, cervical cancer screenings, prenatal care—you name it. The need's greater than ever, and Lord knows we're in a state that doesn't make it easy for women to get the care they need."

Missy shook her head in disgust. "There are so many women falling through the cracks, especially those who are underprivileged. This could make a real difference."

I felt a swell of pride for both of them—Aunt Hattie for using her influence to push for change, and Missy for being the steady, guiding hand behind so many of Hattie's efforts.

"Do we have a venue yet?" I asked, already thinking about the logistics.

"The estate, of course." Hattie gestured around her. "Who else in Savannah has a garden that could accommodate half the city and still leave room for a dance floor?"

"You're not wrong," I admitted. It was not difficult to picture the sprawling grounds filled with guests in their summer best, sipping champagne and pretending not to sweat in the Savannah humidity, still raging in the autumn.

"We'll also need you on the finance end, Pearl. Someone needs to manage the budget and all of that," Missy added, her sharp eyes meeting mine. "We're going to auction off some big-ticket items—a trip to Paris, a private dinner with a Michelin-starred chef, that kind of thing. Hattie's good at shaking the tree, but you're the one who has to make sure every penny ends up where it's supposed to."

"I'm all in." This was one of the things I loved about being back in Savannah, working with people like Aunt Hattie and Nina Davenport to help the community. In Los Angeles, I worked a corporate job and nothing more—here, I had the contacts and network to do more.

Aunt Hattie reached over and patted my hand. "I knew I could count on you, darlin'. And who knows? Maybe we'll even find you a dance partner that night."

I rolled my eyes, but I couldn't help smiling. "Let's focus on the fundraising first, shall we?"

"Fine, fine," Aunt Hattie chuckled.

Missy raised her glass. "To women's healthcare—and Miss Pearl, for putting up with us."

"To women's healthcare," I echoed, clinking my glass against hers.

We were discussing guest lists and catering when the doorbell rang. Shortly after that, Rhett walked in, following a maid.

"Well, well, two of my favorite people with me at the same time." Aunt Hattie rose and hugged her nephew.

"And what am I, chopped liver?" Missy complained.

"I think she meant you and Pearl, Missy." Rhett leaned down to kiss Missy's cheek.

I was grateful he only smiled and said hello to me, keeping his hands to himself. I was on shaky ground with Rhett—my feelings were all over the place.

"Have you eaten lunch?" Missy asked.

Rhett looked strained. He had dark circles around his eyes. "I'm fine, Missy. But I wouldn't say no to some of that iced tea you got there."

Missy didn't need to be told twice. She headed toward the kitchen, muttering about fixing him a plate, whether he wanted one or not.

I poured him a glass of iced tea and set it in front of him. He sat in an armchair across from Aunt Hattie while I sat next to her on a loveseat.

We were surrounded by greenery both inside and out, making the garden room feel like a tropical paradise but cooler.

"Thanks, darlin'," he murmured. He drank half the tea and set the glass down, looking pensive.

Aunt Hattie tilted her head, narrowing her sharp eyes at Rhett. "Well, you look like you've been through hell, darlin'. What's happened now? Don't tell me your father has driven you to drink before sundown."

"Only tea," Rhett joked weakly.

"You want to talk about it?" Aunt Hattie offered.

Rhett gave her a weary smile, running a hand through his hair. "I called off my engagement with Josie last night."

The air seemed to shift in the room, a ripple of surprise followed by silence. My heart stopped for a beat, my breath caught in my throat.

Aunt Hattie's lips curved into a broad smile. "Good for you. I'm assuming the shit has hit the fan?"

Rhett laughed in self-deprecation. "Not yet, but it's

going to. She didn't take it well. I wanted to do it quietly, but she insisted we eat at Elizabeth's and—"

"Please tell me you didn't dump her in a public place, Rhett Vanderbilt," Aunt Hattie chided.

"I thought we'd talk, but...she's fuckin' delusional, Aunt Hattie. I'm telling her we're not working out, and she's telling the server she can't eat bread 'cause she needs to fit into a wedding dress." Rhett ran a hand through his hair. "Next thing I know, my temper ran away, and I told her we're done. She threatened to sic my father on me."

"Well, she will," Aunt Hattie remarked calmly. "But, son, we both know that he doesn't have the power in this relationship; you do."

"I do?" Rhett obviously didn't believe that.

"You hold the purse strings," Aunt Hattie stated triumphantly. "And in Savannah, the one with those strings, is the puppeteer."

"You *have* met my father, haven't you?" Rhett commented sarcastically.

"George Vanderbilt is a pompous ass, and I feared for a long time that you'd end up like him." She looked at me when she said that, and I knew why. What Rhett had done to me was most definitely on the path to pompous assholery.

"And now?" Rhett prompted.

"Now, I think you're going to be fine, as long as you don't let George bully you into living a life that isn't meant for you."

"What *is* meant for me, Aunt Hattie?" Rhett asked

wearily. "I don't know anymore." He turned to look at me then, his eyes bleak.

I didn't say anything. What could I say? *Hey, real glad you ditched that bitch, now, how about you and I shake it up like old times, without the pool scene?*

"Oh, please!" Aunt Hattie scoffed, waving her hand dismissively. "We're all figuring out who we are, *and* all the time, that's called growing. In any case, *that* girl wasn't right for you, and deep down, you knew it. Took you long enough to get rid of her."

Missy returned with a plate of ham and pimento cheese sandwiches for Rhett, the edges of the bread perfectly golden from a quick toasting in the skillet. She set it down in front of him, the aroma of melted cheese and smoky ham wafting up, before settling back into her seat with a satisfied look.

"He broke off the engagement," Aunt Hattie announced.

"Thank God," Missy exclaimed with noticeable relief.

Rhett raised an eyebrow at her. "You too, Missy?"

Missy shrugged, utterly unapologetic. "Couldn't stand that Vance girl. Pretty face, but that's about it. No depth. No heart. And don't even get me started on her mother. *Now,* eat something."

Dutifully, Rhett picked up a sandwich, and I could almost see the energy flow back into him as he chewed.

Aunt Hattie smirked at Missy's bluntness. "Well said." She then turned to me. "What do you think, Pearl?"

"Not my place to think about this, Aunt Hattie," I replied flatly.

I couldn't even fake a smile.

He was free.

Rhett Vanderbilt was no longer engaged. No longer tethered to Josie Vance.

And suddenly, all the feelings I'd been trying to suppress —the attraction, the confusion, the pull I felt every time he was near me—came rushing to the surface like a tidal wave.

But along with that came darkness and a chill that went all the way to the bone.

He doesn't want you, a voice in my head whispered, cruel and familiar. *Why would he? You're damaged, Pearl. A mess. You've spent years trying to fix yourself, and even now, you can barely hold it together when things get messy.*

The voice grew louder, sharper, as if it had been waiting for the perfect moment to strike. *You're not beautiful like Josie. Why would someone like him want someone like you?*

I swallowed hard, my throat dry, and my hands trembled slightly as I reached for my glass of iced tea. I took a sip, but even the cool liquid felt wrong, like my body was rejecting it.

Putting anything edible inside me felt impossible now, the familiar knot of anxiety tightening in my stomach. The room seemed to close in around me, the conversation fading into the background as the voice in my head kept going, relentless. *Don't eat or drink any more*, it whispered. *You don't deserve to, not after indulging in such ridiculous thoughts.*

I placed the glass back on the table.

"Pearl?" Rhett's voice pulled me back, and I looked up to find him watching me, his brows furrowed in concern.

"Hmm?" I tried to sound casual.

"Are you okay?" he asked, his gaze holding mine.

"I'm fine," I said, and because I needed everyone not to focus on me, I added, "You made a rather big decision. Are you sure you weren't hasty?"

What I wanted to ask was: *Why did you do it? Why now?*

"No. In fact, I think I've been too slow in doin' this," he affirmed confidently.

Hattie and Missy chimed in, offering more words of encouragement. I nodded along, forcing a smile when it seemed appropriate.

By the time Rhett left and the house quieted again, I felt raw and exhausted. Aunt Hattie touched my arm gently as I stood to leave. "You alright, darlin'?" she asked, her eyes searching mine. "You're looking rather pale."

"I'm fine," I lied. "Just tired."

"Stay for dinner," she suggested. "Missy is making—"

"I have dinner at home," I lied. Just thinking about eating made me nauseous.

She studied me for a moment longer before nodding. "Alright. Get some rest."

When I left Aunt Hattie's place, I saw Rhett leaning against the porch railing, as if he had been waiting for me.

"Hey." He fell in step with me as we walked to my cottage. "You good?"

I nodded, forcing another smile. "I think that's my question."

Rhett shrugged. "I'm...*relieved*. I never wanted to marry her."

"Then why did you propose?"

"She was pregnant. She said it was mine. She told my family it was mine. Not much I could do."

"Doesn't it bother you to keep being a good ol' Southern boy?" I asked acidly. "And this is 2024, you don't have to marry someone 'cause you knocked them up."

"I know. But *then* I felt the pressure to do the right thing."

"And *now*?" I asked as I bent down to lift a fake rock where I kept my cottage keys.

"Now," he paused and waited until I straightened, and then brushed his lips against my cheek, "Now, I want to be more like you."

"What?" I gaped at him, clutching the house keys.

He grinned. "You inspire me, Pearl, to be a better man. You always have."

He had rendered me speechless.

"Once"—he looked uncomfortable as he tucked his hands in his pockets—"the dust settles, so to speak, do you think...we could...you know?"

I cocked an eyebrow. "I don't know."

"Yes, you do." He smiled.

I sighed. I did know.

"Let's wait for the dust to settle first," I quavered.

Instead of replying, this time, he brushed his lips against

mine, soft and deliberate. A spark shot through me, sharp and unexpected, leaving a sizzle in its wake—one I hadn't felt in a long time. It caught me off guard. I hadn't had sex since moving back to Savannah, and the idea of swiping through Tinder or Bumbl, and stumbling across someone I knew, was mortifying. I was just horny, I decided, which made far more sense than the earth shifting beneath me simply from his touch.

"Let the dust settle, Rhett," I whispered, unlocking my door with shaking hands. I shut the door on his face, not bothering to invite him in. I had to process this shift—even if it was one that I'd been secretly hoping for.

I sank onto the couch.

I'd promised myself I wouldn't let Rhett affect me like this. But now that he was free, now that the possibility of a *possibility* of *us* loomed, I didn't know how to stop my thoughts from spiraling. And then there was that stupid kiss.

Oh my God!

That had rattled my brain for sure.

CHAPTER 19
Rhett

I t was Sunday, and I knew I'd have to face the music at my parents' house soon enough. I'd been bracing myself for the final showdown there, but I was completely caught off guard when my father showed up unannounced. I should've known—this was classic George Vanderbilt, always appearing when you were least ready for him.

I opened the door when he rang the bell as I was home alone, despite my mother's constant nagging about why I hadn't hired a full staff to maintain the house.

Sure, I had a team of gardeners who kept the grounds in shape and someone who came by to check on the essentials —smoke detectors, light bulbs, and things like that—but I didn't have a live-in staff. I did have a housekeeper who came in the mornings and left in the afternoons. She kept the place clean, made sure my clothes were laundered, and put away the groceries I ordered online on delivery days.

I cooked my meals and handled most of my affairs, and the only reason I needed even the help I had was because the house was massive. Ostentatious, unwieldy, and as much of a burden as it was a legacy. It was the family home. And yet, every time I looked at it, the thought crept in: *What the hell am I supposed to do with this place? Can I get rid of it?*

"Son." He stepped past me into my house without waiting for an invitation.

"Good morning, sir," I replied, barely suppressing a sigh as I shut the door behind him.

I thought about Pearl's little cottage as my father and I walked to the family room; a giant fucking space with every piece of designer furniture you could imagine. My mother had decorated this house—no wonder it felt like a mausoleum.

"Would you like some coffee?" I asked politely when he was seated on one of the sofas, manspreading like he owned the place, which he didn't, not anymore.

George Vanderbilt was all about the show, and he sat, exuding his overbearing glory, dressed, at eight in the fucking Savannah *summer* morning, in a crisp navy blazer, white shirt, and gold cufflinks that gleamed with what I mused was disapproval since I was still in my running gear.

"I don't want coffee," he snapped, looking more pissed than a cat in a rainstorm. "I want to know what in the hell is going on with you and Josie."

So, it hadn't taken long for Josie to rally the troops. At least he hadn't shown up last night. *Small mercies!*

"I spoke with Suellen this morning," he continued, his

voice cold. "Josie is devastated, Rhett. She told Suellen that you're havin' doubts. How could you have blindsided her with this nonsense?"

"I am not having doubts," I corrected him. "I'm damn certain that I'm not marrying her."

I decided not to sit, refusing to let him think this was some kind of leisurely chat. Not a chance. Instead, I leaned against the wall, casual but deliberate, my posture toeing the line between ease and defiance. He wasn't used to seeing me like this, and I caught the flicker of confusion and surprise on his face. To be fair, I was a little confused and surprised myself.

I'd been raised to respect my elders—to nod, smile, and stay polite no matter what. And for most of my life, I'd followed those rules without question. But somewhere along the way, I realized respect had to be a two-way street. If my so-called elders expected me to marry a woman I couldn't stand just to uphold their sense of tradition, then maybe they weren't so deserving of my respect after all.

My father narrowed his eyes. "What exactly do you think you're doing, Rhett? You're engaged to a perfectly good woman from a perfectly good family. Do you know what it looks like when a Vanderbilt calls off a wedding? It's not quiet, I'll tell you that much. It's headlines, hushed phone calls, and a string of well-dressed relatives scrambling to save face. For a Vanderbilt, it's not just a decision—it's a scandal and a goddamn embarrassment."

It wouldn't do to let him see I was angry; he'd use that to his advantage. I forced myself to remain calm and fought to keep my temper in check. "I guess I'm saving us from the future embarrassment of a divorce."

"What nonsense. And if you felt this way, why did you propose to her?" he shot back, his voice rising. "You knew exactly what you were doing when you put that ring on her finger. Or are you telling me that, once again, you acted impulsively and now expect everyone else to clean up your mess?"

All of a sudden, my anger evaporated.

I realized I was just too tired to feel that strong an emotion. I was tired of living my life on *his* terms, and worse, I was *tired* of living life without knowing what the hell my terms were. I was thirty-two years old, and I didn't know who I was or what I wanted to be. Oh, I knew who Rhett Vanderbilt was, but he was a persona, a mask I wore, and I didn't want to do that any longer.

"Sir, there's nothing to clean up," I replied, my voice hard.

"That's what you think. Huck and Suellen are not going to let this go unanswered. You're insulting their family name."

"It's a pity they feel that way when they should appreciate the fact that I'm simply not entering a marriage I know for certain will fail." I straightened and decided that the hell with it. *I* needed coffee.

I walked out of the living room as I heard my father call out, "Where the hell do you think you're going, young man."

"I'm going to make myself some coffee." I didn't bother to see if he followed.

In the kitchen, he glared at me as I worked the coffee machine. Since I wasn't a complete asshole, I made two cups. He sat at the island and drank his grudgingly. I knew he was feeling off-kilter. I didn't usually behave in this manner. I was usually overly polite and solicitous. But the plain truth was that I used to let him bully me.

"Just tell me why you think you can do better than Josie?" he demanded after a long silence.

There was a shift in his tone—not quite commanding, but almost pleading. Well, as humbly as my father was capable of pleading, anyway. After a lifetime of being an entitled, pompous ass, it wasn't like he was going to suddenly change because I'd pulled the rug out from under him.

"I don't love her," I said plainly.

His face darkened, and his lips pressed into a thin line. For a moment, I thought he was going to shout, but instead, he shook his head, his disappointment radiating off of him.

"You're making a mistake, Rhett," he stated coldly. "And I can only hope you'll come to your senses before it's too late. This family has a legacy to uphold, and if you think you can just throw it all away because you've suddenly decided you don't feel like playing your part, then you're more foolish than I thought."

I took a leisurely sip of my coffee and, with just enough insouciance, said, "Sir, let's agree to disagree on this matter."

"Josie thinks you're balling some other girl. Is that what this is about? Look, we all have dalliances, and there is—"

"Sir, I don't mean any disrespect, but there is no fuckin' way you and I are having a conversation about my sex life."

The look on my father's face was comical. I'd never sworn in front of him before.

"And *I* don't cheat," I added for good measure.

"What does that mean?" He glowered. "Are you accusing me of something?"

"Sir, just as I won't discuss my sex life with you, I won't be making any assumptions about yours."

I almost wished I'd been recording this conversation, because Aunt Hattie would have gotten a kick out of it. What had started as tedious and difficult was now teetering on the edge of entertaining. There was something incredibly liberating about being authentic, about speaking honestly and not swallowing every retort I'd been biting back for a lifetime. I could tell him to go fuck himself—and, well, I was doing exactly that, just dressed up in more polite words.

My father gawked at me. Then he brushed the coffee cup hard, and it crashed against the tiled floor of my kitchen.

Christ! Why had I been afraid of this man all my life? He was sixty-five years old, and he was behaving like a toddler throwing a tantrum.

Then, as if surprised by himself, he rose, turned, and walked out of the kitchen—and then the house. I even heard the front door slam behind him.

I drank some coffee, feeling much lighter than I had *ever* felt in my life. A few days ago, my father's disappointment in me would have suffocated me, but now, one walk on the beach with Pearl, learning what she'd overcome and seeing her courage, showed me that I could be brave, too.

I looked at my watch and grinned.

Now that I'd pissed off the patriarch, I didn't have to endure the interminable Vanderbilt-Vance Sunday lunch. The Beaumonts would probably be there too, as they often were. I could avoid them all, and that felt like a small victory

A few hours later, I was on my porch, reading the news on my iPad under the whir of the ceiling fan, trying to savor the last bit of cool before the afternoon heat took over Savannah. That's when my phone rang.

"Mama," I greeted.

"How could you?" she shrieked.

"How could I what?" I inquired innocently. It was petty, but I was all out of fucks.

"Rhett Vanderbilt, I expect you to come over and make up with Josie and end this foolishness."

"You can tell Josie she can keep the ring," I drawled, ignoring what she'd just said. Then, because I was still furious at Josie for thinking my parents could bully me into submission—and they would have, if I hadn't finally grown a spine— I added, "She can add it to her collection of engagement rings."

"*Rhett.*" Mama sounded like she was clutching her pearls.

"Yes, Mama?" I asked patiently.

"Are you coming over for lunch or not?"

"Not."

"What?"

Hey, no one was more surprised than me that I was giving my whole family the proverbial finger.

"Mama, you're upset and yelling at me. Josie's probably fake crying her way through a whole river, and Father's most likely strategizing how to chop my balls off. So, no, I'm not coming over for lunch."

I don't think I'd ever experienced Dolores Vanderbilt speechless. *However*, she recovered quickly enough. "Your father is going to disown you," she warned me.

"Okay. Tell him that I'll get the paperwork ready, and he can move all his accounts from me to some other wealth manager." I was now starting to enjoy myself.

"Well, that's what he'll do, Rhett," she sneered.

My mother had no clue that the life she was living was not because of my father but me.

"Tell him that my assistant will be in touch with—"

"Rhett, let's not mix personal with business," my father, as predicted, took over the conversation, which I suspected had been taking place over the speaker for all to hear how my mother was going to *manage* my recalcitrant ass like I was a spoiled teenager.

The irony wasn't lost on me. Back when I actually had *been* a spoiled teenager, running wild and desperately in need of parenting, no one had bothered to manage me at all.

Instead, I'd been left to my own devices, strutting around like I was king of the fucking world.

If my son—assuming I ever had children—did to someone what I'd done to Pearl, I'd have whaled his ass. Then again, maybe the real lesson was not to raise your kids to be assholes in the first place. This was exactly why I didn't want to get married or have kids. I didn't want that kind of responsibility. I could barely manage my own life—how could I possibly take care of others without screwing it all up?

"Sir, let's talk in my office." I threw down the gauntlet.

Silence.

"You can call and make an appointment with my assistant," I continued. I mean, if I was going to insult my father for being a jackass, I should go all out.

I *always* came to my father's home to talk to him about his business, but that was *before* he and Mama decided to take the "I'm disowning you" path. *Now*, Mohammed would have to come down the fuckin' mountain.

"Son, I'm *still* your father."

"I thought we were keeping the personal and business separate," I retorted. "I normally conduct business in my office. You know where it is. Have a good day, sir."

I hung up on him, feeling mightily satisfied.

CHAPTER 20
Pearl

One of the challenges of having an eating disorder was that socializing often revolved around food and drinks, which sometimes made me hesitant to go out with friends. But when Luna and Aurora invited me to join them for Friday evening drinks, I didn't hesitate. I eagerly agreed. I was feeling good—better than I had in a long time. I felt free, like I was finally stepping into the kind of full, vibrant life I'd always wanted. I felt invincible, like all my dreams weren't just possible—they were within reach.

We went to The Peacock Lounge, a Savannah staple that was both historic and trendy. Velvet couches, gilded mirrors, and soft, golden lighting gave it a Gatsby-era charm, while the fancy cocktails, gourmet bites, and after-work crowd gave it a fun, modern vibe.

We sat at the bar, and I ordered, *boldly*, a Southern Living, their riff on the Chatham Artillery Punch, according to the menu. I didn't know *that* cocktail either, but this

Peacock Lounge signature drink sounded delicious, made of bourbon, pear brandy, black tea, and some brut bubbles. I threw further caution to the wind and requested some small bites for the table. Edamame gyoza, spring rolls, and shishito peppers.

It felt liberating to order without scrambling to make excuses for not eating or drinking. Even now, though I was thin, a part of me always worried that people might figure out I had an eating disorder. The thought of anyone knowing terrified me—because I was ashamed and couldn't bear the idea of being watched all the time. The people were wondering if I wasn't eating because I simply didn't feel like it or because I'd weighed myself that morning and decided a quarter of a pound was too much.

Of course, I didn't even own a scale anymore—one of the boundaries I'd set to manage my condition. It had been a small but significant act of reclaiming control. I did have a long mirror in my bedroom, though. For the most part, I avoided it—full-length mirrors were their own kind of torture. Sometimes, on my better days, I'd catch my reflection and allow myself to really look, just for a moment. To see not the flaws but me. These were basics in most people's lives. Checking how you looked after you got dressed. Putting on makeup without wondering if your cheeks were suddenly too chubby, or you were getting a double chin, or if your nose had somehow gotten larger during the night.

But right now, as I picked up my cocktail, I felt like I'd overcome all that, and I could do even more. It was a fantastic feeling, one I hadn't had...well, *ever*. As much as I knew that this was the result of therapy, of me facing my demons by coming to Savannah, I also knew that speaking with Rhett, telling him my truth, and getting validation from him, along with his apology and sincere regret, had helped accelerate my healing.

The workday had been long, but I felt light—like I was finally getting somewhere. My hair was behaving, I liked my dress, and Luna and Aurora were talking about a meeting with a client that went off the rails, that had me laughing so hard I thought I might spill my drink.

Aurora, who was always poised and just a touch reserved, smiled at me over the rim of her Sauvignon Blanc. "You know, Pearl, I think I've heard you laugh more in the past few days than in all the time since you started working at Savannah Lace."

"That's because I've been hanging out with you two." I raised my glass in a mock salute. "You're a terrible influence."

"Damn right, we are," Luna said proudly. She was the opposite of Aurora—bold, brash, and unapologetically herself, dressed in a leather jacket over a black silk blouse.

I had eaten one gyoza, and there was no nausea. It was a victory. I sipped my drink and wondered if this could be one of the times that maybe I'd order a second. I was giddy at that idea. I almost felt normal. Just like everyone else at the restaurant, having a good time after work.

"Pearl, darlin', imagine seeing you here." And because the universe was shitting on me, I heard my sister-in-law's voice.

"Pearl," another voice chimed. I didn't even have to look

to know it was Josie. Her tone was faux sweetness with a sprinkle of condescension. It made my stomach twist, which was annoying since I was doing so well.

I heard my therapist in my head: *You have both internal and external triggers, remember that. The external ones you can zone out—they're the things you can't control, like other people's comments or situations you find yourself in. But the internal ones? Those are the thoughts and beliefs you carry about yourself, and that's where your work lies—to challenge them, to question their truth, and to remind yourself that they don't define who you are.*

This was an *external* trigger. I could rise above it. I wouldn't let this ruin my Friday evening, I promised myself.

I glanced over my shoulder and saw, to my chagrin—Josie, my sister-in-law Caroline, and, of course, Dixie May. They had just walked in and, as bad luck would have it, were going to sit at the bar. I wanted to ask Luna and Aurora if we could find a booth, but that felt like defeat, so I smiled. "Hello, ladies."

Everyone did the hi, hello, air kisses nonsense with Luna and Aurora. After all, we were all part of the same Savannah society circles, and appearances had to be maintained.

"Aurora, we're so looking forward to Betsy's party next week!" Josie exclaimed, then looked pointedly at me. "Rhett and I always love coming by the Rhodes Estate. It's so inspiring as we work on our future home."

Now, I knew that Rhett had broken the engagement, or at least that's what he'd told me. Had they already made up? Well, that was fast, I thought bitterly and set my cocktail glass down without thinking about how suddenly I didn't want to consume anything.

Tune her out, Pearl, I told myself sharply. *Let her go. You don't need her thoughts, words, her poison inside your head. And who cares if Rhett and she are back together, yeah? It doesn't concern you.*

I was going to get up to use the restroom, even though I hated restaurant bathrooms where there were mirrors on every fucking surface, but I needed to get away, even if for a moment.

But before I could, a woman came by to where we were all clustered, Savannah society girls—those with careers and those without—the lines were drawn.

Annabelle Radcliffe was Savannah royalty. Old money, old power, old grace. She was one of those women who could silence a room just by walking into it, and for reasons I'd never fully understood, she'd always been kind to me.

She nodded to everyone, who gushed and said hello. Although she nodded politely, her focus was on me, to the chagrin of the Caroline contingent.

"Pearl Beaumont," she said warmly, her Southern drawl as silky as honey. She looked me over, her eyes bright. "You look lovely, my dear. Absolutely radiant. That color suits you."

I flushed under the compliment, stammering a soft, "Thank you, Mrs. Radcliffe."

"Oh, darlin', call me Annabelle. I just heard from Hattie Odom the amazing job you're doing for the women's health initiative." She put a hand on my shoulder. "You, my dear, are an asset to our community. Beautiful, charming, kind, and smart. We're lucky to have you."

She smiled, giving a slight nod to Luna and Aurora before heading back to her table. For a fleeting moment, I felt untouchable. Seen. Even admired. I may not believe in the society hoopla. However, even I knew that Annabelle Radcliffe giving me her stamp of approval in public was a big fucking deal, especially to the ditzy women standing in front of me, malice and envy in their eyes.

"Good thing you lost all that weight, yeah?" Caroline was the first to reveal her green-eyed monster. "Everyone knows that Annabelle Radcliffe *hates* fat girls."

"Cut it out, will you, Caroline?" Luna drawled. "And, if you don't mind, we'd like to have our drinks in peace. So…I recommend the booth at the other fuckin' end."

I was about to smirk when Josie spoke loud enough for most of the bar to hear. "Well, of course, she's thin. After all, she throws up everything she eats; *if* she eats, that is."

Her words hit me like a slap, my breath catching in my chest.

Aurora gritted her teeth. "Really, Josie, I don't think you know what you're talking about."

"I do, too," Josie protested, her tone syrupy. "I mean, poor Pearl. Didn't you almost die once? I sure hope you're taking better care of yourself now."

Luna froze mid-sip. "What the fuck, Josie?"

I was starting to shake. I could feel my stomach hollow out.

"Oh, I didn't mean anything by it." Josie feigned innocence. "I'm just worried about Pearl, that's all. You know how hard it can be for people with...eating disorders."

Dixie May snickered, and Caroline shifted uncomfortably, clearly not willing to intervene.

I couldn't move. Couldn't speak. All I could do was sit, frozen, as the blood rushed to my face. People were staring now, weren't they? Everyone had heard. I could feel their eyes on me, feel the weight of their pity, their curiosity.

I wanted to speak, say pretty much *anything* to negate Josie, laugh at her, but I couldn't. I was triggered, as my therapist would say, and all because I hadn't done a good enough job of not letting Josie get to me, and I'd done a piss poor job of trusting someone *again*. Rhett must've told Josie. This was worse than fucking me for a bet. This was...*unforgivable*.

"Why don't you mind your own damn business, Josie?" Luna snapped, her voice cutting through the room like a whip. "Not that it's any of your beeswax, but Pearl's doing just fine. Better than you, clearly, if you need to dig into someone else's personal life to feel important."

Aurora stood too, quieter but no less firm. "It's disgusting, the way you talk about someone's health challenges like this." Her icy glare locked on Josie. "You should be ashamed of yourself."

The humiliation burned through me like wildfire. Everyone in the room was watching now. I could hear whispers and feel the tension radiating from every corner. I couldn't breathe.

"I need to go," I managed to say, pushing back my barstool so abruptly it bobbed a little.

"Pearl—" Luna reached for me, but I shook my head.

I didn't even grab my purse. I just bolted, weaving through the tables and out the side door into the alley, the muggy evening air hitting me like a slap. My chest was heaving, and my hands trembled as I stumbled to the far side of the alley, and sank to the ground behind a dumpster.

My breaths came fast and shallow, each harder than the last. My vision blurred, and the world tilted as I pressed my back against the cool brick wall, trying to steady myself.

Everyone knows now. The thought looped in my head, relentless and crushing. *They'll ask if I'm okay. They'll look at me like I'm broken. They'll pity me. Now, they'll all know I'm weak.*

I clenched my fists, my nails digging into my palms as I fought to stay present, to keep the spiral from pulling me under. But I couldn't.

I didn't realize I was crying until I felt the tears streaming down my cheeks, hot and silent. My chest ached, and the edges of my vision darkened as panic took hold.

"Pearl!" Luna's voice cut through the haze, sharp and worried.

A moment later, she and Aurora appeared, their faces etched with concern as they crouched beside me.

"Breathe." Luna put her hand on my shoulder. "Just breathe with me, okay? In through your nose, out through your mouth."

Aurora sat on the ground beside me, her presence calm and steady. "Just take your time, Pearl; we're here for you."

I tried to follow Luna's lead, focusing on her voice, on

the rise and fall of her breaths. Slowly, the world began to settle, the crushing weight easing just enough for me to pull in a deeper breath.

But even as the panic subsided, humiliation lingered, heavy and suffocating. And deep down, I knew that tonight had undone so much of the fragile progress I'd made.

CHAPTER 21

Rhett

Over the weekend, I was busy fixing a client's systems that had gone haywire, so I had to make an impromptu visit to Atlanta, where I worked with my team. I had sent a few texts to Pearl but hadn't heard back, and since I hadn't had time to call her, I was eager to see her when I came to Savannah Lace on Monday morning for a meeting with the finance team there.

The meeting was routine, the kind I could usually navigate on autopilot, but today I couldn't focus. My attention kept drifting to the door, waiting for Pearl to walk in. She always sat near the back, her laptop open, poised, and attentive. Her quiet energy balanced the room, the way she listened so intently, offering an insight that cut through the noise like a scalpel.

But today, her chair was empty.

I told myself not to overthink it. Maybe she was running late. Maybe she was tied up in another meeting or project.

But as the minutes ticked by, the nagging knot of unease in my gut tightened. By the time the meeting wrapped up and she still hadn't appeared, I couldn't shake the feeling that something was off. Something wasn't right.

I lingered as everyone else filed out, nodding distractedly at a few passing colleagues before turning to Nina, who was packing up her things at the head of the table.

"Hey, Nina." I kept my tone casual. "Where's Pearl?"

Nina glanced up, her sharp eyes appraising me for a moment before she answered, her voice cool and clipped. "She's taken a leave of absence."

"A what?" Pearl wasn't feeling well? Panic set in. Was this why she hadn't responded to my messages? What happened? Why hadn't Aunt Hattie called me? "What happened? Is she okay?"

"That's not for me to say," Nina replied, closing her laptop with a deliberate snap. "But whatever it is, I suggest you tread carefully, Rhett."

Her words were pointed, her gaze heavy with warning.

Before I could press her further, she slipped past me, her heels clicking against the polished floor as she disappeared down the hall.

I stood still for a moment, my mind racing, and then I pulled out my phone.

I called Pearl, no answer.

I called Aunt Hattie, no answer.

I texted them both. No reply.

I grabbed my backpack and headed for the exit, my steps quickening as unease bloomed in my chest. I had another meeting in an hour, but to hell with it—I was going to Aunt Hattie's to check on Pearl.

Maybe she had the flu. Maybe....

"You son of a bitch." Luna charged at me when I was out of the building. She had followed me out.

"What?"

"You're one devious creep, Rhett Vanderbilt, and to think I thought you'd turned a new leaf, you can take the teenager out of the asshole, but you can't take the asshole out of the human being."

I raised a hand. "I'm assuming this is about Pearl. I'm headed her way and—"

"Oh, I think not," she snapped, closing the distance between us.

I blinked, caught off guard by the sheer force of her anger. "What the hell is going on?"

She tittered, but it wasn't a pleasant sound. "You really don't know?"

"Luna," I said, my voice tightening. "If you've got something to say, just say it. Otherwise, I need to get going."

"Fine," she hissed, her eyes blazing. "Pearl's gone because of you. Because someone decided to throw her past in her face in front of half of Savannah. And gee, I wonder who might have told Josie all those personal details about Pearl's health challenges, huh?"

The air seemed to drain out of the world.

"I haven't talked to Josie since I ended our engagement, and I've *never* talked to her about Pearl." My heart hammered because I could guess what had happened.

Luna's eyes narrowed. I stepped aside as someone walked up the ramp to get to the door of the building. Once they were gone, I turned to Luna. "I've been in Atlanta all weekend. What the fuck happened?"

"Josie decided to tell everyone and God at The Peacock Lounge that Pearl has an eating disorder and how she almost died. I've never seen someone break...." Luna took a deep, shaky breath.

"Wait," I said, my voice low and unsteady. "You think *I* told Josie?" Did Pearl think that, too? Of course, she did. *Holy hell!*

"Well, who else would have?" she demanded, stepping closer, her fury palpable. "You're the only one she trusted with that part of her life, Rhett. She told us how she'd never told anyone but you and Aunt Hattie, and we know Hattie's a fuckin' vault."

My stomach dropped. Pearl's secrets—her struggles, her pain—they weren't mine to share. I would never, never betray her trust like that. But if she believed I had....

"I didn't tell Josie," I said firmly, meeting Luna's glare head-on. "I swear to you, Luna. I didn't."

Her eyes searched mine, skeptical but wavering slightly. "Then how the hell did Josie talk about it?"

"I don't know," I admitted, my voice breaking slightly. "But it wasn't me. I'd never do that to Pearl."

Luna crossed her arms again, her anger still simmering but tempered now by uncertainty. "Well, Pearl doesn't seem to believe that. She's shattered, Rhett. She thinks you betrayed her, and honestly, I can't blame her for feeling that way."

Pearl thought I'd taken the most vulnerable parts of her and handed them over to someone who'd use them as weapons.

I felt sick.

"Is she at home? Did she...where is she?" I asked, my voice quiet but urgent.

Luna shook her head. "No. I went by her place and knocked and knocked, and no one answered. And Hattie is out of town with Missy, so I couldn't ask them, either. If you care about her—if you're even half the man you're trying to be—you'll figure out a way to make this right."

I nodded, my throat tight. "I will," I said, more to myself than to Luna.

She gave me one last hard look before going back into Savannah Lace.

I all but ran to my car, my mind spinning. This morning, I had felt free. I had finally cut the strings that had been binding me to a life I didn't want. I had been ready to move forward, to see if there was a chance for a real relationship with Pearl.

But now I feared that it was all destroyed before it could even begin. I didn't know how Josie had found out about Pearl's past, but I knew one thing for sure: Pearl thought I'd betrayed her, and that thought alone was enough to break me and probably her.

I had to fix this. Not because I wanted her to forgive me but because she deserved to know the truth. She deserved better than the pain she'd been dealt—not just by me, but by everyone who'd failed her.

I didn't know where to start, but I knew one thing: I wasn't going to let her face this alone. Not this time.

I had tried to call everyone I could think of at Hattie's estate, and no one knew where Pearl was. Her car was by her cottage, but no one had seen her all weekend. My heart sank. Was Pearl alright? Was she hurt?

By the time I pulled up to Pearl's cottage, I was having a full-blown panic attack. The pond shimmered in the bright light, and the air was heavy with the sticky heat of another unforgiving Savannah day.

I parked, climbed out of the car, and walked toward the cottage. I knocked and rang the doorbell, looking through all the windows, but I couldn't see much because the blinds were closed. I tried all the doors, but they were locked.

I remembered, then, where she kept her spare key. I picked up the fake stone, found her key, and opened the door.

"Pearl?" I called out, stepping inside cautiously.

The cottage was quiet. No music, no TV, no sign of the Pearl I'd come to know over the past few months.

The first thing I noticed was the kitchen. An untouched glass of milk sat on the counter next to a plate of Kraft's mac and cheese. The milk had curdled, and the mac and cheese was dry.

My chest tightened. This didn't feel right.

"Pearl?" I called again, louder this time, moving deeper into the house.

I found her in the bedroom.

She was sitting on the floor, her back pressed against the side of the bed, her knees drawn tightly to her chest. Her arms wrapped around her legs like she was trying to hold herself together, and her head rested on her knees, her hair falling in a soft, tangled curtain that hid her face. She didn't look up when I stepped inside.

"Pearl." Her name came out softly, but my voice shook despite my effort to steady it. I knelt beside her, my hand hovering hesitantly near her shoulder. Relief had flooded me the moment I found her, but it evaporated the second I saw her like this—fragile, folded in on herself.

She didn't respond, didn't move. Her breathing was shallow, her shoulders rising and falling with a rhythm that felt off—too quick, too strained. Her skin looked pale, almost translucent, and there was a fine tremor running through her fingers where they gripped her knees.

"Pearl," I tried again, softer this time, inching closer. "Hey, baby, it's me."

Her head tilted slightly, just enough for me to catch a glimpse of her face. Her cheeks were streaked with dried tears, and her eyes...God, her eyes. They were empty. Hollow. Like she wasn't really here.

"How could you?" Her voice came out hoarse, barely audible.

I took her cold hands in mine and looked into her eyes. "I didn't tell her. I'd never do that to you."

"You did then."

I knew she was talking about what I did fifteen years ago.

"Not this time. Please, believe me."

She just stared at me with her lifeless eyes.

"Have you eaten anything?"

She shook her head.

"Since when?"

Luna told me the Peacock Lounge incident happened on Friday evening. It was now Monday morning.

"I didn't eat," she simply replied.

"Oh, baby." I pulled her into my lap and held her close.

"I couldn't," she continued, her words spilling out in a rushed, broken whisper. "I tried. I cooked. I sat down. But it was too much."

I swallowed hard, trying to keep my voice steady. She needed me to be her rock now, not crumble. "Sweetheart, you need food. Your body needs nourishment."

She looked up at me, her eyes glassy with unshed tears. "Josie," she whispered. "She told everyone, Rhett. Now... now they'll all look at me with pity. I can't—I can't do it. I can't be that girl again." Her voice cracked on the last word, and she buried her face in my chest.

This wasn't just hurt—this was devastation. This was Pearl unraveling right in front of me.

"Pearl," I crooned. "Listen to me. I didn't tell Josie. I swear to you, I didn't."

She didn't respond, her shoulders trembling as she cried.

"Pearl," I said again, more firmly this time. "Look at me. Please."

After a long moment, she lifted her head, her eyes red

and swollen. "If you didn't tell her, then how does she know?"

"I don't know," I admitted, the words tasting bitter in my mouth. "But I'm going to find out. I swear to you, Pearl, I will find out. And whoever did this...they'll answer for it."

She let out a shaky breath, her eyes searching mine as if she wanted to believe me but didn't know how.

"It doesn't matter," she whispered. "Everyone already knows. So how does it matter?"

"What do you think everyone knows?"

"That I'm pathetic."

"Pearl, you're not pathetic, not even remotely." My voice cracked despite the control I was putting on myself. "You're one of the strongest people I know."

She shook her head and tried to pull away, but I didn't let her. *Hell to the no was she doing this alone ever again!*

"Why are you here?" she demanded, her voice husky from disuse, from crying.

"Because I'm your person. I'm your friend."

Her gaze flickered, and for a moment, I thought I saw a spark of hope, just a faint glimmer of relief that someone was with her, that she wasn't alone.

But then her eyes dropped again, and she shook her head. "I'm never going to be normal, am I?"

"You already are," I assured her.

She gestured weakly toward the kitchen. "I couldn't make myself eat all weekend. I tried and tried, and then I called Nina and told her I was sick. And tomorrow, it'll be harder. And the day after that, harder still. That's not normal."

"Pearl." I kissed her forehead. "I'm here today and tomorrow, when it's harder. I'm going to take care of you."

I didn't know how because I hadn't done enough research. However, I did know she needed to speak to her therapist.

"Have you talked to your psychologist?" I asked.

She looked at me with raw vulnerability in her eyes. "He's going to be so disappointed in me."

"No, he's not. He's going to help you. Like *I'm* going to help you."

"I don't know how to let you do that. I don't know what I need...want...I don't know *anything*," she admitted, her voice barely above a whisper.

"Then we'll figure it out together." I tightened my hold around her. She felt fragile, like she could break if I squeezed her too hard. "One step at a time. But first...you need to eat. Even if it's just a little."

She lay against me, and I got up, holding her, and carried her to the kitchen. She didn't protest. I set her down on a barstool and kept my hands on her shoulders for a moment, steadying her as she swayed slightly. Her skin was pale, and she looked so drained it was like all the fight had been sucked out of her. But she didn't argue. She didn't push me away.

I opened the fridge, scanning its contents. It wasn't stocked for anything elaborate—just the basics because Pearl didn't eat much on a good day. I knew enough from the little research I'd managed to do to keep it simple, light, and non-threatening. Nothing heavy, nothing overwhelming. Just food that's easy to digest, that she could tolerate without panic setting in.

I pulled out a carton of eggs and a loaf of whole-grain bread. Scrambled eggs on toast—it was simple, light, and exactly what she needed. I'd read somewhere that soft, bland foods were best after a relapse, especially when her stomach had likely been empty for too long. This wasn't about serving up a full meal, it was about getting some nourishment into her system—just enough to stabilize her blood sugar and gently ease her body back toward recovery.

I glanced at her as I cracked eggs into a bowl. She was hunched over slightly, her elbows resting on the counter, her face buried in her hands. She looked small, like she was trying to disappear into herself.

"Hey." I whisked the eggs while looking at her. "You're doing okay. Just stay with me."

She lifted her head slowly, her eyes glassy. "I don't know if I can eat." Her voice was barely audible.

"You don't have to eat a lot," I told her. "Just a few bites. That's all I'm asking. We'll go slow, okay?"

She didn't respond, but she didn't argue, either. I took that as a victory.

I heated a nonstick pan and added a pat of butter, letting it melt before pouring the eggs in. I kept them soft and barely set, stirring constantly to ensure they wouldn't dry out. Once they were done, I popped a slice of bread into the toaster and grabbed a small plate.

When the toast was ready, I cut it into triangles, and

spooned the eggs onto the side of the plate. I wanted to give her simple, manageable portions.

I set the plate down in front of her, along with a glass of water. "Here," I said, sliding onto the stool next to her. I speared a piece of bread and eggs on a fork and held it to her mouth. "Just one bite, Pearl. That's all you have to do. One bite."

She stared at the food on the fork like it was an impossible challenge, her hands gripping the edge of the counter. I could see the fear in her eyes, the hesitation.

"I can't," she murmured, her voice trembling.

"Yes, you can," I coaxed. "Just one bite. For me."

Her gaze flickered to mine, and I held it, willing her to believe me. After what felt like an eternity, she reached for the fork with trembling fingers. I let her take it from me, and she brought it to her mouth.

I held my breath as she chewed slowly, her movements cautious, as if she were bracing herself for a terrible thing to happen to her.

"You're doing great," I spoke gently, watching her swallow.

She set the fork down. I picked up some food with it and held it to her as I had before. "One bite at a time."

She nodded faintly, and after a long pause, she took the fork from me.

We kept the rhythm going.

After four or five bites, she set the fork down, her shoulders sagging. "I can't do more." Her voice was tinged with guilt.

"That's okay," I assured her immediately. "You ate plenty. You did great, Pearl. That's all your body needs right now."

I picked up the plate and set it aside, not wanting her to feel any pressure to finish it. I handed her the glass of water instead. "Take a few sips," I urged.

She did as I asked, taking small, careful sips of water. Her hands were still shaking, and I placed mine over hers to steady the glass.

"That's it. No rush."

"I hate this," she moaned, her voice breaking. "I hate that I can't even eat, which is like the simplest thing in the world to do. A baby can do it. It feels like...I'm failing at being a person."

"You're not failing." I wanted to cry because my heart broke for her, but I couldn't, not now when I was her pillar of strength. "Pearl, this isn't a failure—it's a battle. And you're fighting. Even now. Even when it's hard, and that's courage."

Her eyes filled with tears, and she looked away, her jaw tightening as she tried to hold back the tears.

"Hey." I reached out to tilt her chin, so she had to look up at me. "It's okay to feel like this. It's okay to cry. Letting yourself feel is a sign of strength, not weakness."

And that was it. The tears spilled over, and she let out a soft, broken sob. I pulled her into my lap, holding her as she cried into my chest, her body trembling against mine.

"It's going to get better," I murmured, stroking her hair.

"I promise you, Pearl. We'll take it one step at a time, and I'll be here for all of it. You're not alone in this."

We stayed like that for a while, her tears eventually slowing, her breathing evening out. When she finally pulled back, her face was blotchy, her eyes red, and yet she looked peaceful. I was grateful for that.

"Thank you," she whispered.

"You don't have to thank me." I brushed a strand of hair from her face. "This is what I'm here for. Whatever you need, whenever you need it—I'm not going anywhere."

She nodded, her lips pressing into a faint, shaky smile. I felt a glimmer of hope. She'd eaten a few bites. She'd let herself cry. And she'd let me stay.

I carried her to bed after that, and sat beside her, holding her hand as she fell asleep.

"You'll never have to deal with any of this on your own. Not ever again," I vowed to her sleeping form and brushed my lips against her cold cheek.

CHAPTER 22

Pearl

The cottage was quiet, save for the occasional chirp of crickets outside and the low hum of the ceiling fan. I was curled up on the couch, wrapped in a blanket, even though the summer heat was thick and suffocating. But I was cold. No surprise there. I had no reserves in my body to maintain my temperature.

I wasn't sleeping—not really—but I wasn't awake, either. It was the kind of restless dozing I'd come to know too well in the past few days.

Rhett, Aunt Hattie, and Missy came and left all day every day. I barely noticed. I didn't know how many days had passed since I relapsed. I had resisted talking to my therapist—which I knew was frustrating my caregivers. But they were also relieved that I ate small bites of food, I don't know how many times a day, but it felt like whenever I was awake, someone was making me eat or drink a little. I fought my instincts to hide away, and, instead, ate as much as I could.

Sometimes, it was only one bite of food. I kept waiting for one of them to get aggravated with me. Instead, all I got was encouragement.

"*You're doing great, darlin',*" Hattie said.

"*You ate half a slice of bread. Awesome job.*" That was Missy.

"*You're the strongest person I know, and I'm so proud of you.*" Rhett said some version of that to me all the time.

I hadn't touched my phone since I texted Nina and Layla to tell them I needed some time off. I didn't want to. I was almost afraid to see messages or missed calls from my mother or brother. Or people I knew, people I thought liked me but would now pity me. So, I stayed quiet and burrowed into Rhett whenever he was around. Why he was the one to offer me the comfort that I felt safest with, I didn't know. I was sure my therapist would have a field day with that when I finally worked up the courage to talk to him. I had canceled my sessions or, rather, had just not shown up. Rhett had assured me he'd taken care of letting my therapist know I was *out of commission*—his words.

I heard muffled sounds drifting through the windows, and I groaned when I heard my niece Maddie's voice. I didn't want Alice or Maddie to see me like this. I'd told Rhett, Aunt Hattie, and Missy that I didn't want *any* visitors. I mean, I had enough with *them* hovering over me already.

I snuggled further into the couch and under my blanket, like a child, hoping that if I couldn't see them, they wouldn't be able to see me.

Talk about age regression!

I tried to block them all out by putting the palms of my hands over my ears, but I could still hear them. So, I gave up and just let it go. Eavesdropping felt childish, but everything I was experiencing felt that way—like I wasn't a mature grown-up any longer.

"I didn't mean to," Maddie's voice trembled, barely audible. "I swear, Aunt Hattie, I didn't mean to hurt her."

"I know, darlin'."

My ears perked up.

"Are you angry with me, Rhett?" Maddie's voice was tremulous, and I didn't like that at all. I wanted to get up, go out, and protect her. But Rhett was there, I told myself, he'd take care of her like I would.

"Like Aunt Hattie said, Maddie, it's not your fault." I heard his voice climb up a notch on the sharp barometer. "But you have to be careful about what you say about whom in the future. You really, really have to because words are powerful, and they have consequences."

"She's just a child, Rhett," Hattie interjected, her tone firm but calmer. "She made a mistake."

"I know I made a mistake!" Maddie's voice cracked. "But Josie was being awful about Aunt Pearl, talking about her weight, and I just lost it. I was defending Aunt Pearl."

She sounded like she was crying now, and I closed my eyes tightly. I didn't have the strength to be there for her when I could barely be there for myself. I felt even more ashamed of myself.

"Shh! It's okay, Maddie." I heard Rhett soothe her.

"I told her about Aunt Pearl." Maddie sounded so sad. "I told her about...about the anorexia. I wanted her to stop making fun of Aunt Pearl. I didn't think she'd tell anyone, Rhett, I swear. I just wanted her to stop being so mean."

"How did you even know about this?" Aunt Hattie asked.

There was a long pause, the kind that felt like it stretched across years. My heart thudded painfully in my chest, my hands clenching the blanket tightly as I waited for Maddie's answer.

"I overheard her talking to you, Aunt Hattie. It was a while back and...."

"Damn it, Maddie," Rhett sounded weary.

I wanted to rage at him, tell him to stop guilting my niece. It wasn't her fault her aunt was a frail, fragile basket case, was it?

I pushed up from the couch, ready to go and defend Maddie no matter what. Sure, she made a mistake, but she was only trying to protect me the only way she knew how.

"Can I see Aunt Pearl?" Maddie asked.

I stiffened.

"Sweetheart, I promise the minute she feels better, I'll make sure you see her," Rhett soothed. "Now, why don't you go back to the house? Missy will take care of you."

"Will you tell Aunt Pearl that I'm sorry?"

"There's nothing to be sorry about," Rhett replied. "Now, don't worry about anything, okay? It's all good."

There was silence for a moment, and I heard Rhett growl. "Damn it!"

"She didn't mean any harm," Hattie soothed. "She's a child, Rhett."

"A child who just blew up Pearl's life," Rhett snapped. "Josie humiliated her, Aunt Hattie. She weaponized her trauma. What kind of person does that?"

"You were engaged to her, you tell me," Aunt Hattie remarked saucily, and my lips curved despite myself.

"I extricated myself from that shitshow, so give me credit for that, will you?"

Aunt Hattie chuckled. "It's probably because you ended the engagement that Josie went on the attack."

"Oh God! You're right. This is my fault."

"No," Aunt Hattie said firmly, "not yours, and not Maddie's. This is Josie's lack of decency. Who makes fun of someone who almost died because of an eating disorder? A vile and horrible human being does that. You can't be held responsible for her actions."

My vision blurred as tears filled my eyes.

"At least now we know how Josie found out. But I can't tell Pearl, Aunt Hattie, that'll crush her, that it was Maddie."

"Does she still think it was you?"

"I don't know."

"Then, you should tell her and—"

"I'd rather she thought it was me than Maddie."

At that moment, I felt completely safe with Rhett. He'd carry the blame for something he didn't do to protect my feelings.

I couldn't be annoyed with Maddie. She was just a kid. She didn't understand the ripple effect of her words, the way they'd crack open a wound I'd spent years trying to stitch closed.

That evening, as usual, Rhett fed me a little, this time, it was potato-leek soup. Then he insisted I take a shower—or rather, threatened me to take one or he'd give me one. By the time I went to bed, I was exhausted.

Rhett slept with me, and I accepted it like it was the most natural thing in the world. I didn't want to be alone like I'd been the last time—and it felt good to have his arms around me, his breath next to mine.

I knew he was being a good friend. I couldn't imagine he'd want to date someone as fucked up as me. I'd have to be satisfied with just being his friend.

But what about that kiss?

I ignored wanting Rhett because it wasn't like I could do much about it. I was barely able to brush my teeth most days, so sex was a tall, impossible order.

The nightmares started that night, after I overheard Maddie.

They weren't coherent—just flashes of images and feelings that tangled and twisted in my mind, until I couldn't tell what was real and what wasn't.

In the dream, my reflection in the mirror was distorted and monstrous. A plate of food was sitting in front of me, growing larger and larger, until it consumed the entire room. Josie's cruel and mocking voice echoed endlessly in my head.

You're not enough. You'll never be enough.

Fat Pearl.

Can't even eat to save her life.

"Hey, baby, come back to me. Come on, wake up." Rhett's voice pierced through.

I woke up gasping, my body drenched in sweat, my heart racing so fast it felt like it might explode. The room was spinning, my chest heaving as I tried to pull in a breath, but it felt like there was no air left in the world.

Rhett pulled me to him and held me. I resisted, and he let me go.

"I...I need to use the bathroom."

I stumbled into the dimly lit room, gripping the sink as I leaned over it, my body trembling violently. The face staring back at me in the mirror didn't look like mine. The dark circles under my eyes, the paleness of my skin, the sharpness of my cheekbones—it felt like I was staring at a stranger.

I was slipping. I knew I was slipping. But I couldn't stop it.

I didn't know how long I stood there.

By the time Rhett came up behind me, I was crying *again*. I was such a weakling.

I washed my hands and let Rhett take me to bed.

"You want to talk about it?" he asked me, my head resting on his chest, his arm around me, holding me like no one ever had before.

I didn't know what to say, so I kept silent.

"Pearl," he persisted, his voice filled with worry.

"I had a nightmare," I finally whispered.

"I gathered. You want to talk about it?" he asked again.

I shook my head, the motion slow and heavy.

"Okay."

He was so understanding that it unraveled me. I was falling in love with Rhett, my nemesis, my friend...my...it was all too confusing. My stomach twisted with anxiety, and I knew what I had to do, what I had been avoiding.

"I need to talk to my therapist, I think."

I felt him kiss my hair. "I'm glad to hear that, sweetheart. I'll make it happen."

How he knew who my therapist was and how he could make appointments, I didn't know, and I didn't want to. I was merely glad that someone else was handling the logistics. The times before, having to do everything myself, meant that my recovery was slower.

"You think Nina is going to fire me for abandoning my job?" I asked as a thought rose in my head. In the past, I'd pushed myself to work, no matter what. This time, I had just fallen apart. And maybe I had, I acknowledged, because there was someone there to catch me. Rhett. Aunt Hattie. Missy. Even my misguided niece, if it had come to that.

"Of course, not." He looked down and raised my chin so I'd look at him in the dim light of the bedside lamp that he kept turned on all night because it comforted me and took me away from the darkness that was inside. It was like Rhett had quickly figured out how to care for me. It was disconcerting and comforting, all at the same time.

"You sure?" Panic flashed through me. What would I do if I didn't have a job? How would I pay my bills? Sure, I was fortunate enough not to have to pay rent, but I had other expenses. What about my healthcare?

My breath got short.

"Shh, darlin'," Rhett mollified, "you're not getting fired. I talked to Nina and Layla, and they're happy for you to take the time you need, with full pay."

My breathing settled. How did he know I was worrying about money?

"They think you're a stellar employee."

I snorted.

Some stellar employee I was. I'd just had a nervous breakdown in front of my colleagues by a dumpster, for God's sake.

"They also love you like family." He kept stroking my back gently as he spoke. "Many of them call me every day to check on you. I'm thinking of just having a group call with the Savannah Lace team so I don't have to deal with them one by one. There's Layla, Nina, Luna, Aurora, Stella, Nova...and even Rachel. Your new colleague, Zahra, actually showed up at Aunt Hattie's house with a box full of cookies."

Nausea churned inside me. I didn't know why, but when I had an episode, I couldn't eat sugary things.

"Don't worry, between Missy and Aunt Hattie, there was nothing left. I got a few crumbs."

I smiled at that.

"And, darlin', even if you lost your job, you're so good at what you do, you'll find one right away. I'll hire you any day. But I know that Nina will break my legs if I steal you away from Savannah Lace."

He kept talking slowly, without pushing me to contribute to the conversation. He was making me feel better by telling me I was valued, and it made me feel better.

It made me feel loved and cared for, and it made the wounds hurt less.

"So, baby, it's all goin' to be okay."

I wanted to believe him. But I didn't feel *okay*. I felt like I was drowning, like every part of me was rebelling against the very thing I knew I needed to survive.

"Rhett." I gripped his T-shirt. He slept in a shirt and boxer shorts, probably to make me feel comfortable, because I had a feeling he usually slept in the nude.

"Yeah, baby?"

"What if I *never* get better? Will I...will I die?" It was a fear I had, and voicing it made it somehow less potent, but I also wondered if I sounded like I needed to go to the funny farm.

"No." The tempo and tone of his voice didn't change. He didn't push me. He just kept taking care of me. "You're going to get better. It just feels like a lot now, but time is a great healer, *and* you're going to talk to your therapist. Also, I'm here, Pearl, *always*."

"What does that mean?" I whispered, afraid of the answer.

"It means exactly what you think it does," he replied calmly. "I'm here with you, for you, and when you're feeling better, we're going to start dating."

"You mean *if* I feel better?" I wanted to kill hope with my words.

He wants to date me even after all this? What's wrong with him?

"No, I mean *when*, because you're already better than you were a day ago, two days ago, a week ago."

"How come you're here all the time? Don't you have to go to work?"

"I took a leave of absence."

Hope soared, giving me the middle finger. "What?" That was the only word that managed to slip out, considering my shock.

"It's my company, Pearl. I can take time off, and I am."

"Why?" I was one hell of a conversationalist; just look at my articulate wit!

"Because you need me, *and* I need you." He kissed my forehead. "Now, sleep, darlin'. Everything is going to work out. I promise."

I believed him.

CHAPTER 23

Rhett

M
issy was on Pearl watch. We were taking turns: Aunt Hattie, Missy, and me.

I felt like a gigantic asshole whenever I saw Pearl, wondering how she'd gone through this alone when I'd ripped her life apart, and later, when she'd first been diagnosed with anorexia after her heart stopped. She thought she was weak? A failure? I didn't think so! In my book, anyone who got through what she had on her own was the strongest motherfucker out there.

To help Pearl, I knew I needed to better understand her condition. Since I couldn't talk to her therapist about her, which was unethical and impossible, I found someone who could teach me to be a better caregiver.

Aunt Hattie suggested I talk with her friend, a therapist, Dr. Monica Ryan. We were meeting at The Sentient Bean near Forsyth Park for coffee and a *free* education session.

I used to frequent the Bean often when I was younger. It was a Savannah staple on a cobblestone street, cozy and unassuming. It was populated with locals, college students, and the occasional out-of-towner who stumbled upon it while looking for a decent cup of Joe.

The wooden tables were scratched but polished, evidently both lived-in and loved. I chose a table by the window, where the scent of coffee mingled with the faint tang of magnolia blossoms drifting in from the park despite the summer heat that killed pretty much anything green in sight.

Dr. Monica Ryan walked in right on time.

She had the kind of presence that instantly put you at ease, and her warmth and demeanor were inviting. Yet it was clear there was a sharp intelligence beneath her friendly exterior. Her salt-and-pepper curls framed her face, softening the sharpness of her eyes. She wore a neatly pressed teal linen blouse—a surprise, given Savannah's humidity, which had most people surrendering to wrinkles by midday.

"Rhett," she greeted warmly as she set her leather bag on a chair.

I rose, shook hands with her, and gestured for her to sit across from me. Once she was settled, she told me, "I have to admit, I was a little surprised when Hattie said you wanted to talk, but not as a client. She made it sound important."

"It is," I admitted. "Thanks for making time."

A server came by to take our orders—an iced tea for me and a cappuccino for her. Dr. Ryan adjusted her chair, folding her hands on the table and tilting her head slightly as she studied me. "Alright," she said with a small smile. "Tell me what's on your mind."

I wasn't used to feeling helpless. It wasn't in my nature. But watching Pearl slip into a world I didn't fully understand left me feeling raw and desperate.

"I have a friend," I began. "She was diagnosed with anorexia nervosa about a decade ago. A week ago, she relapsed. I want to make sure I'm taking care of her the right way—that what I do actually helps and doesn't hurt her, whether that's now or in the long run."

"Does she have a therapist?"

"Yeah, but she refused to talk to him until last night. I've set up an appointment for her later today."

She arched an eyebrow. "*You* set up an appointment?"

I sighed and then explained the situation. Pearl was in no condition to handle logistics, and I was adamant that she didn't have to because she had me.

"Can you give me some insight into your relationship with the patient? Is she just a friend? A girlfriend?"

The server came with our drinks and the check. I dropped my credit card immediately, and she pulled out a card reader. We finished the transaction, giving me time to think about how to tell Dr. Ryan that I *was* Pearl's friend but *also* the monster who had changed her life when she was young.

"This is confidential, I assume."

"Rhett," Dr. Ryan admonished.

I raised a hand and nodded. "Sorry. I don't mean to be

insulting, but let me explain what happened, and maybe that'll help you understand why I'm so jumpy."

She listened silently, her face blank of all emotions, occasionally sipping from her drink. She didn't take notes, just nodded and made small, assenting sounds.

I started from the beginning, telling her about sleeping with Pearl and how she'd overheard me. Dr. Ryan wasn't judgmental—she radiated calm curiosity, asking the occasional question to dig deeper and understand more. She didn't rush or interrupt; she simply let me pour everything out.

"Are you having sex with her now?"

I shook my head. "But we're sleeping together...that's all."

She looked at her coffee and then at me.

"Can you help me?" I pleaded.

Dr. Ryan nodded compassionately. "Anorexia is a complex illness. It's not about eating—it's about control, fear, and the stories people tell themselves about their worth. Supporting someone who's relapsed is incredibly hard, especially when you're close to them."

I took a deep breath, the memory of finding her in the cottage still fresh, still painful. "She's not eating. Barely drinking. She's...shut down. She lets me help her take a few bites of food, but even that feels like it's killing her. She's so tired, so fragile. She has nightmares. I hold her when she sleeps. She lets me."

"First," she said after a moment, "you need to understand that you can't fix this for her. I know that's not what you want to hear, but it's the truth. Anorexia is deeply rooted. It's about the beliefs Pearl has about herself, her body, and her value. Those beliefs don't disappear overnight, and you can't reason them out of her. Recovery is a process, and it's one she has to want for herself."

"She does. I know she does. She was doing so well until what happened with Josie. I'm to blame. I started this, and now Josie went after her because of me. I keep hurting the woman I love."

Dr. Ryan smiled at me. "When you were teenagers, yes, you triggered her, and what you did was inexcusable, certainly, but that was then. You've grown, and so has she. Josie's actions are not on you, only on Josie. The thing is, Rhett, if you were the monster you claimed to be, you wouldn't have spent a decade wanting to apologize to Pearl, and finally doing it in a way that, regardless of what she says, she has accepted. A monster would have rationalized it as teenage behavior and moved on. You didn't do that. Give yourself credit for that."

It was hard to do so when I could see the damage it had done to Pearl.

"Pearl's problem started long before you came into the picture. It sounds like her mother pressured her about her weight, and from what you said, her brother ridiculed her, as did children in school. All these factors coalesced for Pearl."

I nodded slowly. "Will she get better?"

"Of course, if she gets help, which she has been and is," Dr. Ryan confirmed. "You can support her the way you already are by being present, creating a space where she feels safe, where she knows she's not being judged or pressured. People with anorexia often feel an overwhelming sense of guilt or shame—about their eating, their appearance, and even about burdening the people who care about them. If you approach her with frustration, it will push her further into that shame."

I swallowed hard, the knot in my chest tightening. "I'm patient with her. I promise. No matter what, I stay calm."

"I know," she said gently, "but, Rhett, what you're doing is more than patience; you've shown her that you're there for the long haul, no matter how slow her progress is."

I stared at the condensation on my glass of iced tea. "What you're saying is that I'm doing a lot of the right things?"

"Absolutely," she affirmed.

"What else?"

Dr. Ryan leaned back, her eyes thoughtful. "Don't make food the focus of your interactions. Talk to her about things she enjoys, things that remind her of who she is outside of her illness. Anorexia has a way of consuming someone's identity—Pearl might need help remembering who she is beyond it."

I nodded, thinking back to the moments when I'd seen glimpses of the Pearl I'd once known—the way her eyes lit up when she talked about books, the sharp wit that surfaced when she felt comfortable.

"And when it comes to meals," Dr. Ryan continued, "don't push too hard. Offer, but don't force. If she can't eat, don't make her feel worse about it. Instead, focus on keeping her hydrated. Dehydration is a serious risk during a relapse, especially if she's been avoiding fluids as well as food. Encourage her to drink water, tea, broth—anything she can tolerate."

"That's what scares me the most," I admitted. "The physical toll. What if something happens to her heart again?" Her heart had stopped for one hundred and ninety seconds once —she'd almost died.

Dr. Ryan reached across the table, placing her hand lightly over mine. "I know it's terrifying. But Pearl is getting professional mental health help. That's very important. I recommend including a dietitian and maybe even a doctor on her care team to monitor her physical health. You can be her support system, but you can't be her entire recovery plan."

"She's finally talking to a therapist, which is a relief. Next step, I hope she'll let me take her to her doctor."

"Understand this," Dr. Ryan cautioned. "When she pushes back, it's not personal. Resistance is part of the illness."

"Thank you," I said quietly, meeting her steady gaze. "I don't want to screw this up."

"You won't," Dr. Ryan assured me with a small smile. "You care, Rhett. That's half the battle right there. But this is a marathon, not a sprint, and that means you're going to have to pace yourself. But the fact that you're asking these questions, that you're trying to understand, says a lot about the kind of support you are for her."

"I can't thank you enough, Dr. Ryan."

She studied me thoughtfully. "How are *you* doing? Taking care of someone like this is not easy. Are you giving yourself time to take care of yourself?"

I blinked. "I'm fine. It's Pearl who is—"

"Let me put it this way: always put your oxygen mask on first, then the child's. If you're not healthy, you can't take care of Pearl."

She wasn't wrong. "What do you suggest I do?"

"I'm glad you asked." She dug into her bag and pulled out a business card, sliding it across the table. "Here is someone I think you should speak with. He's an excellent therapist."

"Why not you?" I asked, genuinely curious. Talking to her felt easy and natural, like she already understood the weight of everything I was carrying.

She smiled kindly, folding her hands in front of her. "I'm afraid I simply don't have the bandwidth to take on new clients right now."

"Are you saying that you're too busy to take on Aunt Hattie's favorite nephew as a patient?" I teased.

"Exactly," she replied cheekily.

"Thanks, Dr. Ryan," I said, picking up the card. "I'll reach out."

"I want you to know that you're doing a lot better than you give yourself credit for. I'm very impressed with your dedication to your friend, and I believe she is going to come through this, and so are you, stronger than before."

When we were ready to part ways, Dr. Ryan gave me a reassuring pat on the shoulder.

"Oh, Rhett," she threw over her back as she walked away. "Tell Hattie she owes me a bottle of Krug for this."

I laughed, the sound feeling almost foreign. Damn, but Dr. Ryan was right; I hadn't been taking care of myself. I was tired and cranky. Confused and belligerent. Yeah, I needed help myself.

CHAPTER 24

Pearl

R hett told me he'd be in the gazebo by the pond so I could talk to my therapist in private.

The light coming through the cottage windows was warm, golden, and alive—the kind of sunlight that felt like hope.

Gah! I was so maudlin these days!

It had been three weeks since the night Rhett found me crumpled and hollow in my bedroom. And though I was still shaky, today I felt steady enough to talk to my therapist.

I sat cross-legged on the couch, a blanket draped over my lap. My laptop rested on the coffee table, and my therapist, Dr. Bryan Allen, was on the screen. We'd been meeting virtually since I left California, and despite the distance, his presence grounded me. We'd been working together for nearly ten years, and he knew pretty much everything there was to know about me.

"How are you doing?" he asked.

"I'm so sorry," I gushed. "I know it must've been weird for you to have Rhett cancel our appointments, but I just couldn't, you know? And then...I just don't...and—"

"Pearl," he stopped me from speaking in his gentle voice. "You have *nothing* to apologize for. And just in case you're worried, I didn't speak with Rhett or anyone else you know. He spoke to my assistant, and *she* conveyed to me that you were canceling your appointments."

"Oh, I never worry about confidentiality with you," I murmured. "And the truth is that, even if you spoke with Rhett, though I know you wouldn't, it would be okay."

"Alright." He leaned back. "Let's start there. Rhett is with you?"

"He's out by the pond," I explained inanely. "He wanted me to have privacy." I shook my head. "But that's not what you're asking. You want to know what he's doing *with* me."

He waited.

"I don't know what he's doing with me," I exclaimed. "No fucking idea."

"Why don't we back up, and you tell me why you canceled our appointments? Not that you ever have to explain, but I feel like there's something here we should explore."

I took a deep breath. "I relapsed."

"Tell me about it."

So, I did. I told him *everything*. I hadn't talked to him since before I'd been in Newport Beach, so I meandered there in between—and I hoped that my word vomit somehow made sense to him.

"Why didn't you want to speak with me?" he mused.

I bit my lower lip. "I was ashamed...I felt like I let you down."

He smiled. "Pearl, you can *never* let me down. I'm *always* on your side, always there for *only* you. There is no judgment between us."

"I know, but I'd been doing so well, and I was so excited to tell you how I went to The Peacock Lounge and ordered food and a cocktail. I didn't think about it, I just ordered and ate. And then...I collapsed. So, I was never *really* doing well, was I?"

"That's not how this works, and you know it. In that moment, it was your truth and reality."

"And now?"

"You're talking to me. You've been eating, albeit sparingly. You've allowed yourself to trust Rhett, even when you suspected he might have betrayed you. That, Pearl, is amazing progress. You're trusting yourself and your instincts, and I couldn't be prouder of you."

Tears filled my eyes.

"It means a lot to me that you say that, Dr. Allen, because I don't feel it. I don't feel like I've done anything to be proud of. Rhett keeps saying that to me as well."

"Tell me more about Rhett."

I smiled. "He's been...he says we're friends, and he's my person. I've never had a person. Well, except Aunt Hattie."

"What does that mean to you? That he's your person?"

I smiled faintly, brushing a strand of hair behind my ear.

"He showed up. He was here with me and for me. He

took time off work, and between him, Aunt Hattie, and Missy, I'm never alone. They keep trying to feed me but never pressure me. It's...I've always done this alone, this recovery...stuff. But to have people is...it's.... I don't feel normal. But I feel better. It doesn't feel like the world is caving in on me anymore because he's with me. *They* are."

Dr. Allen nodded thoughtfully. "What does *feeling better* mean to you right now? Can you name anything specific that feels different?"

I thought about the past few days. About the little victories that might not mean much to anyone else but felt monumental to me. "I ate breakfast this morning. Scrambled eggs and toast. And I didn't cry afterward, or...or feel like I needed to punish myself for it."

"That's an important step, building back your relationship with food as nourishment and not a reward you have to deserve." Dr. Allen's tone was encouraging without being overbearing. "How did it feel?"

"Weird," I admitted. "Like I was waiting for the guilt to kick in, but it didn't. Not completely, anyway. It was still there, but it was...quieter."

"That's progress, Pearl," he said gently. "It might not feel like much, but all these small moments add up. Every time you push back against the disorder, even just a little, you're building resilience. You're proving to yourself that you can do it."

I nodded, though a part of me still doubted myself. It was hard to trust this fragile sense of peace I was making with my psyche; hard to believe it wasn't temporary. "It still feels like a fight. Every bite, every meal. It's like...there's that awful voice in my head, telling me I'm not enough. That I don't deserve to feel good or happy or full. And even when I tell it to shut up, it doesn't go away. It's exhausting."

Dr. Allen leaned forward, his face filling the screen. "That voice isn't going to disappear overnight," he warned me. "And as you know, it may never go away completely. But what you're learning to do—what you're doing right now—is taking away its power. You're not letting it control you. And that's huge."

I swallowed hard. "But what if it gets loud again?" I asked, afraid. "What if I slip?"

"You might," he told me simply, not sugarcoating it. "Recovery isn't a straight line, Pearl. There will be hard days, even hard weeks. But you've been here before, and you've come out the other side. You're learning how to recognize the signs and how to reach out for help when you need it. And you have people who care about you, who want to support you. You're not alone in this. *That* is the thing that is helping you heal faster this time."

I thought of Rhett then, of how he'd been there every single day since my relapse. How he'd moved into the cottage without me even asking, quietly taking up space in my life as if he belonged here *with* me.

"Am I...am I foolish for letting him back in? Weak? Stupid?"

"You know how I feel about you using words like that to describe yourself," he admonished. "Now, let's change the question: how is Rhett?"

"What do you mean?"

"How is he to you? Who is he? What have you learned about him?"

I smiled faintly. "He's...incredible," I admitted, my cheeks warming slightly. "He's been patient, steady. He doesn't push me, but he doesn't let me disappear into myself, either. He makes me tea at night and stays up with me when I can't sleep. And somehow, he's learned how to make scrambled eggs exactly the way I like them."

Dr. Allen's lips curved into a small smile. "It sounds like you feel safe with him."

"I do," I said, the truth of that statement settling warmly in my chest. "I feel like he sees me. All of me. And he doesn't run away from it."

Dr. Allen nodded, looking pleased. "It sounds to me that you're letting yourself accept what he's offering, which is another step forward. And regarding what you said earlier, no, I don't think you're weak or stupid or any of those things. I think you're brave. You dare to forgive, accept that people can change, and give them a chance. A weak person would, out of fear, not let Rhett back in. You're not doing that."

Later that evening, Rhett was in the kitchen chopping vegetables for dinner while I sat at the table, flipping through a Southern cookbook that Rhett had brought home. He'd started cooking more since moving in, partly because he enjoyed it and partly because he knew I needed the structure. Eating was easier when someone else prepared the food, when it felt like an act of care instead of a battle.

"Did you know there's a whole section in here dedicated to desserts that use bourbon?" I said, holding up the book with a raised eyebrow.

"Bourbon is a Southern staple." Rhett grinned. "You can't bake a decent pecan pie without it. That's practically law in Savannah."

I smiled broadly, and it thrilled me that I could. "Do you even know how to bake a pie?"

"Not really," he admitted, tossing chopped zucchini into a pan. "But I'm pretty good at following instructions. Besides, isn't that what you're here for? To supervise and criticize my technique?"

"Oh, absolutely. It's my favorite hobby."

Talking to Dr. Allen made me feel almost normal, whatever that word meant. In addition to feeling calm and peaceful, the smell of garlic and olive filling the kitchen didn't scare me.

Yes, Dr. Allen was right. I had come a long way in just a few days. Part of it was years of therapy, certainly, but the rest was thanks to Rhett, Aunt Hattie, and Missy—a true support system. I lived in constant fear of having a relapse, how I would recover, how I would keep my job, and how I would *live*. But Rhett made me feel like I could rely on him, that he'd always be there with and for me, and if I relapsed again, he'd be my bulwark.

"Rhett," I said, and waited until he faced me, "are we dating?"

He smiled widely. "I fuckin' hope so, darlin'."

I chuckled then. "Really?"

"Absolutely."

I swallowed. "Even though I'm fucked up?"

"I don't like it when you talk about yourself like that," he scolded me, sounding just like Dr. Allen had earlier. "And I'd date you even if you had two horns."

I laughed then, and he just stared at me.

"What?" I asked, feeling self-conscious.

"You're so beautiful when you're happy. So fuckin' stunning."

I flushed.

"Dinner's almost ready." His eyes met mine, and he lowered his voice. "How are you feeling today? On a scale of one to ten?"

He asked me every day. I thought about it for a moment before answering. "A solid seven," I said honestly. "Not perfect. Not fixed. But good."

"That's all that matters."

As we ate the simple zucchini and pasta dish he'd made, I realized it truly wasn't about being perfect or fixed. It was about moments like this—quiet, simple, and full of possibility. It was about building a life I could live, one small step at a time.

As Dr. Allen once told me, "*You just need to get through one moment and then another, live in the present. The past is gone and the future isn't here yet. Breathe, Pearl, you're bigger than anorexia.*"

CHAPTER 25
Rhett

I didn't want to go to the damn Savannah Soirée for Hope, but Vanderbilt Finance was their biggest sponsor. This was one of the initiatives I'd chosen to back when I launched my company. My CFO liked to remind me it was a great tax deduction, but for me, it was far more personal. It was one of the ways I was trying to atone for what I'd done to Pearl.

Looking back on my life, I was still amazed at how much that single act of cruelty against Pearl had shaped me. At seventeen, I'd been a selfish, careless asshole—one who barely thought about the consequences of his actions. It took me years to grow up. I was more responsible and thoughtful, but now, with Pearl back in my life, it was like I'd leapfrogged to a whole new level of accountability.

I first began to support the Savannah Soirée for Hope annual charity because it was aimed at raising funds and awareness for critical issues affecting the local and regional community. Each year, the event focused on a specific cause, and this year, it was to support reading initiatives for under-privileged children. The soirée brought together Savannah's elite, philanthropists, and local community leaders for an elegant evening of cocktails, dinner, and live entertainment.

This year, it was being held at the Harper Fowlkes House, a stunning Greek Revival mansion built in 1842. The house boasted a grand ballroom with soaring ceilings, elegant chandeliers, and original hardwood floors. It was surrounded by a picturesque garden courtyard, offering both indoor and outdoor spaces for guests to mingle and enjoy the evening.

By the time I got there, I was late because I had to make sure Aunt Hattie was with Pearl, and then I had to go home to put on my monkey suit. Aunt Hattie had declined to attend, so I could. Even four weeks after her nervous break-down, we were taking turns being with Pearl. I was working from her home office whenever needed, but mostly, I'd told my team I was taking time off. Those who worked closely with me were shocked because I wasn't the type who did that—but then, I'd never had a girlfriend who needed me to care for her.

Pearl Beaumont was my girlfriend!

That thought lightened my mood almost instantly. Sure, we were starting weirdly—I *lived* with her and slept beside her—but it felt so fucking right.

This year, the soirée featured a silent auction showcasing art, travel experiences, and luxury items donated by local businesses and sponsors. A live jazz band was playing, and I looked around for the organizer. When I found Emily Latham, I quickly made my way to her.

She hugged me and grinned wide. "Isn't everything amazing?"

"It certainly is. Thank you so much for all that you do."

"None of this could happen without you." Emily was in her late forties and had been doing this kind of work her whole life. I had a tremendous amount of respect for her. She wasn't part of the Savannah elite. Instead, she came from, as she joked, *the wrong side of the tracks* and *fleeced the wealthy and snobbish Savannah elites* for money to help her old neighborhoods. I was all in with her efforts.

I supported this charity because of Emily. She made sure that the Savannah Soirée for Hope was more than an evening of glitz and glamour—it was a celebration of community, compassion, and the power of collective action to change lives. The fact that it was popular as an event at which to be seen, and that the rich came to show themselves off, was fine with me, as long as they were generous with their checkbooks.

After talking to Emily, I wound up near the bar, nursing a glass of bourbon I didn't even want, while I half-listened to Gabe Rhodes and Noah Carter talk about the Savannah Bridge project that Carter Construction was working on in partnership with Savannah Lace.

"How's Pearl doing?" Gabe asked me during a lull in his conversation with Noah. "I hope it's okay that Aurora told me what happened."

"Of course. Pearl's better."

He put a hand on my shoulder. "I hear that you're taking care of her. Took a leave of absence yourself."

My jaw clenched. Savannah was a small fucking gossipy town. I waited for Gabe to say whatever he was going to say. He'd been a mentor of sorts, since he was older than me, but mentor or not, if he said anything untoward about Pearl, I was in a bad enough mood to hurt the son of a bitch.

"I'm very impressed," he finished with a twinkle in his eyes.

"I've been where you are," Noah added but didn't expound. "It's not easy to see the woman you love struggling. So, if you want to talk, reach out."

I felt like an idiot for thinking these men, good men, would insult Pearl.

"Thanks, Noah. I will." I meant it.

I managed to eat some appetizers, but I really wanted to finish the speech part of the evening, where I introduced the keynote speaker, and headed home to Pearl.

I smiled at that thought. I smiled a lot when I thought about her.

"How's it going, Rhett?" Luna found me at my table and gave me a quick hug.

"Good," I murmured, but before I could say more, I heard someone mention Pearl.

"Oh, Pearl, *bless her heart*," Dixie May said, loud enough for half the guests to hear. "She can't hold a man, can't hold a meal. It's tragic."

Luna stiffened.

Rage seared my insides.

Josie, Caroline, Dixie May, and Birdie were holding court in a little circle of snide smiles, two tables away. Their laughter carried across to me like nails on a chalkboard.

Alice was nearby, sitting at their table with her phone. She was scrolling through it, clearly trying to escape the social hellscape Caroline had dragged her to. She glared at Dixie May and was about to get up when I caught her attention and shook my head. She sat down, but grudgingly, looking militant.

"She's always been such a drama queen." Birdie Beaumont, Pearl's fucking mother, entered the melee, and spoke as if the weight of the world was on her shoulders. According to Aunt Hattie, she had called to check up on Pearl, only to complain about how she'd become the talk of the town with her ridiculous disease.

The laughter that followed was sharp and cruel.

I saw Josie smirk as she added, "At least she isn't fat any longer."

I didn't even realize I was moving until I was standing right in front of them, my jaw clenched so tight it felt like it might snap.

"Stop," I said, my voice cutting through their laughter like a blade.

Josie turned, her perfect, practiced smile faltering when she saw me. "Rhett," she said, blinking up at me with wide, feigned innocence. "What's wrong?"

"What's wrong," I snapped, "is the fact that you're tearing down someone who's been through hell, as if it's some kind of sport for you."

The room quieted, heads turned toward us, but I didn't care. Let them all hear.

"Pearl almost died." I was taking no prisoners tonight. "You know this, Josie, because Maddie told you. Did you know Pearl nearly lost her life because of what this disease did to her? Because of the years of cruelty and judgment she endured from people like you and *me*?"

Josie's face paled, but before she could stammer a response, I turned to Birdie.

"And you," my voice hardened. "You're her *mother*, and you have no compassion for your child who almost died and is struggling with a dangerous disease? How many times did you tell her she wasn't enough when she was young? That she wasn't thin enough, pretty enough? How many times did you make her feel like her only value was in her appearance?"

Birdie's mouth opened and closed, but no words came out. However, her expression said, *the nerve.*

I scanned the women. "Where the hell is your decency? You're standing here making fun of Pearl like she's a joke. You say *she's* pathetic. I have news for y'all. The only pathetic people I see here are *you*."

Caroline stepped forward, her face flushed with embarrassment. "Rhett, that's enough," she snapped, her voice sharp.

"Not nearly," I retorted. "People like you keep getting away with tearing people down so you can feel superior. Well, enough is fuckin' enough."

"Rhett, control yourself." Cash used his *I'm a Big Man* voice.

I ignored him.

I looked at Dixie May, who didn't look as smug as she had moments ago. "Do you even hear yourselves?" I demanded. "Do you realize how vile you sound? Or are you so far gone you don't even care?"

The silence that followed was deafening.

I turned, letting my gaze land on Cash, who stood by his wife. He was puffing up his chest to let me have it.

Well, I got first dibs, asshole.

"And you." I literally pointed a finger at him. "Your sister almost died, and you didn't even notice. How does that make you feel?"

Cash's mouth opened, but I cut him off. "Save it. We all know you're not the concerned brother since you've allowed your mother and your wife to take potshots at Pearl. Does that make you feel like more of a man?"

"Hey, behave yourself," someone else said, "You can't just—"

"What?" Betsy Rhodes, who owned Savannah society, stepped in front of the man who I didn't care to look at. "I think Rhett is doing exactly what he should do, what any decent person should. Don't you agree?"

The man just nodded blankly.

There was the elite, and then there was Gabe's mother. She turned to face Caroline, Josie, and Dixie May. "I'm very disappointed in all of you." Then she narrowed her eyes on Birdie. "Especially *you*, Birdie. I expected better."

In Savannah society, having Betsy reprimand you in private or public was a death sentence.

Murmurs climbed across the room.

"Emily," Betsy said regally. "I think this year we should also find and fund some organizations that support mental health issues such as eating disorders. What do you think?"

Emily came up to us and patted my shoulder. "That's a good idea, Betsy. And I'm sure our sponsor here will support that."

I turned to see Gabe and Noah standing behind me. People were glaring at Josie, Dixie May, Caroline, and Birdie.

Alice gave me a thumbs-up sign and grinned wide.

I wasn't alone, I realized, not when the Queen of Savannah Society was standing with me *and* with Pearl.

By the time I got back to the cottage, the adrenaline from the confrontation had worn off, leaving me feeling drained. I pushed the door open and stepped inside, half expecting the house to be quiet. Instead, I was greeted by the sound of applause.

Aunt Hattie and Missy were in the living room, their faces lit up as they clapped like I'd just won an Oscar.

"What the hell?" I muttered, setting my keys down in the bowl on the counter.

"You're famous, nephew," Hattie grinned. "That little

257

speech of yours is already making the rounds online. Alice sent it to me first, of course. Thought I'd appreciate it."

"What?"

"Someone recorded the speech you just gave at the Harper Fowlkes House, and posted it to TikTok, Instagram, X, and...well, everywhere. Hashtag My Hero."

I groaned, rubbing a hand over my face. "Great. Just what I needed."

"Oh, come on, you're having a viral moment," Aunt Hattie teased. "You did good, Rhett. Really good. About time someone called those vipers out for what they are."

Missy's smile was warm. "She's right. That took guts."

Before I could respond, Pearl came into the living room. Her hair was loose around her shoulders, and she was wearing one of those soft, oversized shirts she loved, but it was her eyes that stopped me.

They were clear. Brighter than I'd seen them be in weeks.

"I can't believe you did that," she rasped in wonder.

I shrugged, suddenly self-conscious. "It was nothing."

She crossed the room slowly, her gaze never leaving mine. And then, before I could say another word, she went on tiptoe and kissed me.

It was soft and tentative at first like she was testing the waters, but when I didn't pull away, it deepened. Her hands slid to the back of my neck, and I wrapped my arms around her waist, holding her like she might disappear if I let go.

When she finally pulled back, her cheeks were flushed, and she was smiling.

"Thank you," she said simply.

"For what?"

"For being my person. For standing up for me. For everything."

My heart pounded in a way that felt like it might break me—but in the best possible way.

"Well," I murmured, dropping my forehead to rest against hers. "We're more than friends, darlin'."

"Yes, we are." She brushed her lips against mine.

Aunt Hattie snorted. "We're *still* here."

I wrapped my arms around Pearl, looking into her eyes. "You should go, Aunt Hattie, Missy."

I heard them snicker, and then offer their boisterous *goodnights* and *be good,* while Pearl and I looked into each other's eyes.

CHAPTER 26
Pearl

R hett brushed the hair off my face and dipped his head to touch his lips to mine in a long, slow kiss, like we had all the time in the world.

He dropped his head and pressed a kiss to my collarbone, his hands cupping my ass, rubbing himself against me. Then his hands ascended from my hips, tracing my breasts, to cup my face.

"Baby," he whispered, his lips grazing mine. He nibbled against my lips again, and I leaned in, wanting more.

"More," I moaned.

His tongue slid against mine, and I tasted him, salty, sweet, incredibly erotic. The kiss went from soft to passionate in seconds. My hands were behind his neck, pulling him closer.

I fell into him, trusting him, as our mouths tangled for dominance.

"Pearl," he said my name breathlessly, like I was the most amazing thing in his life. He tilted my head, and this time, the kiss was desperate. We'd been dancing around *us* for weeks.

"I love your kisses," he claimed, running his fingers through my hair.

"They're the fucking best," I agreed.

He laughed.

I brought my lips to his again, and this time, I arched into him, wanting more. His hands ran down my hips and cupped my ass again.

"Oh God, baby," he all but whimpered into my mouth and rocked his erection against me.

"That's my line," I breathed.

He chuckled.

"Can we take your shirt off?" I asked, my hands hungrily wanting to touch his skin. He looked hot in a tuxedo, and I'd enjoyed seeing him take off his jacket casually, and now I wanted it *all* gone. "I want to touch you."

"Yeah?" He didn't sound sure that I wanted him.

"I want you."

"Oh, baby, I want you, too."

I couldn't believe what I was saying and how he was responding. I'd gone from wanting to go into darkness to wanting everything life had to offer...and that, right now, was orgasms from Rhett.

Suddenly, he picked me up, bridal style, and I squealed.

"I think we need a bed for this," he announced.

He kept kissing me as he carried me to bed, his tongue licking mine. He was needy and eager, just like me. He set me down by my bed, and we went at each other hungrily. I pushed his dress shirt up, and he helped me, yanking at his cufflinks, which I heard land on the hardwood floor with a soft *clink*.

His hands gripped my tank top, and I froze. It was for a moment, but we both felt it. He waited, not asking for more.

I licked my lips.

"I don't know how I look," I confessed.

He smiled and smoothed his hands over my torso. "You look beautiful. You always have."

"I have a lot of stretch marks."

"Okay."

I took a deep breath. "And...everything is lumpy."

He circled my waist and squeezed. "You feel so good, Pearl."

He cupped my breasts, and I moaned. He pinched my nipples, and it felt so damn wonderful. He gently pushed me onto the bed, and I opened my arms.

"Lie down with me," I offered.

Trust was complicated for me, but Rhett had shown me who he was over these past weeks. Slowly, I was letting go of the past—of the young Rhett who, as this older and more mature man now admitted, had messed up.

He lay down next to me and pulled me to him for a kiss. His hand slid under my shirt.

Skin against skin.

I whimpered.

His hands were everywhere, touching, feeling, learning. He didn't undress me, and I knew he was waiting for me to take that step. His hands glided under the elastic of my sweats, and...*fuck*...he cupped me.

"Oh God." I arched my back, and my legs opened on their own accord, like I was drugged.

He slipped a finger inside me, and I reached out to cup him through his tuxedo pants. He fucked me with two fingers, and I kept kissing him as he did, wanting his taste inside of me. My hands squeezed his cock.

He was hard, God, but he was.

His thumb came to rest on my clit, and he pressed hard just as he inserted a third finger inside of me.

"Rhett," I cried out as an orgasm slammed into me, crashing through all the walls I'd put up for years. It was amazing. And I wanted *more*.

My hand began to jack him off through his pants, and he groaned. "I'll come, baby."

I began to pump him in earnest, wanting very much to take him where I'd just been. He let go, and I felt his pants dampen as he did, his face buried against my neck.

We both fell onto our backs, struggling to catch our breath. My hand moved away from his sticky cock, and his fingers slipped out of me. I looked over at him and found him watching me, and just like that, a giggle slipped out of me. He quirked an eyebrow, and I grinned. "That was... *wicked*."

He turned sideways and raised himself on an elbow. "Yeah, it was."

"You came in your pants." I couldn't stop laughing. It wasn't because anything was particularly funny—it wasn't. I was laughing because...I was happy.

He chuckled. "I certainly did." He dropped a quick kiss on my mouth. "I'll clean up, and then we can go to bed, yeah?"

I was in awe of how domestic all this was. We would go to bed together, like we had been doing for days, as if it were normal.

"Did you think I was fat when we...you know...the first time?" I couldn't say the words.

"What exactly are you asking, darlin'?" Rhett traced a finger down my cheek.

We lay in bed, facing each other. I was too revved to fall asleep, and so was he.

"You know what I'm asking." I glared at him.

He lifted himself to kiss my nose. "I *always* thought you were beautiful. Even *then*. We were young, it was your first time, and I'd had a few sexual—"

"Few?" I mocked.

"Few," he maintained. "I was seventeen, Pearl." He traced my lips with a finger, his eyes somber. "You were so sensual. I'd never had sex with someone so into it...and, in fact, so *innocently* into it. You didn't make sounds because you heard it on a porn video. You were genuine. I loved that. I loved making love with you."

"Then why?" I asked, my eyes filling with tears.

He looked in pain when he saw that I was still hurt from what had happened half a lifetime ago.

"I didn't want to admit that I'd fallen for the...."

I waited a long moment, but he remained silent.

"Say it," I ordered.

"Don't make me, Pearl," he begged.

I shook my head as tears rolled down my cheeks. "Say it."

He took a deep breath as he wiped my tears. "That I'd fallen for the fat girl."

"You thought I was fat?"

He shook his head, and I saw his eyes were moist as well. I wasn't the only one hurting, and somehow, because he carried part of the pain, it was lighter inside me.

"I thought you were smart, beautiful, fun, interesting. I thought you were special. I wanted to spend time with you. I *enjoyed* talking to you. I hated what I did to you. For *years*, Pearl. The first time I apologized...fuck, I was such an asshole."

I chuckled. "You were."

"I was surprised to see you in Savannah for Spring Break. I...I'd been waiting for years to say I was sorry, and then I bungled it."

I sniffled. "You refused to validate how I felt, Rhett; instead, you focused on how being cruel to me made *you* feel."

"I know." He rolled over so he was on top of me, cradling me with his body. "I'll never hurt you again, not intentionally."

I couldn't speak because my emotions were loud, clanging inside me like cymbals at a parade.

"Please forgive me." He kept kissing me as he spoke. My lips. My forehead. My cheek.

"I do."

"Yeah?"

I gave him a watery smile. "I can't forgive the boy, but I forgive the man."

"I know it's too soon. I understand that. But I need to tell you, Pearl. I love you. I have *fallen in love* with you."

I gaped at him.

He nuzzled my nose. "I've never been in love with a woman. I didn't even know that was what I felt until I saw you in your bedroom that day. I don't want to live my life without you."

I didn't know what to say. I wrapped my arms around him and kissed him gently. "I don't know how I feel."

"I didn't tell you because I want you to reciprocate; I told you so you know to trust me. We're goin' to date. We're goin' to do this right."

"We are?"

"I know it's ass-backward since we had sex fifteen years ago, and I just gave you the best orgasm of your life."

"Someone is arrogant."

"Best orgasm of your life," he repeated with a grin. "But we're goin' to take our time, date, get to know one another.

We're not goin' to worry about what people think or say; we're just...gonna be us."

"That sounds good," I murmured, looking into his brilliant eyes. "When will we start?"

"You're not paying attention, darlin', 'cause we already did."

CHAPTER 27
Rhett

S ince Pearl was going to work, I decided to do the
same. There were things that I couldn't do remotely
and had been putting them off. In all honesty, as
dedicated as I used to be to my job and company, after seeing
Pearl fall apart, it all seemed far less important.

My office was in a building along Abercorn Street, on
the edge of Savannah's financial district. The tall floor-to-
ceiling windows reflected Savannah's historic charm while
carving out its place in the present, thanks to the interior
designer we hired to make the office look and feel ultra-
modern.

Since I was the *boss*, I had a corner office with a view of
Forsyth Park, just a few blocks away.

I had a ton of work to get through, and my calendar was
packed with meetings, but I felt restive, so I watched the
trees in the park, some of which had been there since the
dawn of time, sway in the humid breeze.

The knock on my office door irritated me. Being back at work and available to everyone was usually second nature to me—*de rigueur*—but today, it grated on my nerves. I'd never pegged myself as the type who would enjoy time off, but I had. In fact, I loved it. I found myself thinking things like, *"There's more to life than work."*

Since when? Since I met Pearl again, I thought with quiet satisfaction.

"Yeah, come in," I instructed as I walked behind my desk and took a seat.

My executive assistant, Cynthia Baker, stepped in. She was in her early forties and had been with Vanderbilt Finance since I started it eight years ago. I was a child then, and Cynthia had played a major role in *raising* my business and *me* in my professional capacity.

"Your father has requested half an hour of your time... well, he did that a few weeks ago, but I told his assistant that you were on leave."

I chuckled. "That explains the voicemails he left me."

"He thought I was lyin' since you *never* take time off." Cynthia sat across from me. She was African American and had worked for top executives in the financial world. I'd been fortunate when she decided to work for my company, and all but took me under her wing to make a CEO out of me.

"I had important things to take care of," I said, almost defensively.

She grinned, pushing up her glasses. "Rhett, it warms my heart that you trusted your *very* competent team to take care of things, and as you'll see at the status meeting later today, they have done precisely that."

"Thanks, Cynthia."

"How's Pearl?" she asked.

"Good. She's gone to work today. I dropped her off before I came here." I was keeping an eye on my phone. I'd told her to text or call me if she felt uneasy at all and wanted to go home.

"I can squeeze your father in before your lunch meeting with the marketing team." She flipped through her tablet.

"Sounds good."

She looked at me. "You want to tell me what's going on?"

"Cynthia, you could probably tell me what's goin' on better than I can," I murmured.

She made a face. "Well, I know what happened at the Savannah Soirée for Hope. Good work."

I grimaced. "Pearl's niece recorded it, and next thing I know.... I'm assuming you want to know why my father is coming here rather than me going to him?"

"Yes," she confirmed.

I shrugged. "I felt it was time he understood what my taking care of the family estate means."

"Ah, he bossed you around one time too much?"

"Something like that," I agreed. "He threatened me when I ended my engagement with Josie."

Cynthia didn't comment on Josie. She didn't like her and had told me that, and then said she wouldn't be discussing her with me as my life was mine and her feelings about my fiancée were none of my business. Cynthia had a way of ending arguments before they even started.

"I told him he can take *his* money and do what he wants with it."

"Your father isn't going to do that," Cynthia scoffed. "He lost enough Vanderbilt money when he was managing the estate, and what he has—he knows—is because of your astute investment decisions."

"And yet, he had no problem, as you so aptly put it, bossing me around."

"Oh, Rhett, that's because you let him."

She had a point.

"He's not going to be doing that anymore," I vowed, primarily to myself.

"Good," Cynthia declared and then went through my calendar and made sure I was up to date with regard to everything I needed to know.

After she left, I pondered what Cynthia said about how I'd allowed my father to bully me.

Why had I done that?

I leaned back in my chair, letting my eyes wander over the space I'd built. The walls were lined with custom bookshelves, not stuffed with meaningless leather-bound props, but actual books I'd read—on finance, entrepreneurship, and the psychology of leadership. A sleek desk sat in the center of the room, organized but lived-in, with my laptop open and a cup of coffee cooling beside it.

This office reflected me. Not my family. Not their legacy. *Me.*

I started Vanderbilt Finance with nothing more than my name, my degree, and a hell of a lot of ambition. People (especially my father) assumed I'd be a failure, calling it a hobby and a vanity project.

I'd turned it into a success. And while I was proud of the company's growth, I was even prouder that I'd done it without asking George Vanderbilt for a single Goddamn cent. When he saw how well I was managing my trust fund and building something out of it, he eventually asked me to take over his assets and everything Vanderbilt that was still under his control. And I had.

For a brief moment, it felt like validation—like my father finally trusted me and saw me as his heir, not just a rebellious kid trying to prove a point. It had been a proud moment for me, even if I didn't let him know how much it meant at the time.

Instead of seeing what I had achieved without him, I had been focused on what I had accomplished to gain *his* respect. However, I could no longer remember why George Vanderbilt's opinion of me mattered so much when our values were so contrary to one another.

My phone buzzed, and it was Cynthia telling me my father had arrived—ten minutes early.

Before I could get up to receive him, my door swung open.

George Vanderbilt didn't walk into rooms so much as he *entered* them. His tailored gray suit was flawless, his silver hair slicked back in a perfect wave, and his demeanor carefully crafted—a seamless mix of mild disdain and quiet superiority. He was every inch the arrogant Southern patriarch.

I walked to him, and we shook hands.

"I've been trying to make an appointment to see you... which, in itself, is preposterous." He threw down the gauntlet right at the start, telling me what kind of conversation we were going to have.

"I took a leave of absence."

I waved a hand at a client's chair and took my seat. A part of me wanted to sit up straight, but that was the boy still trying to impress his impossible-to-please father. The man I had become lounged in my leather desk chair, at ease with myself and my surroundings. I wasn't going to behave differently just because *he* was here.

"Leave of absence? What nonsense." He remained standing by the door.

"How can I help you, sir?"

His lips thinned as he strode toward the chair across from my desk and lowered himself into it. "You've been making waves," he reprimanded. "That little speech of yours at the Soirée for Hope has the whole town talking."

"Good," I replied simply.

His eyes narrowed slightly, but he pressed on. "And now I hear you're involved with that Beaumont girl."

"I assumed you're here to talk to me about your account because that's all I intend to discuss with you. My personal life is none of your business."

His nostrils flared with anger. He hadn't expected me to push back—well, he'd call it being belligerent. But after our last conversation, he should have seen this coming. Then again, knowing my father, he probably convinced himself it was a one-time lapse and went right back to treating me the way he always had, assuming I'd do the same.

"I think we should keep the business side of our relationship as is," he snarled.

I pursed my lips and then sighed. "I'm happy to continue to do that as long as you don't feel you have the right to come into my office and berate me for whatever societal crimes you think I've committed."

"*Rhett*," he stressed condescendingly, like I was a child on the verge of a meltdown. "I'm not here to fight you on this. The Beaumonts are a fine family. Good name, old money. In fact, I'd say they're just as respectable as the Vances, except they don't have as much money. If you're serious about this girl, I can't see how—"

"Stop," I cut him off. My voice wasn't loud, but it was hard enough to shut him the hell up. "Don't talk about Pearl like she's an asset or a name on a ledger. My girlfriend isn't a society box to check off. She's not part of some strategy or legacy. She's a person—a woman I care about—and I won't let you reduce her to something less."

His face darkened, the lines around his mouth tightening. "You've always been so quick to throw away what's been handed to you. The Vanderbilt name, our reputation—it's what built this city. It's what built you."

I laughed bitterly, shaking my head. "No, Dad. I built me and *this*." I gestured to the office around me. "This company? This isn't the Vanderbilt name. This is me. My work, my ideas, my effort. I didn't use your connections, your money, or your influence. And let's be honest—you didn't offer any of it, anyway. You told me this was a *hobby*, remember? It was to keep me busy until I settled down into the life you wanted for me."

George's jaw tightened, but he didn't argue.

"And now," I continued, letting years of repressed anger lead me, "you want to give me your blessing to be with Pearl? Let me be clear—I don't care what you think about her or me. Pearl and I don't need your approval, and we sure as hell don't need your judgment."

He let out a slow breath, his gaze shifting to a cold, calculated calm—the place every sociopath retreated to when threats failed. "Rhett, you're part of a heritage, an important one in the state of Georgia. If you think you can just walk away from that—"

"I already have," I interrupted him *again*. I think I'd done that more during this conversation than in my whole life, which was telling. "I've been walking away from it for years. Speaking of which, and for the sake of transparency, I wanted you to know that I'm selling the house...the whole estate."

The words hung in the air like a grenade waiting to go off.

His eyes widened, and for a moment, he looked genuinely shocked. "You're *what*?"

"I'm selling it," I repeated, my voice steady. "I hate living there. I've hated it for years. It's not a home—it's a mausoleum. I'm not going to keep holding onto it just because you think it's some kind of symbol. It's not my legacy, it's yours. And you can keep it."

"You can't sell it."

"It's mine, so I can. If you want to keep it in the family or whatever, feel free to make me an offer." He couldn't afford it, he knew that, and so did I, since I was intimate with his portfolio.

He stared at me, his face a mask of fury barely held in check. "You don't understand what you're throwing away. That house has been in our family for—"

"Many, many generations," I supplied. "Legacy doesn't mean a thing if it makes you miserable. You've spent your whole life trying to control everyone around you, pretending it's about preserving the family name. It makes you happy, so you can keep doing it. I'm not going to live my life that way, and I'm sure as hell not going to let you drag Pearl into it."

The silence that followed was heavy, the weight of unspoken truths pressing down on both of us.

"This doesn't end here." I think he wanted that to be the final blow, but it didn't land. The thing was, nothing was landing any longer, and he could see it, feel that he'd lost me.

"Yes, it does." I stood and looked him dead in the eye.

He rose as well, straightening his jacket with a sharp tug. "I always knew you were going to disappoint me, and you finally have."

"Frankly, sir, I don't give a damn."

CHAPTER 28
Pearl

I was worried about what people would think and say.

I was sure by now everyone at work knew that Pearl Beaumont had lost her shit and had to go on medical leave. It was embarrassing, even though Rhett told me that I should be proud of how I took the time to take care of myself—and wished more people did the same.

Easy enough for him to say since he wasn't the one staring at a simple piece of toast, wondering how to put it in my mouth and then chew.

So, it was no wonder that I walked through the glass doors of Savannah Lace with trepidation.

As soon as I stepped in, Rachel, Nina's efficient EA who managed the front desk, greeted me with a warm, "Welcome back," before seamlessly picking up the ringing phone and answering with her usual curt but cheerful, "Savannah Lace, how may I help you?" It hit me then—everything here was the same. Nothing had changed.

But *I* had.

Even after everything, I realized I was almost back to where I had been mentally before the '*incident*,' as I'd started to call it. *Nervous breakdown* sounded far too severe, even though my therapist assured me that's exactly what it was.

Coming back to Savannah, seeing Rhett again, and dealing with my family—it had all swirled together into a tight, overwhelming stress ball inside me. And when Josie did what she did, it was like the last thread snapped, and I imploded.

As I walked to my office, the buzz of keyboards, the quiet hum of voices in hushed conversations, and the occasional ring of a phone were familiar, and normalized my presence among them. The walls were adorned with the same framed photographs of iconic Savannah Lace designs, their elegant patterns a testament to the company's history. Even the faint scent of coffee and delicious food that Mira Bodine created in the cafeteria made me feel like I was home, even if the thought of food and drink made me just a tad queasy.

I gripped the strap of my bag tighter, my heels clicking against the polished floor as I made my way to my desk. My pulse quickened with every step, the knot in my stomach twisting tighter. I couldn't shake the feeling that everyone was watching me, even though most of my coworkers seemed to be too busy with their screens or conversations to notice me at all.

They know, the voice in my head whispered. *They all know.*

For years, I'd worked so hard to keep the most vulnerable parts of myself hidden. But now, my struggles weren't private anymore. The walls I'd built had come crashing down, and now everyone in this building had a front-row seat to my shame. Hell, Luna and Aurora had to hold me while I laid in a fetal position next to a freaking smelly dumpster in an alley behind The Peacock Lounge.

I forced myself to keep walking, trying to ignore the heat rising to my face.

Just keep moving, Pearl. Don't stop. Don't give them a reason to stare. That used to be my mantra when I was growing up in Savannah. That was how I used to ignore the *fat, nerd, dull,* and after Rhett, *slut* comments.

When I reached my desk, I sat down quickly, setting my bag on the floor, and pulling my laptop open as if burying myself in work might make me invisible. I braced myself for the whispers, the glances, the awkward condolences.

But they didn't come.

"Morning, Pearl!" Stephanie, a colleague, called cheerfully as she passed by, balancing a stack of mail in her arms. "Welcome back."

"Morning," I replied warily. "And thank you."

A few minutes later, Alex from payroll stopped by to drop some documents on my desk.

"Thank God, you're back. Can you take a look at these and make sure they're ready for Layla's John Hancock?"

This was standard operating procedure for Alex when it came to contracts. He wanted me to go through them because I was known to be detail-oriented. He didn't linger,

279

didn't give me a pitying look, didn't ask how I was doing. Instead, he added, "And I'll owe you one more drink."

I arched an eyebrow, falling into my usual pattern with Alex.

He ran a hand through his dirty blonde hair and looked sheepish. "At this point, I think I owe you a couple of bottles of...drinks."

I grinned. "As long as someone is keeping tabs."

Alex chuckled and was on his way.

As the hours ticked by, I noticed that no one was treating me any differently. When I walked by, there were no sidelong glances, no hushed tones, and no awkward pauses in conversation.

It was like...nothing had happened.

I exhaled slowly, the tension in my chest easing just a little. Maybe I'd underestimated these people. Or perhaps they were doing what good coworkers do—giving me space to be me. Either way, I appreciated it.

I got a text message from Rhett around noon.

Rhett: *Did you have lunch?*

Me: *I had an apple.*

Okay, so it was a couple of slices, but it was an apple.

Rhett: *Are you hydrating?*

I scowled because I felt like an errant child, but it was lovely to be taken care of, and for someone to ask if I was okay. I took a photo of the half-empty bottle of water next to my keyboard and sent it to him.

Rhett: *Good work! How's your day been so far?*

Me: *Eh. Nothing special.*

Rhett: *My father came by—I think I may have wrecked that relationship irredeemably.*

I called him then. He answered on the first ring.

"What happened?"

"The usual, only this time I told him that I didn't give a damn," he replied, amused. "You worried about me, baby?"

"Yes."

"You know what would make me feel better?"

"What?"

"If you could close your door, and maybe we can have some phone sex?"

I giggled. "My office has glass walls. You'll just have to wait to get me off in person."

"My favorite thing to do," he drawled huskily.

By the time I hung up, joy swirled inside of me. I had a boyfriend—an honest-to-God, delicious, wonderful, and caring boyfriend. I still couldn't believe it, but I was immensely grateful.

It was almost the end of the day, and Rhett was going to pick me up in a bit, when a message popped up in my inbox from Nina Davenport.

Come by my office when you have a minute. – Nina

I ruminated over my first day back at work as I walked to Nina's office. It had been good. I'd had just enough work to keep me busy but not overwhelm me. Colleagues said hello and checked in on me without making it awkward. My boss told me that if I needed more time, I should take it, and then moved on to talking about work.

Apparently, people finding out I have an eating disorder

281

had not turned me into someone to pity—no one was looking at me differently now that they knew.

Diego Perez was coming out of Nina's office as I got there.

"Hey, Pearl, how's it goin'?" he asked casually.

"Good, and you?"

Diego grinned and winked at me. "Fabulous."

As he walked away, I wondered if I'd seen a lipstick mark on his cheek. When I stepped into Nina's office after she asked me to come in, I saw her redo her lipstick—the same pink color as was on Diego's face.

Well, well, there's an office romance blooming. That thought, for some reason, delighted me.

Nina had her glasses perched on the bridge of her nose as she studied her face on her iPhone camera to check her lipstick. She set it down when she saw me, her face breaking into a warm smile.

She came from around the desk and hugged me. "So good to have you back, Pearl."

Nina had always disarmed me. She was one of the toughest and most demanding professionals I knew, and yet she was ready with a hug, a tissue, or a joke when it was needed.

And she had game since she'd snagged the sexiest man in the building, I thought with a giggle.

I couldn't wait to tell Rhett about having caught Nina Davenport making out with Diego Perez in *her* office. He was the only one I could tell because there was no way I was going to spread gossip in the office.

Nina led me to a chair and then took her seat across from me.

"How are you?" she asked, resting her elbows on her desk.

"I'm good." I was genuinely smiling when I spoke. "I *was* nervous, but...it's been a really good first day back." I felt like I was gushing; I think I was. I'd just not expected it to be this easy.

"Now, don't think of me as your boss's boss but as Hattie's friend when I ask you, have you eaten today?"

That took me aback. She was the first person to bring up my *situation* with food.

"A little." And then added hurriedly, "I can't eat right now; I'm not hungry."

"Okay." She picked up her landline and spoke into it, "Rachel, darlin', can you bring some tea to my office? Mint for both of us. Yes, thank you."

Nina Davenport was a woman of many skills, including somehow knowing that Rhett had been feeding me mint tea when I refused to eat anything. He sweetened it a little to get some calories into me. The mint helped with nausea and made me feel refreshed.

"Oh, don't look at me like that." Nina waved a hand. "Of course, I checked up on how to take care of you. It takes a village, you know?"

Before I could respond, Nina's door opened after a brief knock, and Rachel brought in a tray with tea. She set the teapot and two cups on Nina's table, and left the empty tray on one of the side tables. She'd even put a couple of chocolate chip cookies on a small plate, but I wasn't going there.

Nina leaned back and studied me. "I know you think you're the only one with a big secret and problem, but the thing is, we're all working on ourselves. Let me tell you what I've learned over the years: most of the time, the things we think people are focusing on about us are the ones they barely notice. People are so wrapped up in their own lives and their own problems that they rarely have time to dwell on someone else's. It feels huge to you because it is—but to them, it's just another piece of a much larger picture."

"I've always hated being pitied," I told her.

"Maybe because Birdie made it an art form with you," Nina offered sardonically.

I chuckled. This was why Savannah was a great place to live and also a pain in the ass. Everyone knew everyone and everyone's business. "I hate that people know, especially since I've spent so long trying to hide it."

Once the tea was ready, I served both Nina and me.

I took a tentative sip and was pleased when nothing seemed to offend my system. Nina picked up her teacup and took a sip. "I can assure you that every single woman in this building—hell, every woman you'll ever meet—has parts of her body or psyche she's tried to or is actively trying to hide. Some part of herself she's been told isn't good enough, or worthy enough, or acceptable."

I swallowed hard, my throat tightening. "Do you think I wallow too much and—"

"Pearl, I'm not saying this to minimize your problems," Nina said firmly, setting her delicate ceramic teacup down on her desk with precision. Her tone was warm but laced with that no-nonsense edge she was known for. "What I'm saying is that your struggles are yours. The last thing you need to burden yourself with is worrying about what other people think."

"What *do* people think?" I asked, desperate to know, to be validated, to be told I wasn't a terrible person, a weak woman.

"I can't speak about *people* in general, but *I* think that you are a strong woman, who has overcome some really horrendous shit thrown her way during her formative years. That's not an easy task. I also think you're a good and kind person, who helps people and is there for people. You have solid integrity and high moral standards for yourself." She grinned then. "And now, to the part you need to work on, because I also think you worry too much about the world's opinion of you."

"I am working on it," I remarked. "My therapist told me, the last time we spoke, that sometimes the line between a nervous breakdown and a break*through* is thin."

"And?" she coaxed.

"I think I had a breakdown but...." I paused, suddenly reticent to share matters so personal, but the look she gave me was so warm and kind that I proceeded. "I also had a breakthrough, thanks to the support I got from Rhett, Aunt Hattie, and Missy. And all of you, who told me to take time off. I didn't have to worry about losing my job because I wasn't well. It made me feel like I had the time and space to get better and learn more about myself."

Nina traced the top of her cup with a finger and then looked at me. "In my teenage years, I struggled with my body image, too. My mother was supermodel thin, while I had my father's Italian genes, with big hips, and tits that were already garnering unwanted attention when I was barely fourteen."

You could knock me down with a feather! The super-confident Nina Davenport struggled with how she looked? But why? She was gorgeous and effortlessly elegant.

"I wanted to be like Mama," she continued. "I was so consumed with the idea of perfection that I couldn't see what I already had—strength, intelligence, ambition. It took me a long time to realize that the only person I had to be *enough* for was me. And even now, there are days when I have to remind myself of that."

"How did you realize that?"

Now, she smiled widely. "I had a wonderful friend, Monica Ryan. She's a therapist now, but even then, when we were teenagers, she had a skill. She and Hattie and some others were there for and with me. Monica's mother was a psychologist as well, so she talked to me, not officially, because, mind you, in those days, if anyone found out I was seeing a therapist, it would've been a scandal. Long story short, I got a lot of help, and by the time I was out of my teens, those feelings became rare. I'm aware that I was lucky."

"Getting help at the right time is pivotal," I agreed. "I

took too long for me to get help, and by then, a lot of the damage was already done."

"Isn't it wonderful that we can keep growing and developing and becoming better versions of ourselves despite being late in addressing our issues? That we can make mistakes and continue to have fulfilling lives?"

"Yes," I admitted with my whole heart. "It is wonderful."

CHAPTER 29
Rhett

J ust because we were all but living together and sleeping together didn't mean that we were actually *together*.

"That makes no sense," Royal said when I met him and Noah Carter for a drink at the Collins Quarter.

I swirled the whiskey in my glass. "We're *together*, but I feel as if we skipped a step somewhere."

"Like the dating part?" Noah mused, raising an eyebrow.

"We all but live together. Isn't it weird to be dating now?"

"Nope." Noah shook his head. "Dating is the fun part of the relationship. That's the spark. The part where you learn about each other. You have to court her like she deserves."

I frowned, my fingers tapping against the side of my glass. "It's not that we don't talk or spend time together—we do."

"But is it *special*?" Noah speculated.

"And what does that mean?"

Royal smirked. "What Noah is saying is that you need to romance Pearl. Show her that you're not just roommates with benefits."

I shot him a look. "We're not—"

"You know what I mean," Royal interrupted, holding up his hand. "She deserves to feel like she's the most important person in your life. Like you're choosing her every day, not just because you happen to live in the same cottage and sleep on the same bed."

Noah nodded thoughtfully as he set his beer on the table between us. "Stella and I were engaged *and* living together. She was still pissed as hell with me...lots of good reasons for that—and another story when we all have more time, and I've had *way* too much alcohol."

"I agree." Royal winced. "I don't need to re-live that shitshow."

I surmised this had to do with the scandal about a sex tape of Noah and Stella from when they were dating. I didn't have the details—I doubt many did because Noah had managed to put a lid on it effectively.

"Anyway, I took her out on a date. Not just dinner and a movie or the usual bullshit—it was thoughtful, it felt like *us*."

Royal grinned. "Think romantic and over the top."

"What did you do?" I asked, now curious. Noah didn't look like the kind of guy who was sensitive and romantic.

"I booked the botanical gardens for a picnic," Noah said, surprising me.

"The whole garden?" I gaped.

Noah shrugged. "I mean, I have the resources, and she's a landscaper, and...anyway, I put together a basket of food and wine she loves, even got one of those cheesy red and white picnic blankets. We sat under a magnolia tree." Noah smiled as if the memory was still sweet. "It was a damn good evening. It wasn't fancy, but it *was* intentional."

I mulled over that, imagining Pearl and me at a place like that. Quiet. Intimate. A chance to remind her what we were building together in case she was thinking of getting rid of me. I knew she'd prefer not to go to a restaurant and worry about ordering or freaking out when she couldn't eat.

"It's actually a good idea. Though I may not have the kind of resources you do to book the entire botanical garden," I teased. I didn't have the influence or money Noah Carter did. "*But* I think Forsyth Park could do very well for a date."

"Absolutely," Noah said firmly. "If you need help, there's an event planner at the Rhodes Hotel who helped me out, and I'm sure she can do the same for you. I'll send you her details."

"Thanks," I murmured gratefully.

Royal raised his glass. "Sounds like you've got your work cut out for you, Vanderbilt."

"Just don't overthink it," Noah suggested. "Women don't need grand gestures every time—sometimes, it's the simple, thoughtful stuff that means the most."

"You two fuckers are settled and happy," I muttered.

"So, I guess I have to accept that you are more learned about this shit than me?"

"Learned about *a lot* more shit than you," Royal corrected me dryly.

"Yes," Noah agreed, "we are superior to you."

"You're both assholes," I remarked, amused.

"But superior ones," Royal interjected. "Now, go forth and prosper with your fair maiden, young *Padawan*."

"Don't forget the blanket," Noah warned.

"Noted."

I did exactly as they suggested.

First, I asked Pearl to go on a date with me. Her smile was a thousand-watt one, and it made me realize that those bastards were right; she wanted—maybe even *needed*—to be wooed, courted, and made to feel special.

Then, I called Noah's contact at the Rhodes Hotel.

A week later, when I waited for her on the porch to take her on our first date *ever*, I felt nerves attacking me. I'd faced boardrooms filled with billionaires, I'd ended an engagement in front of Savannah society, and yet courting Pearl without fucking it up, as I seemed to have done way too many times in the past, was the most terrifying thing I'd ever done.

Pearl twirled once she was on the porch. "I'm ready."

She wore a green summer dress embroidered with white flowers.

She looked beautiful—not in the glammed-up, polished way Savannah women like Josie aimed for, but in the quiet, effortless way that was uniquely Pearl. Her hair was pulled back into a loose ponytail. She didn't need makeup or accessories. She didn't need anything.

Why on Earth had Birdie or anyone else made Pearl feel *less,* even in the looks department? Pearl was...well, *pure* in her beauty, almost artless. I found her exquisite.

But then, as Michael Bolton said, "*When a man loves a woman....*"

"You look fabulous."

I kissed her gently on the lips, then brought my hand from behind my back, revealing a small bouquet of wildflowers I'd picked up earlier. They weren't extravagant—just soft yellows and whites, simple and unpretentious, like her. I knew she'd appreciate these far more than any elaborate arrangement from a florist. They were natural, unassuming, and real—just like the connection we were building.

"These are beautiful." She took the flowers and held them close to her chest, a look of wonder in her eyes. Had no one gotten my lovely Pearl flowers before? Fuck me! Noah and Royal deserved bottles of good scotch as thank-you gifts.

"I picked the flowers," I told her.

Her eyes widened in awe. "For me?"

Her vulnerability pierced my heart. "Anything for you."

"I should take them in—"

"No, bring them along," I suggested, draped an arm around her, and led her away from the cottage door toward my car.

"So, where are we going?"

"It's a surprise. A good one," I promised.

"I trust you," she whispered and gave me her heart, which I knew I'd treasure with my life because this was a second chance I didn't deserve, didn't expect—but was damn grateful for.

I almost asked her to blindfold herself as we drove but decided that was a little too over the top, and Pearl was recovering from a nervous breakdown, so I had to step carefully and not trigger her in any way.

I didn't book the botanical gardens, but I did work with the Rhodes Hotel event planner.

So, when we arrived at Forsythe Park around six in the evening, the sun still not ready to set as it was another long summer day, we were greeted by a small table set up under one of the massive live oaks. The hotel had put together a fresh meal—nothing fussy, just a few of Pearl's favorites, so I knew she'd be tempted to eat, even if it was only a little.

She stopped short, her eyes widening as she took in the scene. As Noah had instructed me, the table was covered with a red and white checkered tablecloth. Since I knew that Pearl liked Italian food best, this fit the mood, and when I suggested it to the event planner, she was delighted.

A pair of wrought-iron chairs, with their delicate scroll-work lending a touch of charm that felt plucked straight from a quiet Italian piazza, completed the bistro set. On the center of the table sat a simple water-filled glass jar. I took the flowers Pearl was still holding and slipped them into it, creating an arrangement that was effortlessly simple, perfectly in tune with the easy, unassuming mood of the evening I wanted to share with her.

On the table, a single tapered candle flickered gently, its soft glow just starting to compete with the golden light of the evening sun filtering through the sprawling tree branches.

The air carried the faint aroma of basil, garlic, and tomatoes, courtesy of the carefully packed picnic basket resting on the grass near the table. Inside were Italian dishes: fresh bruschetta, creamy burrata with crusty bread, spaghetti tossed in a light Pomodoro sauce, and, of course, a bottle of my favorite Chianti.

Lanterns hung from the low branches of the tree, their warm light not yet necessary, but still adding a whimsical touch to the scene. A soft blanket was spread nearby, just in case we wanted to lounge after dinner. Hidden inside the basket, a Bluetooth speaker played classic Italian music— Dean Martin crooning about how the moon *hits your eye like a big pizza pie.*

I glanced at Pearl, who stood with her mouth slightly open. Her gaze flicked from the table to the lanterns to the flowers and finally back to me.

"You did this?" she asked, disbelief and wonder in her voice.

I shrugged, trying to play it cool but failing miserably. "Well, I had a little help," I admitted, gesturing toward the setup. "But yeah. This is for you...*us.*"

Her lips parted, and then she laughed warmly, excitedly. "Rhett, this is perfect."

"That was the goal." I stepped closer and pulled out one of the chairs for her.

She took a seat with a flourish. She was smiling. And that made every detail worth it.

"It's just us here." I began to uncork the bottle of wine. "No crowd, no pressure. No menus to order from. Just a quiet dinner under the stars. And you can eat what you want, how you want, and how much you want."

She turned to look at me. "You did this for me?" she repeated as if she still couldn't believe it.

"Of course, I did. I want you to feel comfortable tonight. And I know restaurants can be...complicated for you."

She blinked, and I saw gratitude and bone-deep relief in her eyes.

I brought out the bruschetta and burrata, and arranged it the best I could because I was no chef, just a basic cook who could feed myself. I had considered having a server, but that would have taken the intimacy of the moment away. We were in a secluded area of the park, and the event planner had assured me that we'd be left alone. How she achieved that, I had no idea, but I did plan to send her a considerable tip as a thank you.

We talked as we ate, the conversation light at first, about work and books. I made a point not to bring up anything too serious unless she did. I didn't want her to feel like tonight was about her past or her struggles. It was about her, *period*.

By the time we dug into the pasta, I was happy to note that she'd eaten one whole bruschetta, three bites of burrata with three slices of tomatoes, and now had already taken several forkfuls of pasta and four small sips of wine.

Eventually, I'd have to stop counting how much she ate, but until she was stable, I'd keep track. I didn't comment on it or make a big deal about it. I just kept talking, keeping the conversation flowing.

Dr. Ryan had told me that it wasn't like her eating disorder would show up at every meal. Most of the time, if she weren't in crisis, she'd eat like an average person. But no matter how she ate, it was important not to make the food the focal point, so I didn't. Instead, I entertained her with stories.

"She didn't!" Pearl's eyes sparkled when I told her how Aunt Hattie once tried to bribe a zoning officer with home-made bourbon balls.

"You know she did." I set my fork down. "And she was successful in getting her way."

Pearl laughed *again*, the sound warm and unguarded. I felt like a fucking god for making her happy.

For dessert, I asked the hotel to pack small, petite fruit tarts and tiny chocolate truffles, which wouldn't feel overwhelming to Pearl.

I reached for one of the tarts and held it up. "To new beginnings."

She hesitated for a moment before picking up a truffle and gently touching it to mine in a toast. "To new beginnings," she echoed.

We ate in comfortable silence for a few minutes, the golden light of the setting sun fading into twilight.

"Rhett," she said suddenly, her voice pulling me from my thoughts.

I looked at her, the seriousness in her eyes catching me off guard. "Yeah, baby?"

"I just...." She hesitated, biting her lower lip before continuing. "I want you to know how much this means to me. Not just tonight but...everything. You've been there for me in ways I didn't think anyone ever would. And it's not just about what you've done—it's *how* you've done it. You've made me feel like...I'm not broken. Like I'm enough."

Her words meant so much to me that, for a moment, I couldn't speak.

"You are more than enough," I finally managed to say. "You've always been, Pearl. I saw it back then, even if I didn't acknowledge it. But now, I see it, and I celebrate it. I see *you*."

She looked at me for a long moment, and then she smiled—a real, genuine smile that made my chest ache in the best possible way. Then she gave me more when she whispered, "Rhett, I love you."

"I'm the luckiest man alive," I whispered, humbled by her courage, by her ability to forgive me and love me.

We found our way to the blanket, and I turned on the mosquito repellant, which Pearl said showed I was smarter than I looked.

We lay, looking up at the sky, holding hands. The world was quiet around us, and I felt like we were exactly where we were meant to be—*together* and at peace.

When we went home, we made love, and it was like it was the first time for us together. It wasn't that we wanted to pretend the past didn't happen—but it was necessary to know that the past didn't affect us, and this was a new beginning for both of us. We weren't teenagers any longer. We were new people, better people.

She was already in bed when I got in, slid behind her, and spooned her. We'd become comfortable *sleeping* together, and I instinctively knew having sex, for us, would be organic.

I turned her onto her back and covered her body with mine. Letting her feel me through my shorts.

She cupped my cheek.

"You okay?" I asked.

"Yes," she replied confidently.

"Any time you feel—"

"I won't. I want you."

"Thank fuckin' God, Pearl, because I'm starved for you."

I kissed her, soft and slow, but it turned demanding because we both needed it, desperately.

"Pearl, darlin', I need you naked."

I saw a flicker of worry, and then she nodded as if making a decision. In a way, she was. The last time she'd been naked with me had changed both our lives.

I removed her tank top reverently. Her heart beat fast. Her breathing was choppy. She was aroused; I could see that, but she was also nervous.

I stroked her breasts. "They're beautiful."

Her tits were full, smaller than they had been, but then she'd lost so much weight. She was thinner. There were stretch marks over her stomach and hips. Beautiful silver lines that told the story of her courage, how she'd overcome hell.

I suckled a nipple, and she almost came off the bed. She stroked my back, and I felt the acceptance in her touch. She was letting me in. She trusted me. This was momentous for both of us. I never thought I'd be here, in this place with her, ever again, and that the universe had given me this chance filled me with gratitude. Pearl was my gift, my reward for working to become a better version of myself.

I slid down her body, and she stiffened slightly when I got between her legs. I looked up at her, gauging, waiting to see how she felt. She took a deep, shuddering breath and then smiled at me.

I would continue to seek consent at every step of making love with her—until there would come a day when she would give in because it was natural, and all her fears would be vanquished. I knew that day would come. It could take time, certainly, but I knew we'd get there because Pearl was the strongest person I knew.

I licked her and groaned at her taste. Perfect. My Pearl was perfect.

She writhed as I suckled her clit, and stroked her G-spot until she was screaming her release. I looked up at her, feeling like a triumphant warrior, and she was the rich spoils of my victory.

I shucked my shorts and looked at her, waiting for her to tell me it was okay for me to come inside of her.

"I have an IUD."

I nodded, feeling emotion swarm through me and fill me up. Forgiveness never tasted this good, this sweet, this humbling.

"Do you know you're the most beautiful woman I know?"

She giggled then. It was a full, rich, incredible sound coming from my Pearl, the one who'd had such sadness in her life.

I flipped us, so she was on top of me. She gave me an enquiring look.

"Ride me," I murmured, giving up all control, asking her to decide how, how much, and when.

She looked down at my cock, precum leaking out of it, and then at me. Slowly, her face lit up with wonder, and I knew this was how we'd make love for the first time this time around, with her taking charge.

She sank down on me, and we both felt it...felt the homecoming.

"Rhett," she panted.

"Yes." I couldn't look away from her. She was *everything* to me.

"I'm going to fuck you now," she said cheekily, telling me she was alright, this was what she wanted, this was how it would be—that we'd moved past the past and into the present with a future that was going to shine bright.

I let her set the pace. She was excruciatingly slow, but

there was no rush. I wanted to feel and savor—take our time to explore one another, look into each other's souls, and claim each other.

Pearl leaned back, placed her hands on my upper thighs for balance, and began to rock. She looked powerful as she took me, and I couldn't do anything but watch her as she accepted her sexuality, her freedom, and me.

She became more vocal when I started playing with her clit, wanting to push her over, see her face when it happened. Her moans were cries now as she began milking me. She slumped on to me, tired, and I held her hips as I slammed up into her, letting go of myself.

"You're everything," I whispered as I poured into her.

CHAPTER 30

Pearl

W e fell into a rhythm, Rhett and I, which was nice. I went to work, and then I went home —and it was terrific because I had someone waiting for me. We kept to ourselves, hoarding time together greedily. We made love, took long baths, and sat in the gazebo, reading and talking about what we'd read.

We didn't go out, except for the times we'd been invited to Aurora and Gabe's for a small dinner party with people we knew from work, and we'd been to Noah and Stella's home for a barbecue.

I was an introvert by nature. I used to go out with people because I was lonely, but now, my need for companionship was fulfilled.

"But don't you miss going out and partying?" I asked Rhett. I didn't want him to change his lifestyle because of me. I was sure we could find a happy medium.

"I'm happy to meet friends, darlin', but a big party or those charity galas, they've never been my thing." He didn't look up from his computer when he spoke. He sat on the porch with me, where we both worked on our laptops sometimes. Other times, we lay together on one of the loungers and watched the light of the sunset color our little pond.

"I just don't want you to feel like I'm keeping you from things," I explained, turning on the sofa to look at him.

He looked up, then, and scowled at me. "What the fuck?"

I raised both my eyebrows. Okay, so I didn't expect him to get annoyed. "Well, you're making a lot of changes because of me, and I just want—"

"Cut it out, Pearl," he snapped.

"Hey, I'm concerned, and I have a—"

"What you are is insecure about us, and I get it, so ask what you want to *really* ask instead of dancing around it," he demanded gruffly.

I made a face. He was right.

"Are you happy with me?" I asked sullenly.

He set his computer aside, and pulled me onto his lap. He kissed me tenderly. "I thought I showed you how happy I was last night when you sucked me dry."

I flushed. I wasn't used to this easy sexuality Rhett exuded.

"I remember saying, *fuck, Pearl, you make me so fucking happy* several times," he joked, his hand cupping my breast.

We kissed hungrily.

When we parted, Rhett continued to nuzzle my lips with his. "I'm so happy with you that I feel like my heart is going to burst open any minute."

Tears pricked my eyes at his words. I knew he meant them because I felt the same way.

"Me too."

"That's not going to change. I know you're freaked out that I'm moving in with you, and—"

"You moved in weeks ago," I scoffed and pushed at his chest.

A laugh rumbled through him. "But you're freaking out that I'm selling the house, and this will *officially* be my residence."

I *was* freaking out about that. Mine was a small two-bedroom cottage. Would we get on each other's nerves? Neither of us had ever lived with anyone before, so how would it work?

"How do you know me so well?" I marveled.

"You know me just as well." He kissed my nose. "Our souls connect, darlin', and what we have is magical."

"I know, but I have trouble believing what I know," I confessed.

"We're still building trust. You don't have much for me, and I get it, I messed—"

I put a hand on his mouth to stop him from talking. "No more of that. We've moved past that. It's not you that I don't trust, it's me; I don't think I'm good enough for you."

He was about to respond when we heard voices close to the cottage. I quirked an eyebrow, and we both stilled to listen to who was coming over. Aunt Hattie and Missy texted or called before they came after the one time they found us making out half-naked on the porch. Aunt Hattie also sent us both messages to let us know when the gardener would be around so we wouldn't embarrass him.

Rhett squinted. "Sounds like Maddie."

It did. I squeaked and pulled away from him and checked if all my clothing was where it was supposed to be. I threw a pillow on Rhett's lap.

"Cover that up," I said, mortified.

He only laughed and stood up to receive our guests, with a hard-on that was thankfully hidden since we wearing loose pants as he almost always did at home.

Maddie wasn't alone. Alice was with her. *And* my brother, Cash.

My stomach tightened.

Rhett looked at me, cupping my cheek. "You're going to be fine," he assured me.

"Yeah?"

"You and me, babe, when we're together, we can move mountains."

My nieces bounded up the steps, their excitement genuine and contagious. "Aunt Pearl!" Maddie hugged me.

Alice grinned, peeking at Rhett as he leaned casually against the porch rail. "Hi, Uncle Rhett."

Rhett smirked. "I'm not quite yet your uncle, at least not officially, but I'm working on it." He winked at me. I flushed.

Cash stepped onto the porch and shook hands with Rhett. He nodded at me. "Hey, sis."

"Cash."

He stood with his hands tucked in his slacks, looking very much like a man trying to find the right words but coming up empty. He looked different—not just older, but smaller somehow. Less sure of himself. Or maybe I felt more confident in my skin.

"Could we"—he finally jerked his head at his girls— "talk, Pearl?"

Rhett waited for me to nod at him, saying that it was okay, I would speak with my brother. It took courage to do that because I was scared that he'd hurt me again, say vile things, and what if I relapsed *again*. What would I do then?

But I had to start living, didn't I? I couldn't hide, afraid that I'd get hurt.

And if the worst happened, I had Rhett.

"Alright, you two." I looked at my nieces. "Why don't you head over to Aunt Hattie's and see if you can sweet-talk her into some cookies or whatever she has stashed in her kitchen?"

Maddie perked up. "You think she'll have those lemon bars?"

"If anyone can talk her into sharing, it's you." Rhett ruffled Maddie's hair as he gestured for Alice to follow.

Alice looked at me, hesitation flickering across her face. "We'll be back soon, Aunt Pearl."

I forced a smile. "Bring me a lemon bar if there are any

left." I probably would not be able to eat it, not with how wound up my intestines were.

My nieces turned and followed Rhett down the steps, disappearing into the distance, their chatter fading as they made their way toward Aunt Hattie's. I watched Rhett glance back at me once, giving me a quick nod as if to say, *You've got this.*

Did I?

"Are you going to stand there all night, or are you gonna take a seat?" I said, my voice sharper than I intended as I got comfortable on the sofa Rhett and I'd just been necking on.

Cash blinked, startled, and then made his way to one of the loungers, his dress shoes heavy against the wood.

"Sis," he started, but his voice caught, and he stopped to clear his throat. "I should've come to see you sooner."

"Should you have?"

He nodded, remorse evident in his eyes. "The girls, I know, they came, and they told me how you were doing."

"You know you're always welcome to visit," I lied. He wasn't. My mother wasn't. Caroline, who stood there quietly letting Josie torture me, wasn't. These were not nice people, and they didn't make me feel good about myself, so by the Marie Kondo logic, they needed to be cast off.

But they were my family, and I loved them, still. According to my therapist, that didn't mean I was stupid and weak, it meant I was strong enough to forgive those who had wronged me. I was a long way from believing that.

He nodded, his face tightening. "I didn't know what to

say, and once I figured that out, I didn't know *how* to say it. And honestly, I wasn't sure if you'd even want to hear it."

I folded my arms across my chest and waited.

He took a deep breath, his gaze dropping to the porch floorboards. "I was wrong, Pearl." He raised his face to look at me.

That caught me off guard. Cash Beaumont admitting he was wrong? Well, that was new.

"What about?" I breathed.

"About a lot of things. I haven't treated you the way a brother should," he admitted, sadness lacing his words. "I was part of what happened to you. The way the family ignored you, judged you. I didn't see you for who you were because I was too caught up in what I thought you should be. And I'm sorry for that."

I blinked, stunned into silence. I'd expected excuses, defensiveness, and maybe even anger. But not this.

"When I found out about what happened to you," his voice broke slightly, "that you almost died—it scared the hell out of me. I don't want to lose you. I don't want to wake up one day and realize I never tried to make things right, never got to know you."

"Why now, Cash?" My voice trembled despite my best efforts. "Why, after all this time?"

He met my gaze then, his eyes raw and unguarded in a way I'd never seen before. "I was ashamed that it was Rhett and not me who stood up for you that night at the Soirée for Hope. Ashamed that I let myself get caught up in what everyone else thought instead of protecting you the way I should've. You deserved better from me, Pearl. And I want to do better."

The knot in my chest loosened slightly, but it didn't disappear. I licked my lips and gave him a wan smile. I didn't know what to say to him. I didn't forgive him. I couldn't forget. In the present, there wasn't a way in which we could have a relationship, I knew that, but in the future, if we both worked at it, maybe it would be possible. I just didn't know, right now, if I wanted that, if I wanted to put the effort into building a relationship with my brother.

"When I first told Rhett I wanted to talk to you, he told me to stuff it." Cash raked his hand through his hair in frustration. "He said that words are easy, and it's actions that matter. I don't expect you to forgive me overnight. Hell, I don't expect you to forgive me at all. But I want you to know I'm going to try to earn your forgiveness."

I looked away, blinking back tears that threatened to spill.

"I never thanked you, not *really*, for giving up your part of the Beaumont inheritance so I could recover from my fuck up. But, as my wife likes to remind me, I'm good at ruining her life, and everyone else's, with my incompetence."

Your wife is an idiot, I wanted to say but didn't.

"You made some bad decisions," I murmured, "happens to everyone."

He chuckled in self-deprecation. "You know, you are one of the nicest people I know. Most people would call someone like me who hurt them their whole life a loser for failing, but you don't."

"What would be the point?" I asked, genuinely puzzled. "I don't think there's anything good about kicking someone when they're down. I doubt anyone thinks that."

He leaned over and took my hand in his. "Like I said, one of the best people I know." He played with my fingers and added, "I don't know how to fix what I messed up, Pearl. I'm a total failure."

"No one is a *total* failure," I immediately shot back, gripping his hand in mine. "No one. And don't you dare say that about yourself, especially when the girls are around, Cash William Beaumont."

"Yes, ma'am," he drawled, amused.

Then, almost without thinking, I added, "Talk to Rhett."

Cash looked at me, surprised. "Rhett?"

"He runs a finance consulting firm." I shrugged, removing my hand from his and putting it on his arm. "He knows how to turn things around. If anyone can help you, it's him."

Cash seemed to weigh my words, his pride warring with his desperation. Finally, he nodded.

"Alright," he agreed quietly. "If you trust him, I will as well."

When Rhett returned with Alice and Maddie, each eating a lemon bar, probably not their first, I stood and met him halfway across the porch.

"Cash wants to talk to you." I smiled at him to let him know everything was fine.

Rhett looked at me, then at Cash, and nodded. "Alright."

"Girls, wanna see some trout?"

The girls were old enough to know that I didn't want them to hear their father's conversation with Rhett. They agreed, and we went to the pond, giving Rhett and Cash the privacy they needed.

"Aunt Pearl." Alice looked at me, her eyes serious, when we sat in the gazebo. "Do you think you could talk to some of my friends?"

"About what?"

She looked uneasily at Maddie.

"About eating disorders," her sister chimed in.

"What?" I was more surprised with this request than seeing Cash at my doorstep.

"It's actually quite a common thing among teenagers," Alice explained. "And we don't understand the long-term consequences of body image issues. I think talking to someone who has gone through it will help us young women."

They wanted me to open myself up and talk about the worst parts of me with others? That was a batshit crazy ask.

"The thing is, I think girls my age—"

"And mine, too," Maddie interrupted.

Alice sighed and continued, "Girls *our* age will benefit from talking to someone brave like you. They'll learn that... you know, no matter what we go through as a teenager, we can grow up to be successful like you. High school drama shouldn't define us."

They think I'm successful? That I'm brave? Well, fuck!

"Ah...look—"

Alice hugged me then. "Please think about it. And we can wait until you feel better."

When she released me, Maddie peered at my face. "*Will* you think about it?"

"I will," I promised.

Maddie joined our hug, and we held each other as the sun set on another Savannah summer day.

CHAPTER 31
Rhett

I did *not* want to meet Josie in public, but then I didn't want to see her in private, either. I didn't want to see her, *period*. But I had been engaged to this woman and almost had a child with her, so I felt I, at least, owed her a meeting.

The café Josie chose was pretentious as fuck, where everything from the decor to the drink names screamed, *trying too hard*. I'd barely stepped inside before I wanted to turn around and leave. The scent of lavender lattes and artisanal toast filled the air, and the clinking of overpriced China punctuated the low hum of chatter. It was the kind of place that felt curated, just like everything Josie did. How had I not noticed that before? I knew the answer to that because that was the kind of life I was living as well.

I knew Pearl thought she was the damaged one in our relationship and that I was somehow doing her a favor by being with her. What she didn't understand—despite me telling her more than once—was that *I* was the damaged one, and *she* made me a better person. She inspired me to become a better version of myself, one I was proud of. I knew that a life with Pearl wouldn't just be *good*—it would be *great*. And I wouldn't have to compromise my values to have it.

Josie was already seated at a table at the back. She wore a crisp white dress that most definitely had a designer label. It made her look like the elegant socialite she wanted to be perceived as. Her blonde hair was coiffed to perfection, not a strand out of place, and her lips were painted signature Savannah red, which society women seemed to be born wearing. She looked immaculate and, like the café we were meeting in, screamed, *trying too hard*.

When she saw me, she got up, gave me her practiced smile, and then went on tiptoe to kiss me. I moved away.

"Whoa," I reacted.

"Come on, Rhett, we can hug and—"

"We did that when we were engaged. We're not any longer."

But, since you couldn't take the South out of the boy, I held my hand toward her seat and waited for her to sit before I took my place across from her.

She sat primly, her nails painted the same color as her lipstick. She was always so coordinated. Pearl got her nails done and all that, but she was never this precise in her appearance. I preferred Pearl's business style...well, mostly, I kept wanting to peel her suit off of her—there was something immensely seductive about seeing her go from business serious to sensuous.

Okay, stop thinking about Pearl naked, or Josie will think you're hard for her.

"Thanks for meeting me," she said, and her voice made sure that whatever blood had just flowed into my dick made a hasty exit.

"Of course. What did you want to see me about?" I inquired politely.

Her smile faltered slightly, but she recovered quickly, sitting up straighter. "I wanted to talk. Clear the air."

"Okay." I waited, not sure what was coming my way.

Before she could speak, a perky server came by and, out of no fault of hers, irritated the hell out of me. "Coffee, black," I barked, and then added, "please."

"Oh, sure. And you, Josie, are you good?"

Josie was obviously a regular here.

"I'm fine with my matcha latte." Josie pointed to her milky-green drink.

The perky server left to get my coffee.

"We haven't talked since you...," she paused for effect, "left me. Rhett, you just dumped me in a restaurant, and then...that was it."

Was there any good way of ending an engagement? Maybe I should've googled it.

"You gave me no choice when you decided to behave like I hadn't ended our engagement," I pointed out.

"I could hardly believe it." She pouted. "Can you blame me?"

"I was as explicit as I could be, Josie," I replied softly.

"But Rhett, we're so good together. There is so much between us. Can't you see that?" she pleaded, her eyes moist.

She looked beautiful as she made her case. I wondered, cynically, if she'd practiced in the mirror.

"Josie, the only thing between us is the fact that we *used* to be engaged. And, honestly, we should never have gotten there."

She flinched at that, her cheeks flushing slightly. "You don't have to be cruel, Rhett."

"I'm not being cruel. I'm being honest," I said sincerely. "Come on, Josie, we got engaged because you were pregnant and not because we were in love."

Her jaw tightened, but instead of snapping back, she reached for her matcha latte, taking a measured sip. "You broke my heart, Rhett," she accused.

I sighed and was glad when the server interrupted us with my coffee. When I simply said thank you, she looked at both of us and bounced away.

God, but I wasn't in the mood for perky.

"I didn't break your heart, Josie. What broke is probably your ego." I didn't want to do this. I didn't want to be rude to her. No matter what she did to Pearl, I didn't want to stoop to her level. I couldn't control her behavior, but I could mine, and I didn't want to behave in a manner that didn't match up with my values of being respectful.

"And then at the soirée?" Her voice trembled now, and she wasn't pretending; she was really distraught. "How could you humiliate me like that in front of everyone?"

I hated her sanctimonious horse manure. "Josie, are you forgetting how you, not only announced to the world about Pearl's health issues, but made fun of her at the soirée?"

She cocked an eyebrow, the sophisticated persona slipping. "Look who's talking. Weren't you the one who said you had to roll her in flour to find the wet spot to fuck her?"

I closed my eyes and counted until ten because I didn't want to say or do anything I'd regret later.

"Josie, I'm not here to discuss my girlfriend with you. You said you wanted to—"

"Girlfriend?" she shrieked now. "How could you, Rhett?"

I looked around and noticed a few people watching us with interest. "Calm down, or someone will make a video, and that shit will go viral," I warned.

"You mean like your little speech at the soirée?" she demanded, hostility dripping from her tone.

"Yeah, exactly like that," I confirmed.

"You have no idea what my life has been like since that stupid soirée," she shot back. "Do you know what it's like to be shunned by everyone you've ever known? To walk into a room and feel their judgment, their whispers? Betsy Rhodes won't even look at me anymore. Dixie May and Caroline are scrambling to recover their reputations. I've lost everything."

I stared at her, unmoved. "And what exactly do you expect me to do about that?"

Her eyes snapped to mine, a flicker of anger breaking through her carefully composed exterior. "You could help me." She leaned toward me. "You could tell people I'm not as horrible as they think. Remind them that I was your fiancée, not some pariah. We could say we've made up—that we're together again."

Was she out of her fucking mind?

"First things first, we're *never* making up."

"We don't have to," she said from between clenched teeth. "We could just tell people that until...you know things calm down."

My eyes widened at her insolence. "You want me to pretend that we're still together to save your reputation?"

"Yes."

She had big brass ones, I had to give her that.

"The answer is *fuck* no."

"Language, Rhett, and—"

"Oh, cut the crap, Josie. I can't believe that you think I'll lift a finger to help you."

Her nostrils flared rather unflatteringly. "I don't deserve to have my life ruined because of one bad night."

I chuckled at her lack of self-awareness. "Josie, you didn't have a *bad night*. You publicly humiliated someone with deeply personal, private things you had no right to know in the first place. I can't believe you have the gall to ask me for help. The thing is, even if I wanted to help—and *I don't*—I couldn't."

Her composure cracked then, her face twisting with frustration. "You're such a fool, Rhett," she spat. "You always have been. Always so eager to play the hero, to act like you're better than everyone else. But do you even know what's been going on around you?"

I drank some coffee. It tasted like crap. "What the hell are you talking about?" I asked wearily.

She gave me a bitter smile, her tone drenched with derision. "You're so clueless, it's almost cute. Did you really think I wanted to marry you for love, Rhett? Or that I wanted a family with you? Hell, I wasn't even pregnant."

Her words struck me like a slap with such force that I actually blinked. "What?"

"You heard me," she snapped unapologetically. "The whole *pregnancy* thing? That was your mother's idea. She said it would be the easiest way to get you to propose, and, well, she wasn't wrong. You played right into her hands."

My stomach churned with disgust. "You *lied* about being pregnant? Having a miscarriage? That is fucked up, even for you."

"Oh, grow up, Rhett," she quipped. "Everyone lies. It's how things are done. It's about appearances, about securing your place in the world. But you've always been too naïve to see that. Too busy chasing your fantasies of being some kind of rebel to realize the game everyone else is playing."

I pushed back my chair, standing abruptly. I was utterly blown away. "You and my mother are a piece of work. Lose my number, yeah? And *never* talk to me again. You might also want to tell my mother that you spilled the beans."

Her eyes widened slightly, like she hadn't expected me to walk away so easily. "Rhett, look, your mother...you can't tell her that I...*please*. I lost my temper and—"

"Either you tell her, or I will. You might also want to inform my father. He's an asshole, but even he's going to have a problem with you and my mother pretending that you miscarried the Vanderbilt heir."

I kept my voice low, but I wasn't sure if people could hear me, and if they could, well fuck them. I didn't give a damn anymore.

"Rhett."

"Is getting married into the right family more important than your happiness and a moral code?"

She gaped at me like I'd just asked her to explain quantum physics. As soon as she opened her mouth, I held up my hand to stop her from speaking. "*That* was a rhetorical question."

I dropped a few dollars to pay for the coffee, turned, and walked out of the café.

I drove straight home as my mind replayed the conversation with Josie over and over. By the time I got home, I was positively fuming, but as soon as I saw Pearl on the porch with Aunt Hattie and Missy I felt soothed.

"Did the conversation go okay?" Pearl asked as I climbed the steps, her brow furrowing slightly.

I pulled her into a hug and held her tight.

She stroked my back. "Hey, whatever happened, it's going to be okay. I promise."

She had no idea! Being with Pearl was the best thing in my life. I pulled away and led her to the porch swing where she'd been sitting. I kissed Aunt Hattie and Missy on their cheeks, and then sank onto the swing next to Pearl. She cuddled into me.

"You should never have gone to meet that snake," Aunt Hattie drawled. "She poisoned you with a bite or what?"

"Oh yeah," I admitted.

Missy handed me a glass of iced tea. "You look like a man who's been through a briar patch and back."

"Close enough." I gave her a faint smile and took the glass of tea from her.

"What did she want?" Pearl asked.

I took a long draw of tea, and set my glass down on the little wrought-iron table in front of us. "My help to fix her reputation."

Missy snorted. "That girl has some nerve."

"You have no idea," I divulged. "Turns out, she lied about being pregnant to get me to propose. My mother was in on it; probably hers, too. They manipulated me, and I fell for it like an idiot."

"My sister is such a vicious bitch," Aunt Hattie snapped, enraged. "How *dare* she?"

Pearl's eyes filled with affection. "You're not an idiot, Rhett. You were being honorable, though...probably in a misguided way."

She made me laugh. Even now, when my heart ached that my mother had wanted to ruin my life, Pearl brought me joy.

"Why is getting married so important?" I demanded.

"It's society," Aunt Hattie, who was the epitome of a single, independent woman, remarked. "After all, marriage is a social construct, with no bearing on human nature or respect for it."

"I think marriage can be good if it's between the right people," Missy stated and then frowned. "Though, more often than not, it's not between the right people, hence the high rate of divorce."

"No, that's not what I mean." I stroked Pearl's back as I held her. "I believe in relationships. I believe in monogamy. I believe in partnership. But I don't understand this blinding need to have a ceremony and marry into the right family. My father told me he was fine with me marrying Pearl. After all, she's from a good family, which misses the point that I should be with Pearl because she's fucking awesome and makes me a better person."

"So, what's the alternative?" Pearl ran a hand down my arm.

"To not get married." I felt weary as hell. "I don't ever want to. Not after all of this. The lies, the manipulation, the expectations—it's not worth it. I'm done with the whole idea."

The porch fell silent, and I caught the way Pearl's peaceable expression flickered—just for a moment—before she looked away.

I wasn't sure what it meant, but I wondered if I'd just opened a door I wasn't quite ready to walk through. Did Pearl want to get married, and I'd fucked it up?

CHAPTER 32

Pearl

The porch swing creaked as I leaned back, my legs tucked beneath me. The evening air was heavy with the scent of jasmine. Rhett's declaration was like an unexpected breeze—sharp, surprising, and refreshing.

Aunt Hattie was the first to break the silence, her laugh soft but full of conviction. "Finally." She raised her glass of iced tea in a mock salute. "Someone in this family with a bit of sense."

Missy snorted. "Preach," she muttered, and I couldn't help but smile.

I glanced at Rhett. I was still in his arms.

"I get it."

Rhett turned to me, his brow lifting slightly. "You do?"

"Marriage is bullshit," I said bluntly, earning a grin from Aunt Hattie and an approving nod from Missy. "It's just another way for people like Josie—and my mother—to wrap their lives in pretty little bows and pretend everything's perfect when it's not."

Rhett studied me. "You really believe that?"

"Of course, I do." I kissed his lips.

He looked at me like I was a marvel, and I can tell you that made me feel awesome.

"You look like a man who's finally unbuttoned the collar of a life that was always a bit too tight," I teased.

"You're *really* okay not getting married?" He couldn't believe that there was someone out there just like him, who didn't think the be-all and end-all of life was to wear a white dress and throw a party.

"Yes." I waved a hand toward our guests. "Look at Aunt Hattie. She's been single her whole life, and she's the happiest, most independent person I know."

"Damn straight." Aunt Hattie's voice brimmed with pride. "I didn't need a spouse to build a life worth living. And neither do the two of you."

"I don't want to be single. I want to be with Pearl," Rhett quickly said, worried that I was misinterpreting him.

I glanced at Rhett warmly. "And I want to be with you. But why do we have to get married? I've always thought it was pretentious and, worse than that, boring. I've never enjoyed going to a wedding; I doubt I'd enjoy mine."

"But if you want to get married, Pearl," he hurriedly went on, "we can do it. I'll do anything for you."

I sighed. "Rhett, I'm relieved. I don't want to get married. I don't want to have children. At least, that's how I feel right now. If that changes, we can talk about it. This relationship is ours and should not be dictated by Savannah fucking society."

Aunt Hattie and Missy clapped. I took a bow and gave them a regal wave.

Rhett pulled me into his arms and kissed me, like his aunt and Missy were not watching us.

"Hey, keep it PG, will you," Aunt Hattie remarked, and Missy whistled.

"You are *the* woman for me." He looked into my eyes. "The *perfect* woman. The *perfect* partner. The perfect... *everything*."

"Because I don't want all the hoopla—engagement parties, society weddings, property portfolios that scream old money?"

"Yes." He punctuated his answer with another kiss. He stroked my cheek like we were the only two people in the world.

Vaguely, I heard Aunt Hattie and Missy say goodbye and leave us.

"You know, I thought I wanted to sell my house because I hated it, which I do, but I want to sell it because doing it feels like freedom."

I nodded eagerly. "I don't want to own property. It feels like a weight I'm not ready to carry."

"Then don't." Rhett's smile widened. "For now, we'll stay here at the cottage. Keep things simple. No big plans, no big moves. Just...*us*."

"That sounds...*perfect*." My lips curved into a smile.

"Good." He rose and held out his hand. "Come on, let's fuck to celebrate."

"You're so romantic." I rolled my eyes even as I slid my hand into his and got up from the swing.

Sex had never been easy for me. I mean, my first time was with Rhett, and though the experience had been wonderful, the aftermath had messed it up for me. *But* since Rhett came back into my life as a lover, I'd started to get comfortable with sex and intimacy. I had not expected it with Rhett. I thought that it would be difficult and painful; it would bring back the wrong kind of memories while naked with him. But none of that happened. A big part of that was Rhett. He was patient. He was sexy. He was *very* good with his hands, his tongue, and his dick.

In addition to all that was his sense of humor. I never expected to laugh while having sex—it seemed irreverent, but I did with Rhett. He cracked jokes. He all but made it feel like the most normal thing in the world, even if the sexual act in itself was fireworks.

We tore at each other's clothes as we got into the bedroom. When I was naked, he looked at me, and his rumble of masculine appreciation made me feel beautiful. His hands rested on my naked hips, and I watched him lower himself on his knees until his face was inches from my belly; the one with stretch marks. He kissed down my belly, then ran the tip of his nose up my pussy, breathing in my scent. He lifted his eyes to mine and grinned.

He pushed me backward until the back of my knees hit the bed.

He positioned me so my ass was on the bed but my feet were on the hardwood floor. He parted my thighs and licked me, long and slow. "I'm starving for you, Pearl."

I moaned as I felt every nerve-ending in my body get ready to detonate. He suckled my clit, and I threw my head back, moaning.

"Your pussy is so fucking sweet." He loved talking dirty, and since I got wetter because of it, he knew I liked it as well.

"Make me come," I pleaded as he began to pump his fingers inside me.

Rhett knew how to drive me all the way to the edge, and then calm me down to do it all over again. I wasn't in the mood for that. I wanted to orgasm *now*.

As he ate me, his hands roamed up my torso to pluck at my nipples. I thrashed with need.

"Pearl, you got to stay still, darlin', or I can't enjoy my dessert," he admonished.

I gave him the finger. "Finish what you started, Mr. Vanderbilt, or I may forego dessert."

He chuckled. "You like sucking my dick too much to not do it."

He was right. He went to work, his fingers caressed my insides, stroking my G-spot, while his tongue relentlessly stabbed my clit.

When I came, I screamed, my entire body spasming. He didn't wait for me to settle, he hauled my hips to the end of the bed, lifted me up, and slammed into me. At that angle, he was deep inside of me. We watched each other as we always did when we made love, because it was still new, the intimacy so precious—and I sobbed as I peaked again. I came just before he spilled into me.

After we cleaned up, he cooked dinner, saying that since he'd had dessert, it was time for healthy sustenance.

With every passing day, eating was becoming more manageable. I would never be the one who'd binge eat—but I would be the one who finished a single portion of chicken parmigiana without wondering if my stomach was too bloated after the meal.

"You know if you want to get married, we can—"

"Rhett, I don't," I assured him.

"And babies?"

I shrugged. "Not ready. I've never had a burning desire to have children."

"Me neither," he admitted as he topped off my water glass. "I'd been freaking out when Josie said she was pregnant. I mean, I'd be there as a parent, you know, *but* I can't say I was thrilled, but that was probably because it was Josie."

"Would it bother you if we didn't have kids?" I couldn't believe how easily we were having this conversation. We'd been dating for a short time, but thanks to our history and *us*, our unique relationship had gone from not there to serious in minutes, and it didn't feel strange. My therapist thought that the work we'd done in being open with one another, and him taking care of me, had accelerated the timeline of our relationship, and there was nothing wrong with that.

"No. Like you...I can't imagine being a parent now. I don't know what the future holds, though." He laced his fingers with mine. "But I've become a big believer in allowing for growth and change."

I smiled. Happiness was a hearty emotion, filling me up in the best way possible. "Me too," I agreed.

CHAPTER 33

Rhett

I watched Pearl adjust the delicate silver clasp on the front of her dress.

Tonight, she wore a simple burgundy dress, the color of which made her eyes look impossibly deep. Her hair was swept back into a soft, low bun, with a few loose strands framing her face. She looked beautiful, but what caught my attention was her determination, even if her hands trembled ever so slightly while fastening the clasp.

"You're going to be amazing." I leaned against the doorframe, my bowtie hanging loose around my neck.

She turned to give me a small smile, but it didn't quite reach her eyes.

I stepped forward, crossing the room in a few strides until I stood behind her. I met her gaze in the mirror, resting my hands gently on her shoulders. "You've worked so hard for this, Pearl. Not just the speech but *everything*. The work you've been doing with Savannah's Soirée for Hope, how you talked with Alice and Maddie's friends, the lives you've helped change. You've already done so much good."

It had been a year since her relapse, and since then, Pearl had become a force to reckon with. I was in awe of her, and that she couldn't see how incredible she was. Pearl still needed validation, assurance, and support. But I also was confident that, eventually, she'd start to believe in herself, start seeing herself as who she was, instead of the distorted version she'd been taught to see when she was young.

She tilted her head, leaning into my touch. "What if I freeze up? What if I forget everything I want to say?"

"You won't." I brushed a loose strand of hair behind her ear. "But even if you do, it doesn't matter. You're not there to be perfect, darlin'. You're there to be you. Honest, brave, and wonderful. That's more than enough."

She turned then, facing me fully, her eyes soft. "I don't think I would've made it to this point without you."

"You would've." I pulled her into my arms. "I'm just honored that you let me be part of your journey."

Her hands rested against my chest, and for a moment, we just stood there, the hum of the crickets outside the open window filling the space between us.

"You need your bowtie done." She pulled away and fixed my tie.

"Thank you, darlin'." She had tied a perfect knot, even if I fucking hated bowties...or ties of any sort. But the occasion warranted a full monkey suit, so I had to oblige. You couldn't walk away from *all* traditions—some had value, this one did.

The annual Savannah Soirée for Hope was, once again, being hosted at the elegant Harper Fowlkes House.

Strings of fairy lights hanging from the ceiling transformed the grand ballroom. Tables were draped in white linens, each with lush floral arrangements and flickering candles.

As we walked in, I stayed by Pearl's side, my hand resting lightly on the small of her back. She graciously greeted people, her smile warm despite the slight nervous energy radiating from her.

We made our way to our table, where Cash, Alice, Maddie, Caroline, and Birdie were already seated.

Pearl's nieces lit up when they saw her, hugging her.

"You look amazing, Aunt Pearl," Alice remarked.

"She's right," Maddie added, glancing at me. "Doesn't she look amazing, Uncle Rhett?"

"Always," I said, earning an eye roll from Pearl but a wink from Maddie who had anointed me as the Uncle to her Aunt Pearl.

"You look lovely," Birdie managed to spit out. She was, at least, publicly trying to be kinder to her daughter ever since Betsy Rhodes had told her she had expected better from her.

Caroline, who had not changed despite the backlash from what happened last year, just nodded at us, no polite greeting. At this rate, I suspected that the minute the girls turned eighteen, Cash would file for divorce. Another reason that marriage was a ridiculous institution when it could be so easily dissolved. I wanted to be with Pearl simply because I wanted her—not because we had kids, not because of a piece of paper or a contract binding us together, but because being with her felt right.

"I hear from the girls that you're going to talk about your *issues* tonight," Birdie fretted but kept her fake smile in place in case someone was watching.

God damn, Birdie! She just had to fuck with her daughter. Like fucking hell would I let her distract Pearl with her passive-aggressive bullshit.

I draped an arm around Pearl. "I just saw Betsy, I think we should say *hello*."

As I led her away, she said, "You're subtle as a chainsaw, Rhett Vanderbilt."

"Birdie was going to piss me off, so I thought I'd just threaten her with Betsy."

After what happened at this same event last year, people were on their best behavior, and cattiness was now performed subtly. I was sure the women of Savannah would rise to the occasion and find a way to be bitchy without being called on it.

Aunt Hattie was at Betsy's table, and we greeted them, and then checked in with Emily, the resolute organizer of the charity gala.

I convinced Pearl that we should sit at Betsy's table as it was closer to the stage. The truth was that I didn't want her to be anywhere near her mother or sister-in-law. I had hoped they'd behave, but when Birdie threw down the word *issues*, I knew I needed to get her the hell out of there.

Gabe and Aurora graciously took our seats at Pearl's

family's table. Alice and Maddie, who were fond of Aurora, would be fine and would understand why I needed to keep their aunt away from their grandmother.

As the program began, I watched Pearl's fingers curl tightly into a fist. I reached over, opening up her hand and lacing our fingers loosely. "You've got this," I murmured, leaning close so only she could hear.

She turned to me. She was afraid, but she was also resolute. This was courage. It was easy to do things others thought were brave if you had no fear, but to overcome your worst nightmares and succeed, well, that was my Pearl.

When Emily introduced Pearl, a round of applause filled the ballroom as she stood, smoothing her dress over her belly and hips—an act that told me she was worried about how she looked—before walking to the podium. I didn't miss the way her hand trembled as she adjusted the microphone or the deep breath she took before she began.

"Good evening," she started, her voice soft but clear. "My name is Pearl Beaumont, and tonight, I want to talk to you about something deeply personal, which has shaped who I am in ways I never expected."

The room fell silent, all eyes on her.

"When I was a teenager," she continued, her voice becoming stronger with each word, "I thought that if I just ignored the nasty things people said to me, I'd be fine. What I didn't realize was that words have a way of sticking, especially when you're young. Words like *fat*, *ugly*, and *less-than* seep into your bones until they're not merely words. They become part of your identity."

I felt my chest puff with pride as I watched her.

"I developed an eating disorder when I was young." She smiled, and I knew then she wasn't nervous anymore. She'd said the words, and now she was free. "I thought if I could control my body, maybe I could change the way people saw me. But the truth was, I couldn't—not the judgment, not the cruelty, not even the way I saw myself."

She paused, her eyes scanning the room. "And it almost killed me. I was twenty years old, when my heart stopped because my body couldn't take the damage I'd done to it anymore. You see, I'd begun to starve myself, living on very little food, because no matter what my scale said, when I looked in the mirror, I saw a fat, ugly, less-than person."

A ripple of shock moved through the crowd, but Pearl didn't flinch.

"I survived." Her new demeanor was of a woman with authority. Yeah, she was fine now, I thought with satisfaction. "And I got help. But I didn't do it alone. Recovery isn't a journey you can take alone—it requires support, under-standing, and patience. It takes people who see you as more than just your struggles."

Her eyes found mine then, and for a moment, it felt like the whole room disappeared.

"I'm standing here today because of the people who believed in me, even when I didn't trust myself. And tonight, I want to remind all of you how powerful your words are. They can build someone up, or they can tear them down. So, please—choose kindness. Choose compassion. Because you never know what someone is carrying with them and how your words will either make them feel ten feet tall or so small that they want to disappear."

She finished her speech by appealing to everyone to give generously to the organizations that help young women deal with mental health issues, which we were supporting this year with the soirée.

The room erupted in applause as Pearl stepped back from the podium, her shoulders sagging slightly with relief.

When she returned to the table, I stood, wrapping her in a hug before she could sit down. "You were incredible," I whispered, my voice thick with emotion, and then, because I knew we needed to lighten the mood, added, "I don't think a speech has ever made me hard before."

She chuckled and slapped my shoulder. "Everything makes you...like that."

"Everything about *you*," I corrected.

I heard a sniffle. It was Betsy. Her husband, Atticus Rhodes, handed her a napkin, and she wiped her eyes. "Pearl, that was brilliant. Thank you."

Pearl grinned, her hand holding mine. "I'm so grateful for y'all's support." She then looked at me and winked, her mouth close to my ear. "You think we can find a quiet place to take care of that hard thing between your legs?"

Laughter rumbled in my chest. "Yeah, darlin'."

She slipped her hand in mine, and we went to find a place to have a quickie because my life since Pearl returned to me was fucking baller.

CHAPTER 34

Pearl

"I t's someday," I told Rhett proudly.

"Hmm?"

"Yeah, you said you wanted to go to Patagonia someday. Today is *some*day."

That's how we ended up in Patagonia in late spring when the weather felt like it still had one foot in winter and the other thinking *hard* about summer. The air was crisp and cool, but the sun was warm enough to kiss the tops of the towering Andes mountains with golden light. The wide, untamed expanse of Torres del Paine National Park stretched out before us.

Rhett stood at the edge of the trail, hands on his hips, staring up at the jagged peaks of the Cordillera del Paine. The light wind tugged at his hair, and the blue of the sky reflected in his eyes as he turned to me, grinning like a kid who'd just been handed the keys to a candy shop.

"I can't believe you brought me here." He shook his head in disbelief.

"Why not?" I asked, shrugging casually as I adjusted the straps on my daypack.

"Because I've been talking about this trip for years." He took a deep breath as if sucking in the big, wide expanse. "And you just...you booked it? Just like that?"

I smirked, reaching into my pack to pull out a small travel guide I'd ordered on Amazon. I held it up like it was a mic drop. "It's because I'm fabulous."

For a moment, he looked at me, his eyes softening. He reached out, pulled me into his arms, and rested his forehead on mine.

"You certainly are, and I'm the luckiest motherfucker in the world to have you with me." His voice was filled with so much emotion it made my chest ache.

"Good." I leaned into him. "Because I'm not done being fabulous yet."

We hiked all morning, the trail winding through fields of wildflowers and past shimmering glacial lakes that looked like they'd been painted in shades of turquoise and sapphire. Every turn seemed to reveal breathtaking nature—a waterfall cascading down moss-covered rocks, a herd of guanacos grazing in the distance, their caramel-colored coats blending into the rugged terrain.

By the time we reached Mirador Las Torres, I was out of breath, but it didn't matter. The view was worth every single step.

The three granite towers that gave the park its name loomed in the distance, their peaks sharp and jagged against the bright blue sky. At their base, a glacial lagoon shimmered in hues of green and blue, the water so clear you could see the rocky bottom even from a distance. The wind whipped around us, carrying the scent of snow and earth, and the only sound was the soft rustle of the wind and the distant cry of a condor soaring overhead.

Rhett stopped at the edge of the overlook, his eyes wide as he took it all in. "Pearl," he exclaimed reverently, "this is *perfection*."

I smiled, dropping my pack onto the ground, and sat on a nearby rock to catch my breath. "Not bad for a last-minute trip, huh?"

"It's unbelievable. *You're* unbelievable."

I shrugged, trying to play it cool, but the way he was looking at me made my heart flutter.

Rhett walked over, crouching down in front of me so we were at eye level. "You're full of surprises, you know that?"

I raised an eyebrow. "Hang with me, kid; I'll keep surprising you."

"I can't wait."

Before I could respond, he reached into his pocket and pulled out a small, weathered leather pouch. My breath caught as he opened it, revealing a simple platinum band with a small, glimmering diamond embedded in the center.

"Rhett?"

He took my hand, his grip firm. Looking at me, his blue

eyes reflected the endless sky above us. "Pearl Beaumont," he said with quiet conviction, "I don't ever want to marry you."

I blinked, caught between confusion and amusement. "What?"

He smiled, his thumb brushing lightly over my knuckles. "I don't want the big white wedding, or the society circus, or any of the things we were raised to believe mattered. I don't want any of it. I just want you. *Forever*. No papers, no pomp, no rules. Just us, doing things our way. Will you *never* marry me and make me the happiest man on Earth?"

I stared at him, my heart pounding in my chest, as I absorbed what he'd just said. "This is for life?" I breathed.

"Absolutely." His smile widened.

Tears stung the corners of my eyes, but I didn't bother wiping them away. "No expectations. No one else's rules. Just you and me, building a life that makes sense for us?"

"Yes. So, what do you say?" he prompted, his grin turning playful.

I laughed because how could I *not* be with this man who made me so incredibly happy? "Yes, Rhett, I'll *never* marry you."

The relief and joy that washed over his face was pure. He slipped the ring onto my finger, and pulled me into his arms.

We stayed like that for a long moment, the wind whipping around us, the towers standing silently as witness to our promise.

Later, as we sat by the glacial lagoon, our boots off and our toes dipping into the icy water, I looked at the ring on my finger and smiled. It wasn't flashy or ornate—it was simple, understated, and completely *perfect*.

"You know." I rested on my hands. "A year ago, I never would've thought any of this would be possible."

"Any of what?" Rhett asked, glancing over at me.

"All of this." I gestured to the mountains, the water, the ring. "Being here. Being happy. I didn't think I'd ever get to a place where I felt like I was enough."

Rhett reached over, taking my hand in his. "And now?

I smiled, squeezing his hand. "I'm getting to a place where I believe that I'm more than enough," I admitted. "But it's a process, and, as you know, some days are harder than others."

"And on those days," he vowed, "you've got me. Whatever you need, whenever you need it. Always. Forever. Because, Pearl, you're there for me every day as well, making me better."

I looked at the man who had once been the source of my deepest pain but was now the love of my life. As I gazed at him, I felt something I had slowly grown used to since he reentered my world: *hope.*

"Forever," I echoed, leaning into him as we both stared out at the jagged peaks and the endless sky, the world stretching wide and wild before us.

After all, today was *someday*. And it was just the beginning.

Thank you for reading *Never The Best*. Want more Rhett and Pearl? Read the bonus chapter, **The Road Less Travelled,** on my website at www.MayaAlden.com.

Also by Maya Alden

GOLDEN KNIGHTS

The Wrong Wife

Bad Boss

Not A Love Marriage

SAVANNAH'S BEST

Best Of Me

Best Served Cold

Best Kept Secret

MARRIAGE BY CONTRACT

The Wrong Husband

The Wrong Bride

The Wrong Fiancée

A MODERN VINTAGE ROMANCE

Kiss From A Rose

No Ordinary Love

Against All Odds

IN TROUBLE

Tee'd Up For Trouble

About the Author

Maya Alden is a Top 20 Amazon bestselling author. She's known for her angsty contemporary romances—where charmingly infuriating heroes always find a way to redeem themselves and steal your heart.

CONTACT MAYA

www.MayaAlden.com

Printed in Dunstable, United Kingdom